TORSION

SERA AMOROSO

BEYOND THE
STARS
PRESS

"Full of secrets and intrigue, Torsion will have you constantly guessing what happens next. This book introduces the reader to a fascinating world of science and mysteries that leaves you wanting to know more. Also, Aiken."

—AMELIA E. CLAWFORD, AUTHOR OF
ALL THAT THERE IS(N'T) TO KNOW ABOUT FROGS

"Torsion will have you asking countless questions and desperately turning the page in search of answers. The science and components of this story are immaculately crafted, creating a compelling sci-fi like no other."

—DAPHNE PAIGE, AUTHOR OF RETURN OF EVE

"Torsion is the kind of book that will have you thinking you know what's happening and then pull the rug under you. From the way the characters think to the way everything happens it's a complete roller-coaster of emotions."

—DIG, ADVANCED READER

"Torsion is one of the few books to make me sit still for four whole hours so I could know how it ended. If you like a lovable cast of characters, women in STEM, and a twisty conspiracy that will keep you guessing until the very last page—don't walk, run!"

—ELLIE EMBER, AUTHOR OF THE PAPER CASTLES TRILOGY

"Full of intrigue, mystery, and college kids trying to figure out what's going on, Torsion will have you on the edge of your seat with every page. Amoroso paints a vivid sci-fi world that will have you questioning reality!"

—RILEY J. PERRIE, AUTHOR OF INSPECTOR PIM AND
THE IN THE KING'S ARMY CHRONICLES

To Miriam,
For showing me how to fall in love with books again.

Content Warning

I intended this book to be PG-13. However, please be advised that the cast is 18+ and there is on-page death, mentions of violence, blood and gore, depression, manipulation, anxiety, and other potentially triggering topics. If you are a parent and your child is under the age of 13, I would recommend reading it first.

Table of Contents

Prologue   **1**

The Woes of Traveling   **4**

Prototypes   **10**

New Beginnings   **17**

Castor, Eric, and Morgan   **24**

Accidents and Project Beginnings   **30**

Patterns   **36**

Friendships Formed in Isolation   **40**

Discovery   **46**

Ditching   **52**

Perfect   **59**

Put on a Show   **65**

Clues   **69**

— J   **74**

Dreams   **79**

Ginkgo   **83**

Destiny   **88**

The List   **94**

Second Finals   **99**

Summer   **104**

The Lowest Point   **110**

Headless   **115**

Mourning   **120**

Building   **125**

Nasra Takes a Break (Sort Of)   **131**

Stolen   **136**

Found   **140**

Theoretical Immortality   **144**

Priorities   **150**

To Touch the Stars   **154**

You Believe in Happy Endings?   **158**

Trials   **163**

Androids   **168**

Xavier   **175**

Brothers   **181**

Missing   **186**

Help   **191**

Search and Rescue   **195**

Guilt and Nostalgia   **200**

Unraveling   **206**

Decisions   **212**

Cloning   **217**

Test Tube Babies   **222**

Reflections   **228**

In Loving Memory of Arya Jade   **234**

The Final Stage of Growing   **239**

Waiting   **243**

Cassidy   **247**

Unconventional Ideas   **254**

The Transfer   **258**

Misconceptions About Final Projects   **265**

Epilogue   **273**

Acknowledgements   **i**

Pronunciation Guide and Glossary   **ii**

Bonus Content   **iii**

About the Author   **xi**

Prologue

Light streamed into the room through the gaps in the curtains of the back window, casting shadows across the floor. An old man stared at the computer on the desk in front of him. He had reviewed several hundred files that day, and he hummed thoughtfully as he decided between the last 18 files.

Even though he knew what kind of students he was looking for, there were too many options to consider. He had eliminated most of them already. The program did most of the work for him, however, the ones who met the school's criteria still had to meet his. There could only be nine, after all. They had to be smart enough to survive in the day-to-day academics, but also oblivious enough that they didn't notice the blatant inhumanity of his project.

Yes, if there was one thing he knew, it was that no person in their right mind would approve of what he was doing. No one really approves of weapons in the first few stages. He didn't really care though, and neither did the people who supported him. He did this for the fun of it, and he threatened into compliance those who disagreed. His faculty, of course, knew exactly what he wanted. Some were even eager to help.

He clicked his tongue and opened the last application. He skimmed it, after all, he only needed the credentials. What could this person bring to the table? What could they offer the school? He frowned in distaste at one of the applicant's answers. No, he didn't like this one. *Delete.* Finally, he was left with nine files. Only the best could deal with his precious experiments, he needed the perfect control group.

They weren't perfect, no one was, that much he knew, but they were the best of the best. He nodded and muttered to himself as he finished, clicked the last few buttons, and then left the computer to load. He had trusted that the process would go smoothly, considering he had built this computer himself.

The project was taking way too long. This would be the last attempt; he could feel it. These applicants showed more potential than any of their predecessors. He didn't care about who they were, but he knew that what they could do would help immensely. He was too caught up in his thoughts, because victory was right in front of him... This was his first mistake.

He had failed to notice the small red hard drive at the base of his computer, left by one of his *precious experiments.* This was his second mistake. The drive sent pulses through the computer. With each command, it corrupted the motherboard even further, and error messages popped up all over the screen.

Messages the man would never see. The corrupted files were wiped from the computer, leaving only nine random files intact. The University's new students.

Several floors down, the boy in the lab smiled, knowing that despite the fact that he would forget what he had done in the morning, he'd at least set back the old man's work. Hopefully, the students his program had selected would cause some trouble of their own. He wasn't proud of his role in the experiment the old man was doing. He wasn't happy with the tests, or the problems they caused every student who had been a part of the experiment. He hoped this time would be the last.

In the office, the drive ejected from the computer and fell to the floor, underneath the desk. The error messages disappeared. The program returned to normal, this time with nine random applicants. Automated messages were sent out to every applicant. *'Your application has been rejected,'* most said.

But for those who were selected, albeit accidentally, the message was: *'Congratulations, you've met our requirements. Welcome to Torsion University.'* And that was that. They were coming. Nothing could stop them. It couldn't be undone.

Maybe the boy was lucky the old man never remembered faces that weren't important. Maybe it was his own cunning. Whatever it was, the old man didn't, and wouldn't, know. Not unless someone told him. And the only person who ever knew was a boy whose memories would be gone in the morning.

The boy intercepted the last error message that got sent to the lab computer from the upstairs office. It popped up as footsteps echoed in the hallway outside the door. The boy typed fast, did his best to make sure the message was never seen. He deleted everything he could find. Then he scampered across the room, slid into a pod, and closed the lid. *'Data breach,'* flashed the screen. *'Warning.'* Then it shut off.

The Woes of Traveling

Henry Lee would call himself a patient person. However, that patience went out the window anytime he was sitting on a train, as he was right now. The boy was crowded and jostled, surrounded by people going everywhere, and nowhere. People who looked rich, and those who were poor. And Henry just happened to be seated next to the loudest idiot on the train. He winced. His ears hurt from all the cross-chatter.

It had been a dream of his to go to a college of this caliber, and to have been admitted into Torsion was the highest honor. Applying had been a hassle, to be expected when you're applying overseas. The process required passing a test that would allow the students to do their undergraduate degrees in two years, rather than four. The curriculum was rumored to be hands on and extremely intense. Henry knew there was a less than one percent chance he would be accepted, so it was a pleasant surprise when he got the email. He hopped straight on the next flight out of South Korea, flying to some remote location in the middle of nowhere to be picked up, just to go to the middle of nowhere again.

He thought he was smart, and hoped his family was proud. They wanted that honor, didn't they? He was excited to say the least, marveling at the city and the crowds of people surrounding him. Until the train. He didn't like the train. It made his skin prickle. *'Haven't these people ever heard of personal space?'* he thought. He sat quietly, not wanting to make a scene. *'You're almost there,'* he reassured himself. *'Almost free.'*

Nasra Dabiri had the same feeling. It was the first time she had been outside in a while. She had spent the past few years cooped up in her room studying, isolated, aside from the occasional visits from family and friends. She stood on the walkway, breathing in the cool morning air. It was beautiful. Spend that much time indoors, and you'd forget how lovely the outside world was too. She lived in the Saudi Arabian countryside, though she was close enough to her pick-up location that she could walk there.

Nasra carried her luggage a mile down the road to the bus stop, not caring about the people that passed her, or the cars that honked whenever they got too close. She thought maybe she should be scared. She was scared of many things, but for some reason, today she wasn't scared. Maybe it was the fact that she was curious. She was free of the pressure of her own expectations, for now. It was okay to relax, just a little.

Her feet began to hurt as she trudged along, waving at the birds and whistling happily. She was leaving a lot behind for her education. Her childhood home, her family. She was also leaving many of her insecurities behind. She was leaving her country for a dream that was about to become a reality. For the first time in years, she was excited.

Elena Valdivieso didn't share this delight. Elena was the youngest in her family, living her whole life in the shadow of her siblings. This was her one chance to do something meaningful. Even if she was scared. Elena threw one of her books across her room in anger. She had broken one of her pencils, a petty thing to get mad about, but she was on the verge of crying from stress.

As much as she wanted to go to this school, she wasn't sure if she would make it. She had spent years learning English, and when she got the email she was sure she read it wrong. Then, her official acceptance letter came in the mail. She held it in shaky hands as all twelve of her siblings looked on, congratulating her.

Every second Elena feared the call saying they made a mistake and that she wasn't accepted. She packed all the same, hurrying to get out the door on time. She wanted to go, she needed to go. She needed to get out of her small Spanish town, she needed adventure. And not a chicken-chasing adventure. Of those she'd had her fill. Chasing chickens was exciting, but she wanted, and needed, to chase ideas.

Elena thought her aunt would be proud to have her out of the house, proud of her for actually doing something with her life. As she began her walk to the airport, she tightened her grip on the straps of her backpack. She skipped down the front steps, out onto the sidewalk, and headed towards the bus station. Any doubts she had, any taunts, any worries about being alone in a big city far away from home faded as she walked. *'I'll prove them all wrong.'*

Across the world, another girl shared the same agenda. Zola Reed tapped her feet on the floor of the taxi. She wasn't so sure of herself anymore, now that she'd left for good. She always tried to be strong, for herself, and also for her brothers. Zola anxiously picked at the polish on her left pinky, a bold red to the black her other nine fingers sported.

As she looked out the window, thinking about her new life, scenery flew past her window. Zola sighed. She'd be homesick for a while, but she'd find her place. She had to do this. She had to show them she was ready. She looked down at her hands, trying not to fiddle with her braids, instead focusing on what awaited her. Zola leaned her head against the taxi window. How did she miss home already?

She hadn't wanted to leave her brothers behind. They practically forced her out the door saying that she needed to go see the world for herself. She knew they would always be a call or a text away, and she smiled as she pulled a card out from her bag. *'To Zola, be brave,'* it read. She would be. She'd make them proud.

Katya Leonova had only one goal in mind. *'You have to prove yourself.'* She was going to show the world that she was smart, more than just a pretty face. As she left Moscow, a small voice nagged in the back of her mind. What would her brother think when he found out she moved? That she had chosen against living with him? She thought he might be mad, but she comforted herself. She didn't need him to approve. It was, after all, her dream.

She had always loved astronomy; her father had always hated it. But shouldn't one's family support their dreams?

"Stars don't put food on the table, Katya. Not in the way we need."

She shook her head. Katya needed this. She needed to follow her dreams, to reach for the stars. Inhale, exhale, inhale, exhale. Once she reached the stars, she'd return home, and tell her family all about them. Katya clutched her purse and wrapped her coat tighter around herself. Deep down, she was worried. After all, they only ever wanted her to have a good life. They wanted her to be safe. But she needed to carve a name for herself. Katya exhaled. She could see her breath in the air, and she shivered. She could do this.

Aiken could do this too. He wandered around the airport confused. Having grown up in the city, he was used to the crowds moving very quickly, but it was still overwhelming. He jumped when an insect ran across the floor. Aiken squared his shoulders. *'Calm down,'* he internally scolded himself. *'It's not that bad.'*

Aiken muttered to himself in German. It was a stupid idea on his part to not have practiced speaking English as much as he should have. Reading it wasn't all that hard, but talking? His mouth felt dry. *'It's okay. Just ask for directions. It's not that hard.'* He grit his teeth then tapped a nearby woman. "Excuse me ma'am, I think I'm lost," he said, softly. His accent seemed to betray him.

The woman stared at him. "What?"

"I'm a bit lost," he said louder.

"Oh. Okay, where are you going?"

"I'm supposed to be meeting someone." Aiken stumbled over his words. He was nervous, hands shaking and sweating. He had never done this before, barely ever left his house. Luckily, the woman was more than happy to give Aiken directions, and it wasn't long before he spotted a man with a sign that had his name on it. He breathed a sigh of relief.

Mary stepped off the bus. *'Don't mess up,'* she whispered internally. She scrolled through her text messages, the last ones being wishes for safe travels from her parents and a set of directions. Behind her, Alyssa grumbled about the amount of traveling they had to do, only to arrive in the middle of nowhere. Mary shushed her, trying to get a bearing on their surroundings.

Mary scanned the poster on the side of the bus stop wall. "Looks like the next bus isn't going to come through until 3:00 p.m."

Alyssa groaned. She pulled a bag of sliced apples from her backpack and plopped down on the bench. She offered them to Mary, who took one and chomped down angrily. If she had known the bus wouldn't get there for another hour, she would have taken a different bus. Maybe she wouldn't have had to wake up as early.

The two girls had applied to Torsion on a whim, never once thinking that one would get in, much less the both of them. As childhood best friends, they were rarely apart. How strange and yet familiar it was to be sitting side by side waiting for this bus. Waiting for their lives to truly begin.

Alyssa blew strands of her hair out of her face. "So, we just wait here?"

Mary sighed. "Yep. An hour until the next bus comes, then a train ride to…" she paused and looked at her map. "…Ontario."

Alyssa huffed.

Mary snickered. "Yeah, this might take a while."

Astra hurriedly apologized to the person she had bumped into. "I'm sorry!" The airport was packed, not her forte, and she wanted to get out in the open. She was ecstatic when she found out that she was accepted. It was a great school, perfect for blending in. Though, as she set foot on the ground, leaving the plane behind, it occurred she could no longer be the girl she once was.

Today, she was Astra Aracelli, only Astra Aracelli, and would remain so for the rest of her time in school. It wasn't her idea to come here, and she was rather surprised she had been accepted with no prior intervention. It seemed that everything was perfect. A little bit too perfect.

She sidestepped a man barreling down the sidewalk, barely missing being run over. She blamed her short attention span for this. It's not that she couldn't focus, she could, but she found she was often distracted by details. And as Astra forced her way into her new life, the sun was shining.

At Torsion University, the old man stood by the window and watched as each car rolled up. He was not aware of the switch that his creation had made. The memory-wiped boy did not understand the repercussions, nor did he remember his crime. He did not understand the magnitude. Whereas, the old man liked to think he understood it all. He thought he was in control. Right?

Control was all he knew. He wasn't accustomed to being tricked by the things he had built. He wasn't used to being wrong. The man counted in his head, nodding as the last car drove through the gate. He stole a final glance, then turned from the window. At long last, he would meet his brand-new control group.

2

Prototypes

The old man looked on as the pods opened. Lab assistants scurried around to grab the prototypes, get them dressed, and put them in another room. They looked dead, eyes closed and limbs limp. It was a testimony to his genius, how life-like and real they were. Unfortunately, it was that life that gave him trouble. This time around, the prototypes wouldn't know about the lab. It caused too many problems for them to be aware of the experiment, and there was no longer any room for error. Especially with the student volunteers.

He sighed. He had glanced at the new students in the walkway as he passed above them earlier and noticed how confused they looked. He had watched as a staff member brought them to the front room. He wanted to get the prototypes to interact with the students but wondered if maybe he should have gone to greet them first. After all, he had to make a good first impression. He didn't want them to be suspicious as soon as they arrived.

The new control group was carefully chosen for two main reasons: their intellect, and their record. Plus, the ability to recognize when something was wrong would be vital. Most of the students he had chosen were average in that area, but some were not. How fast they recognized what the prototypes were, if at all, was the most important part of the experiment.

As for the prototypes themselves, the system reboot had done its job. Anything they previously knew, any problems they caused, any failures, they wouldn't recall. All of their memories had been extracted and safely stored on hard drives. Now, the rest of the experiment was up to the current students.

He had thought about letting the prototypes know of their robotic nature this time. The more he thought, the more he decided it was a bad idea. They had already turned against him once. It was better to just let them know nothing. A few minutes later, an assistant called him into the other room. He watched through a tinted glass window as his experiments woke up. They seemed to behave like normal. They had been told they were a part of a smaller experiment, one studying sleep. He had purposefully programmed these new memories into them. They wouldn't suspect a thing.

It was up to the other students to not slip up to the new ones, or the prototypes. He narrowed his eyes. If they did, they'd be expelled, and no one wanted that on their record. The prototypes filed into the hallway. He nodded as he looked over each one, shook their hands, and thanked them for their time. He motioned for the eldest prototype, who took a step forward. The other eight disappeared down the hall. Their new protocols would have them go to their dorms and rest. He made sure the staff monitored their movement, then he turned, and the two marched to meet the new students.

Back in the front room, the group was nervous. Besides Alyssa and Mary, no one knew each other. Astra fidgeted in her seat. Zola picked at her nails. Henry looked around at the others, curious as to who they were. Katya sighed and retreated into herself as she tried to subtly shift away from Elena, who was too close for comfort. Elena didn't notice as she was too lost in thought. Nasra stood up against the wall, avoiding the light that streamed into the room, while Aiken sat on the floor and leaned his head against the chair behind him.

Astra fidgeted again, glanced at the ceiling and walls to see if there were any cameras. Zola continued to pick at her nails, removing the polish entirely from one finger before moving onto the next. Alyssa let out a sigh and laid her head on Mary's shoulder. They waited in dead silence, all thinking that someone would come through that door and tell them there was a mistake. That they were the wrong students, and a car was here to take them back home.

The door opened, which caused them to jump. They each stared with bated breath as they waited for the worst to happen. They found their fear was uncalled for when an old man stepped through the door, a smiling girl trailing behind him.

The dean cleared his throat. "Hello students, my name is Leroy Parkes. I am the Dean of Torsion, and this is one of your fellow students, Nara Arai. She goes by Nicole. You may call me Dean, or Doctor Parkes."

The dean cleared his throat. "Hello students, my name is Leroy Parkes. I am the Dean of Torsion, and this is one of your fellow students, Nara Arai. You may call me Dean, or Doctor Parkes." The group took this in silence, before each realized they were being rude. As one, they stood and greeted the two in unison. Leroy nodded, not smiling. Then he turned to Nara, who was holding a clipboard. She looked up, startled, then smiled awkwardly. "Oh, uh, yes, hi! I'm Nara, you can call me Nicole. You need to get in age order so we can get your IDs, the oldest is, um, Nasra?"

"Uh…" She looked up, startled.

"Your birthday, November 4th, 1998? You're 22, correct?" Nicole looked at her pointedly.

"Yes."

"Stand to the far left please, your left." She pointed and Nasra moved, fast, trying not to trip over her own feet. Nicole looked down again. "Henry?"

"I'm here."

She nodded. "Henry. Stand there, thank you. Okay, Alyssa?"

Alyssa jumped when Mary hit her with her elbow.

"Stop staring," Mary whispered out of the corner of her mouth.

Alyssa nodded. "Uh, yes, I'm here, I, exist."

She moved to stand next to Henry. Nicole looked down at the clipboard again. Alyssa continued to stare. The girl's hair was a bright shade of blue. She always wanted to dye her hair. Maybe she should. Alyssa shook herself to get out of her thoughts as Nicole called the next girl.

"Elena?" She walked over without a word.

Nicole frowned, then quickly recovered, shook her head and glanced down at the board. "Katya?"

Katya smiled and moved into place. "Here."

Nicole nodded and put a checkmark next to Katya's name. "Astra?"

"That is me, yes, I am here."

Nicole nodded. "Marilyn?"

"Here." Mary's voice was soft, almost silent, and she kept her eyes trained on the ground when she moved to stand next to Katya.

"Okay, Aiken?"

Aiken sighed. "Yes."

Nicole nodded again, almost mechanically. "Aiken. That means," she looked up. "Zola?"

The girl nodded. "Present."

Nicole smiled. "That's everyone then. If you'll just follow me, we'll get your IDs. Leave your things, staff will bring them up to your rooms." Nicole marched out the door, and they trailed after her in silence.

Leroy stared after the group. He could have sworn their names were familiar in the worst of ways, though he didn't know why. He had chosen them, so why was he so concerned? Something seemed off, but he didn't have time to dwell on it. They were gone, and he turned away to take care of his prototypes.

—Flash—

Astra winced in the light after her photo was taken. She studied the freshly made ID in her hands. She looked fine, if not slightly annoyed. Her eyes looked almost black in the photo, instead of brown. She frowned. Then Nicole ushered her into the hall, where Henry had gone ahead of her.

Astra flashed a smile at the older boy, who just nodded at her. Then, Katya stumbled out into the hallway. Astra gave a small wave. "Hi."

Katya waved back. "The lights in there are so bright. They remind me of UFOs, and alien ships."

Henry rolled his eyes. "Aliens don't exist."

Katya frowned. "Yes, they do."

"No, they don't."

"Yes, they do."

"No, they don't." Henry took a step away from the wall and glared at Katya, who fidgeted slightly. She hated confrontation.

"Yes, they do." Her voice was firm but soft.

Astra sighed. "Please do not fight. Technically, neither has been proven, so their existence is just a hypothesis. There is no point in getting upset over a theory."

Katya nodded. "Okay." Her voice was barely a whisper.

Astra turned to Henry. She glared at him. "Look what you have done, you hurt her feelings. Not everyone shares the same views, you know."

Henry nodded. "Fair enough. But what if I don't want to apologize?"

"Then please, at least do not do it again," Astra asked.

Henry looked away. "Fine."

Katya looked between the two of them awkwardly.

Astra smiled. "Are you okay? He should have been more considerate."

Katya nodded. "I'm fine, thanks for asking. I won't hold it against him."

Henry rolled his eyes. "Stop talking about me like I'm not here. Alright, I'm sorry Katya."

"Apology accepted."

Then the others were out in the hall and Nicole was leading them down another passageway into a side room. She pulled out yet another clipboard.

'Where is she getting all these clipboards from?' Zola thought.

Nicole set off at a brisk pace. "So, I'm going to be telling you about your dorms. Because there are nine of you, we can split you up into three dorms, three with two, and one with three. I hope you like your roommates because you can't change them. Well, at least not during the semester." Astra snickered. Nicole ignored her. "Dorm 1, Astra, and Zola." The two girls looked at each other.

"Yes ma'am." Astra smiled at Zola. The girl didn't return it. Astra's smile dropped.

Nicole continued to ignore her. "Alyssa and Marilyn—"

"Mary."

"Hmm?" Nicole looked up.

She stared at the floor, trying not to make eye contact. "Please call me Mary."

Nicole nodded, scribbling a note in the margins of her paper. "Alyssa and Mary."

They nodded silently. Both were pretty happy to stay together.

"The last female dorm, Dorm 3 will have Katya, Nasra, and Elena. After I drop them off, I'll take the boys to their dorm room." She put her pen down, holding the clipboard to her chest tightly. "If you'll follow me?"

She showed Alyssa and Mary to their dorm first, then Astra and Zola, and then Katya, Nasra, and Elena. The girls got settled in quickly, deciding on sleeping arrangements almost silently. After making sure they were okay, Nicole led the boys further down the winding passageways to a room of similar set-up to the others and left them.

Henry threw his bags on the closest bunk bed and sat down on the floor. Aiken pulled out a container of disinfectant wipes and proceeded to wipe down on the wooden surfaces, including the headboard and his own desk.

Henry frowned. "Germaphobe?"

"Nope, not really. Just don't like the idea of not having a clean space."

"They probably cleaned before—"

"Doesn't matter."

Henry shrugged. "Suit yourself." He kicked his bags off his bed and flopped down to scroll through his phone. He tried to ignore the noise as Aiken aggressively cleaned everything on his side of the room. Eventually, the younger boy was satisfied and started to unpack. Henry rolled his eyes and sighed.

Aiken took a break to glance at him. "Aren't you going to unpack?"

"Later. Be quiet, will you?"

Aiken glared at him, then returned to his task, while Henry huffed and tried to ignore the homesickness that was setting in.

Back in his office, Leroy watched as the sun set over the hedges in the garden beyond and allowed himself a grim smile. His experiment had begun.

3

New Beginnings

Astra woke early, careful not to wake her roommate. She had always been a careful person, if only in certain ways. She snuck around quickly, getting dressed and leaving the room. She wandered the hallways, light barely coming in through the windows. It was as expected for her 4:00 a.m. stroll. But this outing wasn't a coincidence. Astra knew what she was doing, and she would complete her mission, no matter the cost.

She crept through the corridors, checked every window, every door, every hallway. She counted every camera and made sure to sneak around them. She listed every staircase and every single room. Astra enjoyed this sort of thing. The emptiness in the morning before the sun rose. Even if her reasons were less than innocent, the walk calmed her. At least she had this time to herself.

She had to admit, the school was beautiful. It was a mixture of old and modern architecture, with grayish brick walls for the older buildings, and cream-colored wallpaper for the newer buildings. All of the buildings had darker brown-red bricks for the outside, and inside, it was a mix of dark hardwood and checkered black and white tiles for the flooring. They were all connected by hallways and arches that also served as bridges between the upper floors.

As Astra noted the locked doors on her way through the third floor, she looked for anything that seemed strange or out of place. There had to be hidden passages somewhere, whether behind the statues, paintings, or shelves. The limited decor threw her off, but everyone like Dean Parkes used passages of some kind. She'd find them, she'd just have to explore more later, in between the gaps of her classes.

Their classes. Astra didn't know much about them, and she wondered about them as she counted the classrooms. Finally, she made a mental note to check the library for maps, then slipped back into her dorm.

At seven a.m., the others were woken. They stumbled around getting ready, then lined up in front of the cafeteria. Most were disgruntled because of the early wake-up call, a few were happy and curious about the events of the day. Nasra played with the hem of her shirt. Zola stared at Astra, wondering what was going on with the girl. She had heard her leave the room, coming back right before Nicole arrived to wake them up. She was curious as to where Astra had disappeared for three hours.

Unfortunately, Zola didn't get to think long about it before Dean Parkes arrived. They stood straighter as he surveyed them before nodding and stepping aside to reveal a blond boy holding a clipboard. Then, he went into the cafeteria. Zola rolled her eyes. *'These people must have an obsession with clipboards.'*

The boy stood there awkwardly before realizing what he was supposed to be doing and stepped forward. "Hello everyone. My name is Cassian and I have your list of classes. Once you get them you can go to breakfast."

Astra raised her hand. "Excuse me?"

"Yes?"

"Are we going to be in classes together, stay in one class, have a major class? Please explain? It occurred to me that we don't really know anything."

"You'll be switching classes. You all have at least one class together, and we try to keep you all together, but your major classes are specific. I know you all signed up for some electives, but your first semester classes were chosen for you. I'm sorry, I know we don't give much instruction on our website."

Astra nodded. "Okay." It was a weird setup, but she knew not to question it. Anything to not stand out.

Zola frowned. She, too, knew that it was strange, especially since she was sure she was going to meet with some form of a school counselor. "Excuse me, how do we sign up for next semester's classes? How do we know we're on track with our degrees? How do we add or drop classes?"

"Yeah, and how do we know where to go?" Elena added.

He laughed awkwardly, then shuffled through the papers on the clipboard. "You can make an appointment with a staff member to talk about that, however you are not allowed to add or drop any of your core classes this semester. I've included a map of the school as well, so you don't get lost. Here, Astra, you can have your schedule first." He passed it to her, then Astra left, hurrying down the hall away from the cafeteria entrance. He paused, watching her leave, eyes furrowed in confusion. "Okay then, um, Nasra?"

Nasra took the paper from him then backed up. She didn't look him in the face, instead focusing on her schedule.

Cassian nodded to himself, trying to figure out who was next.

Zola narrowed her eyes. "Why only this semester?"

Cassian sighed as he passed a schedule to Henry. "You can bring that up with the Dean if you'd like. I don't make the rules. I just work here. I'm sorry, it was the same for me too, so I don't know. Take your schedule."

Zola snatched the paper out of his hand. She rolled her eyes and mocked him internally before heading into the cafeteria.

Cassian raised an eyebrow. "Okay then. Aiken, Mary, Alyssa, Katya, Elena, here you are." They took their lists. Whispers of curiosity and comparison over schedules were passed amongst each other as they headed inside. Nasra glanced back for a second at the blond-haired boy before turning and trailing after the others.

The cafeteria was oddly quiet and was pure white with metal tables filling the room. It felt like a prison. Katya picked at her food. Next to her, Elena glared suspiciously at the people around her. Astra appeared shortly after, sitting with the group but not eating. There were whispers from the boys and girls who stared at the newcomers. Zola slammed her hands down on the table, pushing her chair back and standing up.

"Stop staring at us! Haven't you ever seen new people before?"

Astra snickered.

Henry grabbed Zola's hand and pulled her down into her seat. "Calm down Zola, it's not that abnormal." He let go of her and looked down at his plate. "Though I don't think it's normal to stare that long."

"It's not." Alyssa shook her head and elbowed Mary, who nodded.

Eventually, murmurs in the cafeteria grew to boisterous conversation. The nine shared stories of their applications, and journeys to arrive at the school, each trying to forget the odd feeling that they did not belong. Eventually, Astra got up from the table, disappearing into the shadows of the halls of the school. No one noticed her absence.

* * * * * * * *

The first day of classes went by quickly for Nasra, who felt like she couldn't learn enough. Aiken yawned, trying not to fall asleep in his required history class. Henry sat in the back of the classroom every time, trying to avoid stares.

They met new people, who gave off the impression that they were not wanted, and suffered through professors droning on about what they expected in class. No matter how hard they tried to reach out, people turned them away. That is how, despite not wanting to, the nine ended up together again outside at lunch, away from the other students.

Astra huffed. "Social isolation. I'm not a stranger to it, but you'd think people would be more welcoming," she said matter-of-factly.

Henry tossed his jacket to the side. A tattoo of what looked like a small lizard peeked out from under his sleeve. "Well, if they don't like us, they don't like us." He picked up an orange. "Change

is painful, but not as painful as being stuck where you don't belong."

Astra nodded. "People will always fear that which they don't
understand."

Mary threw a plastic spoon at Astra and Henry, causing the two
to look at her confused.

She folded her arms. "This isn't fair! Every time you guys open
your mouths, I feel like my IQ is like, negative 3. Why do you guys
sound so, like, wise?"

Katya coughed. "Technically, it's impossible to have an IQ of
negative 3." She looked down at her lap.

"So, you're just gonna sit here and tell me that I'm too dumb
to exist?"

Katya opened her mouth to respond but Zola cut her off. "Mary,
if you're here, you're smarter than most of the people on the planet. Applicants are automatically smart, and getting in is a process
that selects only the best."

"But Henry and Astra—"

"They're older than you! Besides, intelligence isn't measured
by how much you know about life concepts," Zola retorted.

The two continued to bicker until Astra shushed them. They all
looked up at the sound of approaching footsteps. A boy walked by
and glared at them, muttering something that they couldn't make
out.

Zola glared at him. "Whatcha whispering about? If you want
to say something, say it to our faces!" He didn't make any sort of
indication that he had heard her, continuing to mutter under his
breath.

Zola clenched her fist. Astra grabbed her hand. "Hey, first of
all, you have no idea if he's talking about you. Second of all, even
if he is, it's not worth it." The boy walked away from them, still
muttering under his breath.

Elena frowned. "Why are people so judgmental? We're just sitting here and having fun."

"Kids these days." Zola pulled herself out of the grasp of the girl behind her. "Who does that kid think he is? Why are these people so rude? They're all the same, acting like rich kid robots or something!"

Astra's eyes widened. She dug through her purse frantically, causing Henry, Elena, and Nasra to look at her weirdly.

"What?"

"I just realized I forgot to grab my phone charger."

Zola rolled her eyes. "Seriously?"

Astra ignored her, pulling out her phone. "Come on, this thing is important." She waved it in Zola's face. "I have my schedule on here. My reminders. Important things, understand? Besides, I have to call someone, hang on." She ran away towards the dorms.

Zola threw her napkin on the table. "Hmph."

Henry glanced at her. "Why so angry?"

"I swear, I am not usually like this. However, there is something about this place that makes me…" she hummed and tried to find the right words. "…irritable." She looked at him. "Don't you think? I mean, we've all been pushed together, but even all of us probably won't get along." She waved a hand at Mary and Alyssa. "They came together, Astra's probably one of the sketchiest people I've ever met, and all the older students give me the creeps."

Henry nodded solemnly. "I know exactly what you mean. Well, I mean for the school. First off, be glad you don't share a room with Aiken."

"Hey!" Aiken exclaimed.

"Secondly, I could not sleep last night because I felt like I was being watched."

Zola nodded. "Astra left the room pretty early."

"Maybe she likes morning walks," Aiken said. "I do, it's a lot more quiet, does wonders for my anxiety."

"Or, think about this, maybe she's a spy," Henry added.

"I think you're reading into this too much," Aiken said. "That and you watch too many spy movies."

Zola laughed. "I doubt she's a spy, but maybe Aiken's right. Maybe I am reading into this too much."

"Drink some water, and focus on the future," Aiken quipped. He tossed a water bottle at her. "That's what my mother says. I mean, I'm anxious all the time, but if I focus on what's ahead?" He sighed. "I don't feel so scared anymore."

"I just want some answers to my questions," Henry said.

"In this economy? You're lucky if you get any kind of answers." Aiken shivered. "Not to mention, I go out of my way to try to make a friend, and people just stare at me like I have three arms. What did I do?" he yelled.

"Maybe it's the accent," Zola said.

Henry nodded. "It's probably the accent."

"Oh, cry me a pond."

"River," Zola corrected.

Aiken glowered. "English is a stupid language."

Henry laughed. "You can say that again. Well, I mean, even if we don't make any friends here, we can always make friends with each other."

Aiken shrugged, ignored his racing heart and silenced the thoughts that welled up inside him. "I'm up for trying."

Zola nodded. "Me too."

4

Castor, Eric, and Morgan

Nasra's head slipped off her hand and she jolted. She blinked a couple of times before she realized she had zoned out. The professor droned on, and Nasra gave a sigh of relief that she hadn't been caught. Nasra glanced around the room. Her eyes fell on Astra, who was hunched over what looked like a DS. Nasra frowned. *'Is she playing a game in class?'* She tapped Astra on the shoulder.

"You should pay attention," she whispered. Astra ignored her. "Stop playing video games." Astra rolled her eyes.

"Fine." Astra turned the device off and slipped it into her bag. She stared straight at the teacher, or rather, the place right above the teacher's head. She didn't really like this class. It was boring, partly because of the teacher, whose name she didn't care to remember, and partly because the first few days of classes always leave some sort of impression of how the class would go. She didn't like where this one was headed, and she especially didn't like having to pretend to play games to keep suspicion off herself. Astra glared at the tile, willing it to come off and hit the teacher on the head.

Which, to her surprise, was exactly what happened. The scorned teacher looked up and screamed into the empty space above her. "Get down here!" Three students, one after the other, clambered down and hopped into the classroom. They rushed to stand side by side, heads down.

Astra laughed internally.

The teacher growled. "Would you like to explain yourself?"

The taller of the two boys stepped forward. "In my defense, I was trying to fix the ceiling. They broke it."

"I can and will poison you. Watch your back," snapped the other boy.

"Technically, I broke it. Sorry Professor." A small blonde at the end of the line raised her hand. "It's my fault."

The professor huffed. "It's all of your faults. For that, you will report to the Dean's office, and why don't you take our new students to their classes while you're at it? And Ms. Lee, if I see you break one more thing, I will have your head mounted on a plaque! Dismissed. All of you! Get out of my class."

Students scrambled out of the classroom left and right, desperate to get out of the presence of the angry woman. Astra and Nasra found themselves in the hall, pulled in the opposite direction of everyone else. The two girls were dragged along for a good five minutes until they stopped, out of breath, underneath a portrait of the school's coat of arms.

One of the boys smiled at them. "Hi, I'm Eric, and yeah, it was actually me who broke the ceiling. I would never admit it to her though."

"Hello, I'm Castor, and I want to kill Eric since it's his fault. He keeps getting us in trouble and it's infuriating."

"Oh, shut up!"

The girl ignored them. "I'm Morgan, and I'm the one who's forever cleaning up these two dorks' messes."

"Well then. I'm Astra, and I appreciate the distraction. This is Nasra, she's shy." Nasra nodded, hiding behind the younger girl. "Nasra," Astra glared at her. "You're 21. Face these people like a woman!"

She peaked out from behind Astra's shoulder. "I'm sorry. Meeting people can be awkward for me."

The three nodded. "Understandable," Morgan said. "So, as she said, we have to take you to where you need to go. What's your next class?"

"I have General Chemistry, but Nasra has Biology."

"Oh good, the bio lab is on the way to engineering. Eric and I can drop you off. Morgan has a chem class and all of them are in the same area, so she can take you, Astra," Castor explained.

Morgan nodded.

Astra smiled. "Thank you." She stepped away from Nasra. "Good luck!" She waved as the three of them set off down the hall.

"So," Morgan said.

Astra glanced at Morgan as they started walking.

"Is chem your major class?" Morgan asked.

"No, I'm a computer geek. My major class, or rather classes, are later."

"You double major?" Morgan looked surprised.

"Computer science, engineering, and programming, as well as data analysis."

Morgan whistled. "Clever girl. I wish I could do that."

"I grew up around technology, I guess I wanted to follow in the family footsteps," Astra said flatly. She glanced at the walls as they walked. The statues looked more friendly in the light, and also slightly dusty.

"Not a bad thing to do when you have a good family," Morgan said.

Astra looked at her. "I'm not sure you could really call them good."

"Humans are naturally good, are we not?"

Astra narrowed her eyes. "I think humans are naturally evil, and they find a way to mask it with pride. Besides, who said they were human?"

Morgan laughed. "Sometimes people have twisted views of their family, so it's not abnormal to feel that way. However, that is an interesting take on life. You seem to hold yourself to a very high standard."

"How else do you think I got into this school?"

The two stopped in front of one of the classrooms. Morgan turned to face her and smiled grimly. "I would say a combination of hard work and an impressive essay. That's how I got here. Well, here you are. This is where I say goodbye, I have a higher-level class to go to." She held the door open for Astra. Astra glanced back as the door slammed shut behind her. Morgan waved and disappeared down the hall. Astra smiled to herself. This was her way in.

Across the school, Nasra was terrified. After the two boys had dropped her off at class, her heart rate had lowered, but that was only because she was no longer surrounded by the boys' continuous taunts. They may not have been directed at her, but they still made her skin crawl.

Nasra was lucky that the professor understood her tardiness. She took a seat in the far back corner. She took a deep breath and stared at the front of the room. A few minutes later, she was joined, surprisingly, by Aiken.

"What are you doing here, Aiken?"

"I major in Earth Science, and this is a required course for us. You?"

"I'm a neurobiology/neuroscience major, so this was on the list of suggested supplemental classes. I'm glad I got assigned to it. My major class is much more focused, knowing that everyone in the room has the same major, trying for the same jobs."

"It must be tense, huh?" Aiken asked.

"Very. But wouldn't you know about that? I mean, you have a major class as well."

"Well, no, not really. There aren't that many people in my major. I met all of them. It's weird to think like that. They're all really nice though."

"I'm glad that you had a good experience. I hope mine will go well, too. It's not until the evening." Nasra made a displeased face.

"Oh, wow. Mine was straight away in the morning, and woah, was I worried. It was all for nothing, though."

"Well, imagine how I feel. I have to worry until five p.m.! It wasn't very nice of them to make our schedules without our input, don't you think? I would complain to the dean, except that I can't get thrown out of school this quickly."

"Well, it is only one semester. Who knows? You'll get used to it," Aiken said.

"Just because I'm used to it doesn't mean I actually like it," Nasra retorted.

"Right. Well, just have fun with it, Nasra. It'll be okay."

The two worked in silence after that. They listened intensively to the lecture and dug deep into their books to answer questions. Occasionally, Aiken would pass Nasra notes with jokes related to what the professor said. Nasra relaxed. At least she had a friend.

After class, Aiken bid Nasra goodbye and moved on to his next class, yet another science class. This one was plant science, something that he was incredibly excited about. He settled into a seat in the middle row. He found himself there early, so he laid his head down on the table. Then someone tapped him on the shoulder, and he sprang up. A blond boy waved at him.

"Hi, I'm Castor. I'm the student assistant for this class."

"Oh, sorry, I'm new, I'm Aiken."

"Aiken? Huh, that's weird."

"Is something wrong?"

"I don't think so." Castor skimmed the paper. "Oh nope, I see the problem. Aiken, you're in the wrong class. You're supposed to be upstairs. This is environmental science, you're in plant science. Eric!"

"Boo!"

Aiken screamed and jumped back to see the boy standing behind him laughing.

"That was hilarious," Eric said.

Castor rolled his eyes. "That wasn't funny, Eric. You can't just go around doing that to anyone. Sorry, Aiken. Anyway, your class is across the hall from biological engineering, which is one of the classes Eric helps monitor. Only the engineering part of it, though."

Aiken turned. "You're an engineer?"

He flashed a smile. "I'd like to think that I'm the very best."

Aiken shivered involuntarily. "Okay?" He wasn't sure what else to say.

Eric laughed and motioned for Aiken to follow him. "Come on, I know where you need to go, it's a floor down, so you got the right room, sort of."

Aiken hesitated before following Eric down the hall. This was going to be interesting.

5

Accidents and Project Beginnings

Lab mishaps were not uncommon in the university. However, Aiken didn't know this. So, he was rather unhappy when he got sent back to his room to get changed after one of the other classes spilled some nontoxic chemicals everywhere. The only side effect was that it turned his eyes a bright neon blue for a few hours.

Alyssa and Mary noticed the change when Aiken plopped himself down in his seat. Mary whispered something in Alyssa's ear, and she laughed. Aiken shifted uncomfortably. He didn't like it when people laughed at him. Alyssa tapped him on the shoulder.

"Are those contacts?" she questioned.

"No."

"What happened then?"

"It was an accident. There was a chemical spill in my last lab. It's not harmful, it's just weird."

"Is it permanent?"

"No, it'll go away."

"That's a shame, it's a nice color."

"Thanks?"

"I wish I was there."

"Well, we can't exactly recreate it because we don't really know what happened," Aiken said.

"Oh, a mystery."

"No, as I said, an accident. Not a mystery. We messed something up. If we try to do something like that again, we might hurt someone. There's really no reason to take that chance." Aiken said, annoyed.

Alyssa whistled. "Well, that escalated quickly. Are you okay?"

"I'm fine, just pay attention to the lecture, please."

Literature was the class all nine of them shared. It was another one of the many required classes they had to take. They were seated close to each other, almost as if they needed each other for protection. Sure, the isolation from the other students had pushed them together. However, they weren't too keen on trusting each other that quickly. Katya tapped her fingers on her desk, lost in thought as she doodled stars on her paper instead of taking notes. Zola stared down at her neat notes, before looking across to Astra's.

"You write so..." She clicked her tongue. "Sharply."

Astra looked down at the words on her page.

"I guess?" She sighed. "I write as fast as I think, so I don't care to make them pretty as you do."

"Are they really pretty?"

"Pretty, aesthetic, whatever you call them, they're organized and symmetrical."

Zola shrugged. "If you say so. I hadn't really noticed."

Astra looked up. "They are. I never really had the need for notes. But yours look like something I would want to put on my wall."

"That's a little excessive."

"Writing wasn't something I was praised for growing up. Whether or not I could take apart and put together a computer was more important."

"Hey, that's a good kind of childhood as well."

"You could look at it that way. Or, you could say that art wasn't really encouraged." Astra nodded to Katya. "I can't even really draw stars. Or stick figures. I can sketch plans for any sort of machine, but I can't draw a flower."

Zola nodded. "You could take a class."

Astra looked down. "Maybe. I don't think I have the time for it."

The lesson continued. It wasn't boring—the teacher was a lot more engaging than previous ones—but none of them were really interested in literature, so they soon tuned him out in various ways.

Elena banged her head on her desk. "I want to go to my major class."

Henry tsked. "Isn't it like right after this class?"

"Yes, but I want to go now."

Mary rolled her eyes. "Literally wait 20 minutes. We're almost done."

Alyssa snickered, causing Henry to flick her on the back of her head.

Mary looked down, pretending to take notes. "Let's just get through this and then we can go. Besides, he's glaring at us."

They settled down, and as it turned out, Mary was right. The last 20 minutes did fly by, and as Elena headed off, she held her head high, excited. She entered class early and listened attentively. The professor's name was Charlotte. Elena didn't remember her last name. She did remember how passionately the woman talked about engineering and the process of starting a project.

Elena soon lost herself in the plans that she made. As she looked over the discarded sketches, she thought of what she wanted to build. She tapped a screwdriver against the page. New things were hard to make; the best she could do was make something better. It was then that she finally realized that she belonged here. The professor droned on, and Elena found herself hanging on her every word. Elena found that Professor Charlotte was passionate about it in a way that most people wouldn't understand. But Elena understood. She was passionate about it too.

She was passionate about the way the world worked and moved. It amazed her, how nature gave way to the man-made and metallic structures that overcame it, and the way that nature waited to reclaim its spaces. Elena never really understood why people ever wanted to tear trees down, when there were so many ways to make things that complimented the world they were given. She hummed to herself as she began to piece together her first project.

Across the school, Alyssa still sat at her desk, despite the fact that class had ended half an hour ago. She snapped the gloves over and over until her skin was red from the impact. The girl had spent the last hour dissecting an actual corpse the biological engineering team had made for them. It had never been alive, but it was still creepy. She shuddered. It was so lifeless, and she wanted to keep people alive. Seemed like a bad combination, her and dissection. Unfortunately, if she wanted to be a doctor, that is what she had to do.

Alyssa had never had a problem with blood. She never cared about dissecting animals in high school biology, she had always watched in fascination at documentaries about neuroscience and major surgeries. There were so many things she could name that needed fixing. She tapped her pencil against her health book. Her notebook was open beside her, full of questions and ideas. *'What sort of problem can I solve?'*

As many as there were, she was drawing a blank. It was far too ambitious to take on a famous disease, far too easy to work off of something that already existed. She needed to find some sort of middle ground. Alyssa pulled her gloves off and threw them away. She gathered her stuff, then headed to the library. Time to find some answers.

Three floors down, Mary was in utter disarray. She was still delighted in her major, civil engineering, since it gave her the chance to create. Architecture was her passion, too. It was an art to create buildings and blueprints. Mary had always loved designing. It was something that was in her blood. Art filled her in the way that she painted, sketched, and built. She built a treehouse in her backyard once, and that's when she decided that she was passionate about building, architecture, engineering.

Of course, the process wasn't easy. She had to make it logical. She had to consider the type of materials she'd need, and the time it would take to think of an idea, create plans, and build her project. She knew she wanted a place to experiment, and she definitely wanted to be out of the range of other people's prying eyes. She scanned a map of the grounds they would build their projects on until she finally settled on a plot. Mary signed her name on the paper. She knew this would work out just fine.

The sound of clacking keys filled Zola's ears. It was something she was used to by now. Networking was tiring, but rewarding, and she loved it. Zola watched as code flashed across the screen, allowing her program to run one more time. Connecting all the programs of all her classmates was no easy feat, but she supposed that the teacher knew what he was doing. Well, if he tried hard enough, he could do it.

She thought that he just wanted to show off. *'I'm better than you, impress me,'* he seemed to taunt. Zola didn't like her professor. She had worked with computers and programming her entire life. They were fickle. Machines could malfunction, after all. Machines were not to be trusted, were they? Machines had no feelings, only made logical decisions based on algorithms programmed by humans. In a way, humans were like machines: they had motherboards—their brains, veins like wires, and followed simple commands.

Likewise, humans were more complex than the code that made its way across the screen. They had emotions, and the computers did not. The teacher peered over her classmates' shoulders. Soon he would make his way to her, ask questions, criticize her every move. Zola narrowed her eyes at the screen. She didn't want to be the best, she just wanted to do her best, and that would be enough. Zola entered in a few more commands. A few more people and he would stand right next to her, expecting her to explain what she was doing. Zola sighed. *'I can do this.'*

Katya polished her telescope. Her major class was at night, and though the wind whipped at her cheeks in the cool air, the darkness, the lights above her made up for the chill. *'What are stars?*

Just balls of gas in the vast expanse above?' If it even was above her, since direction was technically a construct made by gravity. She turned the telescope perfectly, centering on the red surface of Mars. Around her, Katya's classmates shuffled their feet, writing down coordinates, answering the questions on their worksheets.

She blocked them out and stared. It was beautiful. A soft breeze ruffled her hair, and somewhere in the back of her mind, she registered that the professor was giving instructions. Katya breathed in the cool air, wishing she was breathing in the stars themselves. To her, it was an honor to know about the stars. It was a privilege to see what they were made of. Maybe she was just a little too attached to the night sky.

She blinked, trying to pay attention. Katya looked down at her paper. There were only a few questions, but it was a wonder that they knew any of this at all. That there were some answers to her questions in the expanse of all that they didn't understand. The unknown was incredible, and maybe, just maybe, if she ran far enough, stretched long enough, jumped high enough, she would reach her goals, reach the stars. But until that moment, she was going to fill out this worksheet, and admire the stars from afar.

6

Patterns

To say that the upperclassmen software development team were jerks would be an understatement. That was Henry's view at least. The older students were cocky, even in the way they passed out papers and walked. They seemed to mock him with their eyes. He sighed, digging a screwdriver into the computer he was taking apart. It was a shame. He used to look up to them, back when he first thought about coming to the school.

Henry pulled out the insides of the computer. It was kind of strange that this was science. The art of discovery, making, and breaking. He used a reciprocating saw to cut the motherboard in half, sending sparks jumping across the table. It needed a new one anyway. He continued to gut the computer until all that was left was its metal cage.

Henry began to sort the parts—wires, boards, ports, chips. He stopped and frowned. Near the bottom of the computer was a small chip. It didn't look like anything he had ever seen before. He felt as if this chip wasn't supposed to be there. Of course, it could be because he didn't have enough experience with this type of computer. He slipped it into his pocket.

No need to get made fun of because he didn't know what it was. If anyone would know, it would be Astra or Zola. He made a mental note to get a hold of whichever one he saw first.

The rest of the class went smoothly, Henry disassembled and reassembled so many computer parts that his fingers had started to go numb. He didn't mind, however. He dug his nails underneath a small metal disk and popped it off. Rules, and computers, were meant to be broken. If you can't see inside of something, do you even know it? And how does one learn without doing it themselves?

He noted random things about the processor and the cooling system. If he was going to make a computer, it would be the best computer the world had ever seen. It was a bit hard to pay attention in class, it seemed everything was going just a little too fast. Despite that, and the language barrier, he knew that with time he'd get used to it. He'd check the pre-recorded lectures that night, just to make sure he didn't miss anything.

Around lunch time, Henry spotted Astra and pulled her aside. For some reason, she and Zola were much better with computers than he was. They had earned his respect rather quickly. Henry pulled the chip out of his pocket and showed it to Astra. "Have you ever seen anything like this?" he asked?

Astra plucked the chip from Henry's palm. "It looks familiar. I'll have to research it."

Henry nodded. "I didn't recognize it. Keep it. You don't have to return it, but I'd like to know what it is when you find out."

Astra nodded. "I'll let you know."

Henry disappeared into the cafeteria, while Astra just stood outside, staring at the small chip in her hand. She shivered slightly, though there wasn't any reason to. Then she pocketed it and went about her day. However, the chip preoccupied her thoughts. Somehow, she knew something was terribly wrong. Astra was good at keeping secrets, she was good at being silent, but the chip in her pocket made her feel something she hadn't in a long time. Fear.

Astra went to her major class in silence, wrote her code in silence, ignoring the other people around her. It wasn't like she wasn't smart enough to be here, but they thought so. She did fake it after all. She pretended like she wasn't meant to be there. They believed it. She sighed, and ran the code again, despite the knowledge that it would fail. It was built to fail, like everything else she had created here. Failure wasn't something to be afraid of, was it?

Her professor just shook his head when he looked over Astra's shoulder to see her progress. She knew he was disappointed in her;

she had shown a lot of promise at the beginning. As he walked away, Astra smiled. Her game had only just begun. Astra's last class was data analysis, and that was something she was incredibly good at. Data was logical, something that could be worked through. Something that laid itself out in patterns, complicated patterns, but patterns all the same.

Patterns were easy to read, code was easy to manipulate, and so were people. In that sense, humans were no better than machines. All things can be manipulated if you say the right things. It doesn't matter if you are human, or machine, you give it away in the way you act, how you talk, how you walk, those are patterns. Patterns that can be memorized, exploited, and erased.

Everyone in the school had a pattern. Everyone in the school had a goal, a mission of some kind. No one really trusted each other, except for the small alliances between the desperate. Of course, that meant everyone had a weakness. She just had to figure them out.

Later that night, Astra sat on her bed. Her computer was open, running one of the few codes she wrote that actually worked. Her notebook was open, filled with notes, data, and the chip Henry had found. Next to it, a similar chip lay. Astra knew what it was, but what could she do about it? Nothing. Nothing but wait. She sighed, tucking Henry's chip into a bag full of the same chips, then burying it at the bottom of her bag.

Technology? That was no challenge for Astra, she knew it inside and out. Computers? Data? She had learned them quickly. She could recognize those types of patterns in her sleep. The thing that was really a challenge was the overwhelming realization that she had been outsmarted once again. And she didn't like that.

Astra sketched the outline of the chip Henry gave her and noted its properties. She had found a second one earlier that day, of the same build, though slightly larger. She was more accustomed to these. She guessed that whatever Henry had found was a model, built to be more efficient. Easier to hide, or plant if need be.

It wasn't much, but those chips were proof. Evidence. Data. Just another number on the page. Another mistake to add to her report. She couldn't afford more mistakes. Astra sighed. It was best to ignore it for now. It was best if no one found out, it was better to know but not be known, right? Her bag moved slightly, and she slapped it, trapping the scrambling thing underneath the palm of her hand. Astra was ready. She knew how to hide in plain sight, and she could put on a show better than anyone.

7

Friendships Formed in Isolation

Alyssa crunched on her chips. Next to her, Mary had her nose stuck in her notebook, frantically scribbling down random notes next to her sketches. Two seats down, Katya was creating an entirely new star map while Nasra recited the properties of poison ivy underneath her breath.

It was always like this in Literature, with only Henry and Aiken actively paying attention. The past month at the school made them attentive, helped them hone their skills, and above all, made them rely on each other. They were an odd group. They came in together, but it was like everyone expected them to isolate themselves like the rest.

If anything, that was what fueled the need to stick together. Even though they didn't fully trust each other, the shared notes, food left on desks, water bottles stuck in backpacks, and smiles from across rooms were enough. Friendly, but not quite friends.

Aiken held his breath. He felt jittery. It was normal for him to be apprehensive, but the environment always made him feel like he had to be on high alert. He had almost grown comfortable with others, yet there was always the fear of betrayal. Though, as he watched them, they didn't seem very dangerous.

Elena messed with gears underneath her desk, Zola completely lost in thought next to her. Katya switched back and forth between her map and her notes, trying to take in everything at once. Nasra didn't even bother to hide the fact that she wasn't paying attention. Astra tapped away on her computer, creating yet another useless code.

One thing that Aiken knew was that Astra had almost perfect grades in her major class. It confused her teachers. She followed the instructions to the letter for projects, but on her own, code never seemed to obey her. Aiken admired her dedication. He knew Henry did too. They had discussed the girl outside of class one day, when Henry moped around after she beat him in an in-class exercise.

Henry thought Astra's codes were amazing, as he saw the ones that Astra never showed the teachers. Henry often wondered why Astra never displayed that talent in class, but he didn't ask. It was her choice to fail if she wanted. He told her that, and she had ignored him. Henry smiled to himself.

The teacher continued to talk, and Henry's eyes drifted around the room. He hissed at Alyssa, telling her to stop eating in class. The girl begrudgingly put her snack away, annoyed at being caught. He didn't really want to deal with this anymore, but he did anyway. Soon, class was over. Henry met Aiken's eyes as the boy left the class.

Henry flagged him down. "Hey."

"What?"

"I know you've got to go, but some of us are going to be in the study rooms later, around three p.m., come if you want, or don't, but we'll have snacks."

Aiken nodded. "I'll see what I can do."

Aiken watched Henry leave before heading in the direction of his next class. He took a seat near the back and opened his notes. He had drawn a set of Punnett squares, as well as several species of plants that he had cross-referenced.

A whole new plant. Growing it would be hard, but the results? Astounding. As it turned out, Environmental Science was a good choice of an extra class. As his classmates began to file in, Aiken mapped out the seeds he'd need to make this. The wheels in his head were already turning.

Elena shaded in the edges of her sketch. Machinery wasn't anything new to her, but she found herself becoming confused over what she wanted to make. What would make the world a better place? What sort of technological advancement would make life easier?

She'd need a lot more than just heavy machinery, games, or high-speed computers to impress Dean Parkes and the rest of the school board. She looked down at her paper again. *'Would this be enough?'*

Katya gently lifted the glass out of the telescope. She nestled it in the box beside her, replacing it with a thicker lens. The telescope itself was being completely remade. She felt a bit bad for stealing it, but her classmate shouldn't have left it in class, should they?

She lifted it onto its stand, tightening it, so it was perfectly bolted in place. She glanced down at the star map on her desk. Katya was confident that her calculations were correct. Aliens were a childhood love that spilled into her adult life. Katya adjusted the settings on the telescope, moving it ever so slightly. She looked into the lens, changing the settings and zooming in. She knew she was right. There wasn't any other way.

* * * * * * * * *

Henry looked down at the pieces on the table. Chips were scattered across the surface, wires stuck out randomly from the command block he was building. Next to him, Mary was working on her blueprints, shoulders tense as she shaded in the sides of a building on the sheet. Alyssa sat across from the two, a chart of the Periodic Table in one hand, a list of medicine in the other. She frowned and silently wrote down the ideas that she had.

Mary sighed, laying down her pencil. "Don't you think something around here is off? Like, I get the feeling of being watched. I think that's normal when you're in a place like this, but for some reason everything is just wrong."

Henry nodded. "It is a little too uptight, too weird to be normal. Then again, this isn't a normal school."

"We shouldn't talk about this." Alyssa looked down. "Anything we say could get us in trouble."

Henry scoffed. "I wonder why that is."

"You know why." Alyssa refused to meet his eyes.

"What do you mean, *'I know why?'* I don't know why, don't be cryptic."

Alyssa sighed. "Torsion University earned its place through manipulation. They twisted the system, and it's one of the top schools in the world, simply because the board of directors never took no for an answer. Don't you think it's just the slightest bit strange that they chose our classes for us?"

"I mean, yeah."

"And what about the fact that it's a cut-throat, don't trust anyone, if your work is stolen that's your own fault environment?"

"Maybe they want to prepare us for what goes on in the rest of the scientific community," Henry said. "Stolen work is common in the real world, just look at history."

Mary shook her head. "No, no, Alyssa's right."

"Of course, you would agree with her."

"I'm not saying this just because she's my best friend. I'm saying this because I know you agree. This isn't a normal environment. You're right, it is too uptight, and kind of scary."

"It's not like they're going to get rid of us if we do something they don't agree with," Henry said.

"You don't know that," Alyssa retorted.

Henry raised an eyebrow. "Seriously? You think that a teacher, or like, the dean would kill someone?"

"I'm not accusing them of anything, I'm just saying, it's possible."

"You're reading into this too much. It's one of the most acclaimed schools in the country."

"And they are in some kind of alliance with the other ones," Alyssa said.

Henry frowned. "How do you know that?"

"Because I did my research."

"Wha—hey! So did I!"

"Did you dig deep enough though?" Alyssa looked at him, determination in her eyes. "The minute we got here I knew something was wrong. I've been doing my best to figure it out, and guess what? Did you know that the college doesn't compensate families if their kid dies in a lab accident? That the graduation rate here is one of the lowest in the world? Sometimes they make students sign NDAs for certain classes or projects."

"Really?"

"Yeah, for an acclaimed college, they really aren't doing well. They've got drop-outs all the time."

"Woah, wait a second," Mary cut in. "Can we go back? The college won't what?"

"Compensate our families if we die. It's in the application. Did any of you read the fine print?"

Mary looked down. "No…"

"Mary, I expected better from you!"

"I did the application with you! I thought you would have told me if something was weird."

Alyssa rolled her eyes. "It doesn't matter. The point is, something about all this makes my skin crawl, and I can't put my finger on it yet. But if any of you ends up hurt, I will laugh and say I told you so."

Henry started sorting his computer chips. "Well, let's just not get hurt."

"Easier said than done," Alyssa said bitterly.

Henry sighed. "Just"—he paused—"do your work and try not to get in trouble."

"Again, easier said than done."

"What do you want us to do then?" Henry questioned.

Alyssa shrugged. "I want to find some answers, but honestly, I don't think that's happening any time soon."

"Yeah." Henry chucked a motherboard in his backpack. "But

hey, lighten up. Have a little patience. It's not like we're going to straight-up drop dead any time soon."

Alyssa pursed her lips. "Hmm, I guess you're right." She pointed her pen at Henry. "But no funny business. If we go down, we go down together."

"That's fine by me." He tossed her a bag of chips and raised his water bottle in the air. "To not dying and actually passing classes."

Mary laughed. "Cheers."

8

Discovery

Elena tapped her fingers on her leg. The rhythm was calming for the girl, whose stress levels hit the ceiling about ten minutes ago. Being caught by a hall monitor was not something she wanted to deal with. She had been in the lab after curfew. It wasn't like she would get in too much trouble if she had been noticed, given that the after-hours staff were easily bribed, but she didn't want to risk it.

Once Elena was sure the monitor was gone, she crept out from underneath the table. She grabbed the miniature flashlight she had kicked underneath one of the desks in her hurry to hide. She was only missing a few parts for her blueprints, but each one was essential to the process of building. Elena narrowed her eyes. She wondered if she could get Henry to pull parts from the computer lab for her.

Then she sighed, head falling into her hands. *'Henry is a goody-two-shoes, there's no way he'll steal parts for me. But Astra might.'*

Elena hurried into the hall, blueprints in hand. She had to get two floors up to return to her dorm. The only problem was that Katya might still be awake. The girl was a night owl who spent her time watching the stars.

She hoped Katya would not notice her coming back into the door. Of course, it looked like that wasn't going to happen.

"Where were you?"

Elena stared at her. "Where were you?"

They were at a standstill, facing each other in the hallway outside their dorm.

Katya opened and closed her mouth. Finally, she rolled her eyes and opened the door. "Just go inside."

Elena entered the room and turned around. "That doesn't answer my question."

"Fine." Katya flopped down on the floor. "I was outside."

"You can see the stars from the window, you know."

"It's not the same. Besides, you never said what you were do-ing."

"I was in the lab."

"Doing what?"

"Working on school, what do you think?"

The lights turned on. "I think the both of you shouldn't have gone out."

Elena froze and turned around to see Nasra, standing there in her pajamas, glaring at them.

Katya winced. "Sorry, Nasra."

"Saying sorry wouldn't do you any good if any of the teach-ers saw you. Why can't you just follow the curfew and wait until morning?" It wasn't the first time Nasra watched them leave. She had only started caring when it became a nightly occurrence. Ev-ery time she'd watch them leave and return, waking her up in the process, and she had had enough. "You can't just leave whenever you want, there are rules you know."

The two girls nodded, muttering apologies. The two got ready for bed in silence, avoiding Nasra's gaze. As Elena drifted off, she thought about how she was going to talk to Astra. She wondered and feared what the girl would say to Elena's request.

"You want me to do what?"

Elena flinched. "I know it sounds bad, but I need them."

"I'm not going to question why you need them. Couldn't you just ask a teacher?"

"I was kinda not gonna let them know."

Astra raised an eyebrow then shrugged. "Alright."

"What?"

Astra reached over and patted Elena on the shoulder. "I'm not gonna question you El, we all have our secrets." Elena nodded.

Astra continued, "Getting these might take a bit, so, when I do get them, good luck with whatever you're doing." Astra took off down the hall, leaving Elena to contemplate what she had just done.

* * * * * * * * *

Alyssa and Mary left their dorm, heading towards one of the open study rooms. The girls had decided to work together, which wasn't uncommon for them, and what better place than a study room?

Normally, the two girl's majors wouldn't collide, but today they would be combining them. Or so they hoped. Mary spread her blueprints across the table, noting key elements, such as the doors, locks, and overhead lights.

Alyssa carefully wrote down the materials that Mary rattled off, she would try each one to make sure they wouldn't rust or melt with her project.

They were so caught up focusing on their work, they didn't hear the pounding footsteps in the hall next to them. The door swung open with a bang, causing the girls to look up, startled.

A boy stood there confused, then left, or tried to. A girl, one that the two recognized as Nicole, threw him back in.

"You can't just leave without apologizing for interrupting!"

The boy nodded. "I'm sorry ladies." He smiled awkwardly at them. His smile dropped when he heard a yell of his name out in the hall.

"Castor!"

Mary leaned back from the table to try to see around him. She spotted a boy dressed in all black behind the door. Castor waved at them then ran out. Nicole followed, closing the door behind her, but not before she gave them an apology of her own. Their voices faded as they walked away, and Mary turned back to her work. She met Alyssa's eyes and the two dissolved into giggles.

Alyssa sighed. "Ahh, that was funny."

Mary nodded. "It was. We should get back to work though. I'm sure the others are doing exactly what we're doing right now. Motivation! We have to get this done."

Alyssa rolled her eyes. "Really?"

"Really."

"What about breaks?"

"No breaks!"

"Come on, you don't seriously think that we're going to fall behind, do you? It's not like everyone is almost done with their projects or anything."

"They could be."

Alyssa scoffed. "Whatever. You can be the overachiever. I don't think I'm the only one struggling right now."

Alyssa was right. Across the school, in one of the science labs, Nasra was staring down at her notebook. Her brain was useless. She groaned, leaning back in her seat. Biology seemed like an easy thing to her in school, but how could she ever measure up here? Life had always fascinated her. Scared her sometimes, but the curiosity won out in the end. She spent many hours trying to discover the many intricacies of life and how the mind worked.

The problem was that life was already uncovered here. Nothing she could figure out would not already be known by the higher-level students. Nothing impressed them. Nasra facepalmed. She must have made a terrible mistake. Nasra glanced down at her notes. The human nervous system was mapped out across one of the pages.

Nasra only had one idea. She didn't know if she could do anything about it, or if she could actually use it, but she wanted to. It would be hard, but with the right tools, maybe, just maybe, her research would get her somewhere. Nasra started adding to her notes. She was no doctor, but the bioengineering students were nice enough, and they would probably let her look into their lab.

According to Alyssa, they grew humans, ones that had never breathed, and never lived. But if there was one thing that Nasra was, it was curious. Humans were interesting. They had to have brains, thoughts, to be considered alive. What if she could get one of the bioengineering corpses to live? It would be almost impossible, but Nasra was up to the challenge. If anything, the least that her research would do is give the scientific community a new understanding of the nervous system. Nasra flipped to the next page in her notebook and began to formulate a plan.

In one of the nearby computer labs, Zola turned the lights on. The computer lab was available until curfew, so she had to start working now. She couldn't risk getting caught by Astra again when she tried to leave the room. That had happened a few nights ago, and Zola could have sworn that Astra must have read her mind.

Zola turned one of the computers on. That was one thing she and Astra agreed on, the fact that computers were all networked together. They were like a hive mind, reacting the same way to the same commands, using the same basic code. However, they were also different. They didn't automatically share information. That was something you had to figure out how to do on your own.

Zola intended on doing that. Her professor had thought so highly of himself the day that he had edited all their programs to work together. How humble and embarrassed he would be when he found out what she had done. She entered the parameters, entering the variables from the page she had brought with her. The base code would settle into the network, even if she was unable to activate it now, it would stay there.

She had to work fast. If curfew came before she finished, the computer would recognize the code as a virus, because technically, it was. Zola would be kicked out of school for it. If she managed to get it in just a few seconds before curfew, the code would bury itself so that the security scan wouldn't recognize it. Zola's heart beat faster as she watched the download tick ever closer to a hundred percent.

The screen blinked momentarily, showing the download complete screen for a second before it disappeared. Zola smiled. It had worked. She clicked open the file on the desktop, just to make sure that it didn't show up there.

She scanned the whole computer, double checking that the file was safely stored away. That's when she saw it. A Word file. There was nothing really special about it, except it had no name. Not even *'Untitled Document.'* Zola narrowed her eyes. That wasn't a normal document. Without thinking, she clicked it. A small black screen opened, green text running across its surface.

'Are you sure you want to run this program?'

"Yes," she whispered. Just before she clicked enter, the computer shut off. "No, no, no, come on!" she yelled.

The speaker on the wall whined before turning on. "All students have five minutes to get back to their dorms before curfew."

Zola glared. She hated the PA system. Whoever was in charge of announcements was extremely annoying. She huffed, slamming the door as she left the room. Whatever was in that file, she would figure it out. Even if it was nothing. Because it couldn't be a coincidence. Someone had put it there, on a school computer, hidden in plain sight. Whatever it was, Zola wanted to know, and she would do whatever it took to find out.

Ditching

Katya wasn't one for fights or arguments, but this time she had had enough. She had dumped water on the head of a pretentious upperclassman, which had gotten her removed from class for the day. She was currently sitting out on the school grounds, sun washing over her as she sketched more of the new telescope she was planning on building.

"Hey, are you okay?"

Katya jumped. She turned to see Astra sit next to her. "I'm fine. What are you doing? I thought class doesn't get out for an hour?"

Astra sighed. "Thanks to the three stooges, I got kicked out of class. I should say the same for you though, you're here, same as I am. What are you doing?"

"Kicked out for dumping water on an upperclassman."

"Ah yes, you go girl!"

Katya smiled and looked down. "It isn't that good."

"Yes, it is! You're finally standing up for yourself. The world is a cruel place, and being soft is not the same as being weak. Don't forget that."

"I guess."

"Guessing is reserved for a hypothesis. That is not a guess, it is a fact. A law of nature, if you will. What doesn't kill you will try again. Toughen up Katya, but don't lose your kindness."

Katya raised an eyebrow. "I never knew you were so wise."

"I wouldn't say that about myself, just that I learned how to survive."

"Didn't we all?"

Astra sighed. "Sometimes, childishness is forced out of us. People are trained to fight, kids are made into weapons, whether for good or for evil is up to their superiors to decide. Often, it's hard to tell which is which. Cruel leaders made cruel followers."

"That's… dark."

"There are a lot of dark things in this world. It's like you decided to switch off the lights one day and never figured out how to turn them back on."

Katya shrugged. "I guess that's why I like the stars then. Darkness. Easier to hide."

Astra shook her head. "No. You like the stars because they're the closest light source you have in your life. If anything, you hate the idea of being alone, because you think you won't be if you get to reach them, right? It's hard to really love darkness. As for those who do, well, nothing good ever comes of it." Astra stood up. "Now, if you'd excuse me, Eric Huang's face has a date with my fist."

Katya laughed, pulled out of the scene that Astra had helped her envision. "Good luck!"

Astra smiled and ran inside, leaving Katya to her thoughts. Katya sat there in silence for a while, before turning back to her work. She looked down at her unfinished sketch. Katya picked up her pencil and began scribbling with a newfound fervor. There was a new, or rather, refined sort of longing for what was ahead. She hoped it wouldn't take long to get there.

* * * * * * * * *

Unlike the other two, Zola purposely skipped her noon class. The computer lab wouldn't be in use until later that afternoon, but she still had to be quick if she wanted to get in. Zola's curiosity almost always got the best of her. It was one of her flaws, the fact that she had to know everything. That, and of course, her general fearlessness. Though, she didn't like jumping spiders or piranhas.

She wouldn't say that she was curious to the point of being idiotic, she knew her limits, but the unknown scared her more than anything. She just had to find out. The thought of being helpless without knowledge almost paralyzed her.

So, she went to find some answers. Zola wasn't surprised that the door was locked. Obviously, someone was hiding something, though it also could be because the third-year Chemistry students tried to steal the computers last week to spite the Communications majors.

She hacked the lock hurriedly. This was her only option at the moment. Zola knew that if she got caught, especially if it was something important, she could get kicked out of school. Of course, it wasn't like she hadn't tried to access the computer a different way before choosing to break into the lab. Unfortunately, the app acted like it was built into the computer, making it locked to the mainframe. She couldn't access it remotely.

She had been so angry when the program persevered, almost jeering at her as she tried not to scream. Zola hadn't wanted to leave her dorm right away. But the questions had begun to gnaw away at her mind. She sighed. Her curiosity was going to be the death of her someday.

There was a soft beep, and the keypad lit up green. Zola rushed inside, closing the door slowly and silently behind her. She stopped and caught her breath, trying to calm her racing heart. Then she ran to the computer, turning it on, waiting anxiously for it to load.

To her surprise, the program was still there. Internally she expected it to be gone. So, as anyone else would do, she ran it. She half expected an alarm to go off. The computer whirred and beeped, before a string of numbers streamed across the screen.

The monitor turned black, then turned back on, revealing a white open tab with coordinates on it. Zola frowned. She hadn't known what to expect, but she knew that she wasn't expecting that. She took out her phone all the same, and snapped a photo of it, shut the computer off, and cleaned her fingerprints off the desk and monitor. Then, she left the lab, making sure to lock the door. She smirked to herself as she ran down the hall. Whatever this was, wherever it was, she would find it.

* * * * * * * * *

Nasra sighed. Her sketches seemed almost perfect, but to bring her vision into reality would be a little tricky. The human nervous system was something that she knew well. If she could tap into it, which she knew she could, she could intercept commands from the brain and rewrite them. Of course, she just needed a program to do that. But that meant she'd have to teach herself to code, something she wasn't entirely sure she could do on her own.

She stared at the wall, resisting the urge to fall asleep. A person has all the inherent energy they need to be stronger and faster than what people think of humanity as a whole. That was one law of the body she had never forgotten. *'You have enough strength in your jaw to bite off all of your fingers if you want, but the brain has barriers in place to make sure you don't.'*

Adrenaline made people do superhuman things when in all reality, anyone could do it. She could use that knowledge to her own advantage. Nasra was no stranger to the sinister side of science; she spent months in her dark bedroom by herself piecing together spare ideas and experimenting on herself.

Like the others, she was curious, but her curiosity just so happened to lead to a pretty painful place. The scars on her arms were a testament to that, small squares filled with even tinier holes. Adrenaline patches. Unfortunately, they weren't as successful as she hoped.

Nasra knew that one way or another, whether it be by essay or a prototype of her own design, her research, if proven to be true, would be a major discovery. The only problem was keeping it from falling into the wrong hands. The government had a nasty habit of taking things that didn't belong to them. Luckily, she had enough time to create a backup plan, just in case. She glanced over at the mess of things she had managed to get from the bioengineering students. Time to get to work.

* * * * * * * * *

Mary sprinted down the hallway. Alyssa was waiting for her in one of the study rooms, and she left all her blueprints in their dorm room. She rounded a corner and crashed into Henry, causing them both to fall down.

"You okay?"

Mary nodded.

Henry chuckled. "Stop running the halls and you'll be safer. Good luck kid!"

Mary smiled and waved, turning and speed walking towards their dorm. She collected her papers and headed to the library. As she got closer to the room that Alyssa was in, she spotted Astra sitting on the floor tinkering with some wires.

"Hi, Astra!"

She looked up. "Hello Mary," she said softly.

"What are you doing?"

"Trying to figure out this." She held up the tangled mess of wires. "It belongs to the motherboard of one of my latest failures, the least I can do is try to fix it."

"Well, I mean, every failure is a learning experience, am I right or am I right?"

"You're right. I'm just a little frustrated."

"Hey! You'll figure it out. I mean, everyone has one class that they struggle with."

Astra raised an eyebrow.

"Oh, Henry told me. Said that you weren't doing well with stand-alone coding projects," Mary said.

"I've been practicing." Astra turned back to her mess of wires. "It won't be long before I can do it better, without help."

Mary laughed. "That's the spirit! Good luck with your project."

"You too, on whatever it is you're doing. Also, don't run in the halls! Henry told me that you almost fell flat on your face, what were you thinking?"

Mary snorted. "It's fine. I'll try not to run too fast anymore. Bye!" She sprinted out the door.

Astra sighed. "Great."

* * * * * * * * *

Meanwhile, Elena was starting to bring her inventions into reality. She had started by building a base for the machine, then built parts that would fill it. But it was hard, and it was time-consuming, and she wanted it to go faster. She couldn't rush. She had to take it slow, or it wouldn't work. It might even explode.

She snickered at the thought. It would be kind of funny to take out a part of the building, but that not-so-fun part would be the re-building of her already fragile machine. That's what she got for handling plutonium. A super-charged battery yes, but it had the potential to be a nuclear bomb.

It was a good call on her part to put it in only after she had finished the tests. Micro-radiation was not guaranteed to work, but she thought she might as well give it a chance. Well, try building a super battery smaller than AAA. Elena was going to lose her mind.

It wasn't a terrible idea, volatile though the batteries might seem. She'd have to build a bigger version first, then scale it down, that was, if it worked. She grabbed a screwdriver and started attaching another plate to the bottom of the frame.

Elena huffed. She grabbed her notebook and added changes to her design. It had to be perfect. Well, as perfect as perfect could be. Here, there was no room for failure. Especially not with a tiny battery that could be a bomb. She threw a microwave on the table and started dismantling it. Her work had just begun, she just hoped she could finish it in time.

* * * * * * * * *

Aiken was having about as much luck with his work as Elena was. He had grafted the seeds together, but he wasn't even sure if it would grow. To say that it was a weird combination would be an understatement. The plant he was trying to create was filled with antibodies. Technically speaking, it was a medicine in plant form. Synthetic, and yet perfectly safe. Far safer than radiation.

Radiation. From x-rays to helping treat cancer, the toxic energy came in many forms. All he wanted to do was find a replacement, or maybe ease the side effects. There weren't many choices though. He was taking a risk, tackling such a severe problem, something that he knew the rest of the group wouldn't even think about trying to solve.

He knew of thousands of plants that could poison you in an instant, no known cures, just a painful death. So why couldn't there be plants that could heal you? He was sure that at the very least, a plant could make the effects a little less deadly. Unfortunately, plants take forever to grow, and he didn't have that kind of time. So, he found a solution.

In his mind, the only way to know if what he made would work was to make a serum that would make it grow faster. He spent several weeks perfecting it on random flowers and vegetables. Today, he would try it on his plant. He tipped the vial carefully over the pot, watching as the liquid spilled lazily over the dirt. Now all he had to do was wait.

10

Perfect

Aiken's serum worked. His plant grew to full size overnight. It was perfect, exactly the way that he had envisioned it. Aiken didn't want to leave it in the lab, so he moved it to his dorm, placing it safely on the windowsill. He even put a small dome over it, holes poked into the sides to let oxygen in, and a note with a threat to Henry that if he ever touched the thing, Aiken would stab him with a fork.

Speaking of Henry, Aiken heard him yell his name, so he left the room trusting that his plant would stay safe until his return. Aiken followed Henry down the hall, something about Nasra calling a meeting in one of the smaller study rooms. The two practically ran, a bit worried about what would get Nasra so frazzled that she wanted to talk to them. Well, all of them.

It was a bit unusual. When they weren't eating meals together, or gathering in their designated alliances, they simply ignored each other. Whether it was to keep from calling attention to themselves, or simply due to dislike and maybe even miscommunication, Aiken didn't know. All he knew was that when Nasra called you, you came running.

Astra and Zola were already in the room when they entered, whispering angrily over something that the two didn't catch, quieting as soon as they stepped in. Mary, Alyssa, and Elena arrived soon after, and Nasra closed the door, locking it behind them. Nasra marched to the head of the table and sat down, folding her hands and looking at the group sternly.

"We have a problem." She pulled out a computer, turning it on and facing it towards the girls. "Someone is spreading rumors about us, saying we're a problem. Saying that we're going to steal other people's projects, or that we're bullies, so on and so forth."

Astra hummed. "So that's why the senior girls were glaring at me today. Either that or because I put spiders in their purses for making fun of me." She tapped the side of her bag.

Aiken shuddered. He wouldn't like to get on Astra's bad side.

Elena frowned. "This is a little soon, don't you think? I mean, we have barely been here a few months, what makes them want to hate us?"

"We're new, that's the problem. Easy targets. As soon as other new students arrive, we'll fade into the background," Henry said. "Though, I do not like being accused of bullying, that is a bit new."

Nasra rolled her eyes. "Hush. That's not the point. The point is, we have to stick together now until this all settles down. That means no more fighting." She looked pointedly at Astra and Zola. "What even were you two arguing about?"

"Nothing," they chorused innocently.

Henry raised an eyebrow. "Obviously it was something. Considering you two seem to have become pretty close friends."

Zola scoffed. "No! That's not it either. We were—" she paused. "Discussing computers in a debate-like manner."

Astra rolled her eyes. "If *'debate-like'* means insulting my codes then yes, it was debate-like."

"That's because your codes are trash."

"I already know my codes are trash, you don't have to bring that to the public eye."

"If you knew your codes were trash, then why did you come here? I don't think you deserve to be in this scho—"

"Enough!" Elena stood up. "Nasra is right, we need to get along. Which is a bit hard for me to say honestly, but it's true. The only way we'll ever survive the rest of this school year is by working together. So, are we all friends here?"

Henry nodded. "I'm like, 30 percent sure you all are my children, but yes. Friends."

Mary looked up and nodded firmly. "Alyssa and I will be honored to be friends with you all."

"Who said you could speak for me?"

"I did, I'm older."

Alyssa sighed. "Okay and?"

Mary rolled her eyes.

Nasra laughed. "That's settled then."

"I didn't agree," Zola said.

"No one cares, Zola, we know you like us."

"Astra, I will whack you with this notebook."

"Astra, Zola, finish your argument outside please," Nasra said.

Astra rolled her eyes and stood up. "Fine." She left the room without a second glance, Zola on her heels.

Nasra sighed. "Alright, so now what?"

* * * * * * * * *

"Why would you do that?" Astra asked.

"Do what?"

"Argue with me in front of everyone."

"Because. Just like you, I don't need people knowing that I actually like them." Zola smiled.

"Softie."

"Disrespect me one more time—"

"Hey, wait up!" A familiar voice called out to them from behind.

The two stopped and turned around to see Morgan and Castor running towards them. They came to a stop, catching their breath as they did so.

"How are ya doing?" Morgan grinned. "Haven't seen you in a while." Morgan nudged Astra. "How are all the techies treating you?"

Zola rolled her eyes. "Shouldn't you be with all the other people who are complaining about us causing trouble instead of being here annoying Astra?"

"Nope!" Castor giggled, running ahead of them and turning

around to skip backward. "We've caused a whole bunch of trouble in our days. We know you guys aren't half bad, cause we had that exact problem when we started out. They like starting rumors, it weeds people out. Which, by the way, I know you already met Cassian, Nicole, and Eric, but do you want to meet the rest of our group?"

Astra shrugged and looked at Zola.

"Sure," Zola said.

Castor smiled. "Great! Let's go!"

They followed Castor and Morgan down the hall, curious to meet their friends. The two seemed to know the building well, leading them through several passageways and secret stairwells.

Morgan chattered as they went along. "The school was built over a mess of tunnels, there are tons of hidden rooms and passageways everywhere. We managed to find one that we liked and have been hanging out there ever since. Here we are."

It was a small dusty room, with a single, circular window that allowed light to pour in. The walls were made of bricks, grey, though, they could have been black before. Astra drug her finger along the wall, leaving lines in the dust. She sneezed.

"Hey guys!" Castor yelled to get the attention of the seven people sitting on a carpet in the corner of the room. Zola recognized Cassian, Nicole, and Eric, as well as the boy who had glared at them when the group ate outside.

Zola was glad for Astra's presence at that moment, otherwise, she might have jumped at the boy and tried to rip off his head. They sat down and Morgan and Castor introduced them.

"Guys, this is Astra and Zola. Girls, this is David, Willow, William, and Isaac, you already met Cassian, Nicole, and Eric." The boys nodded at their names, and Zola felt cold as they stared at her. She shivered.

Astra smiled primly, trying to ignore her own unease. "So. What do you guys do?"

William, the one wearing all black, spoke up first, surprising Astra with his cheery manner. "Well, I do accounting, Willow and Eric do engineering—"

Morgan cut him off. "So do I!"

"Yeah, but you do chemical engineering, and Isaac does computer engineering."

Astra smiled. "So do we."

Isaac nodded but didn't say anything.

Nicole laughed awkwardly, trying to diffuse the tension. "David and I do physics, but his is a more focused major than mine."

David grinned. "Molecular physics."

Astra scoffed. "That's insane, it's so difficult! How do you manage?"

David shrugged. "Dunno, I just think it's fun."

Cassian raised his hand. "I do chemistry."

Astra smiled. "Awesome, do you like it?

Cassian nodded. "It can get annoying sometimes, but I never get tired of it."

"It can be hard, too," Astra said.

Castor pouted. "You're making me feel left out dude, all I do is environmental engineering."

Zola raised an eyebrow. "That's still important. Our friend Aiken does Earth Science, you two would get along. I mean, plants are essential to survival. Most of our oxygen comes from them."

Castor nodded. "I guess you're right."

Astra slapped Zola on the back. "She usually is."

"Besides," Zola picked at her nails. "I think you'd get along with Aiken very well. He really loves his plants."

Astra quieted down and let Zola do most of the talking. She let her thoughts wander, taking a break from the usual assessment she did for all the other students. She felt wrong, like something, or someone, was not what they said they were. As the others and Zola got more comfortable talking, she zoned back in and memorized the information they were sharing. She knew they were hiding something. Soon, they had to slip up. Nothing was this perfect.

11

Put on a Show

Astra knew a lot of things. She knew she was hiding in plain sight, spending every moment tense, worried that someone would find her out. She knew she could trust her new-found friends, at least a little bit. She knew the school was hiding things, some of which she was aware of, others she wasn't, though they wouldn't be too hard to figure out. She just never anticipated that the school was hiding this.

The day started normally, as one would expect. The same classes, same chatter from the others, same droning and disappointed looks from her professors, who knew nothing, not like she did. She was smarter than them, playing dumb, playing prey in a school full of predators. She couldn't wait to watch them fall apart. Today, however, it was her turn to be caught off guard.

It happened at lunch. Henry and Nasra were walking ahead. Mary and Alyssa trailed behind the group, chattering about whatever it was the two liked to talk about. Eric and Willow came over to them to talk to the others, smiling and waving, giggling with them, joking around.

Astra began to relax, letting her guard down around her friends. William came not long after, dragging Isaac and Morgan behind him. Isaac walked lost in thought, Astra wondered if he was okay. She could tell he didn't seem to be all like the others. Morgan passed out candy that she had snuck out of one of the calculus professor's offices.

Then she heard it. A shrill, high-pitched, familiar, female voice. "Isaac, come on, you said you would help me with homework." And Astra froze.

The girl introduced herself as Delilah Hayes, all smiles and sweetness, carrying herself in a poised but down-to-earth manner.

Astra didn't believe a word she said. Then, Delilah and Isaac disappeared, leaving Astra hurriedly trying to piece together her old shattered theory.

"You okay?" Elena's voice pierced Astra's thoughts. She smiled. Fake.

"Just peachy. Look, I have to go grab something from my dorm. I'll be right back; you guys go ahead."

Elena nodded slowly and turned back. "Right, let's go find a place to eat."

Astra watched the group leave, then scurried off. She had to work fast if only to make sure the others didn't suspect her. Or rather, the other group of students: Morgan, Cassian, Nicole, William, Willow, Isaac, Eric, Castor, David. What about them? Her theory had been way off, they knew nothing. They were safe. For now.

She arrived at her dorm out of breath, grabbing her bag as soon as she entered. Everything that she had carefully calculated was ruined. Everything she thought she knew about this school was wrong. Astra had constructed several theories. Things had been stolen from her and her family, but she didn't think they would be repurposed, not like this.

She couldn't let her friends know what she had learned. Coming to this school, taking this job was a mistake. On both the school's and her end. She stopped. *Take a deep breath Astra. You can still do this.* She sighed. She'd finish the year, figure out what was really going on at the school, and then she'd take what she needed and leave. It was still the original plan, just with a small detour. She wasn't supposed to make them crumble from the inside, but plans change, and sometimes they need to be altered.

Astra slung her bag over her shoulder and left the room. Time to do some research. Thanks to Morgan and Castor, Astra knew her way around several of the school's secret passageways. It wasn't long before she found her way to Dean Parkes' office.

She tapped on the door and pushed her ear up against it, closing her eyes and listening for any sound of a person inside. Then, she picked the lock. Astra opened the door carefully, silently swinging it shut behind her and locking it again. It was ironic, that he was smart enough to not trust students to not hack an electronic lock but failed to expect someone to actually know how to pick a lock.

Astra moved over to his desk, slipping gloves on as she went. No fingerprints. She removed her shoes, dumping them in her bag. No shoe prints either. Her socks muffled the sounds of her feet hitting the floor. Astra carefully moved the chair aside and turned on the computer.

She searched frantically for evidence of their entrance. The reasons why she and the others were chosen. As she typed, scrolling through the other candidates, she realized: It truly was a glitch. They weren't meant to be there. Especially not her.

Astra opened another folder, digging deeper, curious. There had to be a reason for the mistake. Then she found it. A small file, easy to miss. An error remnant. Whoever had hacked the computer had missed it. She clicked on it. It opened a screen with nine other applicants. The real students that were supposed to come to Torsion.

Astra heard a sound out in the hall, quickly, she closed the file, clearing the history and code of the computer so it wouldn't register that she was even there. Footsteps sounded just outside the door. Astra hesitated. *'Do you want to delete this file?'*

What good would it do them, For the others to know that they weren't good enough for the school? Astra sighed. The footsteps got louder. A key was inserted into the lock. Astra made her choice.

'File deleted.'

She shut the computer down. The door opened. Dean Parkes stepped into his office, not realizing what had just happened.

Outside, Astra pressed herself against the brick wall, barely keeping herself on the ledge outside the window. She turned around carefully and started climbing up towards the roof.

There was no turning back now. She made her decision. She had to remove suspicion from herself. There was no doubt that if she failed her midterm, she would be kicked out. Astra reached the top, throwing herself over the ledge and onto the roof.

She couldn't fail anymore. Astra picked the lock on the service door and made her way down the stairs. The others would be wondering where she was. *'Put on a show. Figure out what's going on in there, and then come home. If you can get the tech back, that's perfect, otherwise it's a job for another day. Oh, and do your best to not get caught, okay Little Star?'* Her orders were so simple, but this was putting a bit of a block in her plan.

She hurried out into the hallway, passing teachers, students, and doorways. They were all so full of secrets, weren't they? These people had no idea what was going on right underneath their noses. Astra smiled. Well, they were about to find out.

She stopped halfway down the steps to the courtyard. What if she was wrong? What if everyone knew? What if they weren't safe? What if— Astra's heart began to beat faster. She had been wrong about everything so far. What if she was wrong now?

Astra narrowed her eyes and continued down the steps. She couldn't be wrong. Not this time. Because by this point, if she failed, she wouldn't just be expelled. No, she'd finish the job. She was going to figure out what was going on underneath the surface, or she'd tear the school apart trying.

12

Clues

Zola sat on top of her bed, not feeling the fatigue that had long since sent her roommate to sleep. She stared down at the photo on her phone. What did these coordinates have to do with anything? Why were they so hidden? Who put it there? Was it important? This school was so secretive that it could be anything.

But why that one computer? And why that lab? Why this specific program, and why was it put there? Those questions clouded Zola's mind until she couldn't focus on anything else. She spent the night researching and testing theories on ways to disguise a program as another file. Suffice to say, she didn't sleep that night.

The next morning, Zola dragged. She barely got by with a C on her test, while Astra passed with flying colors. It was her code that worked while Zola's didn't. She was beginning to think that they had switched places, but she didn't think that Astra would sabotage her.

No, Astra wasn't like that. Zola frowned. Astra could have just been practicing, she wasn't the only person who saw the girl pouring over coding books in the library. At the beginning of the year, Zola wouldn't have thought that Astra was talented enough to put that kind of code in the computer. But at this point, she wasn't so sure. It could have been anyone. Still, she didn't think Astra would have put the code there because Astra wasn't at the school long enough to have put the file into the base code. But there was still a possibility. After all, like everyone else, Astra was hiding something. In fact, Zola was sure she was hiding a lot.

Astra was one of the few people that Zola knew could help her. Still, Zola wasn't quite sure she could trust her, especially not with Astra's seemingly immediate, and definitely suspicious change in skill level. Astra could probably tell her about the school and there

was no doubt that she would get the answers quicker than anyone else. But Zola would have to watch her a little longer before
she could let Astra know. Luckily, there was another person who
would know how to read the coordinates, even if it took a bit more
time.

"Well, I have good news and bad news. Well, it's not really
bad news unless you expect to go there." Katya waved the phone
around. "Good news is the coordinates are close. The bad news is,
they're somewhere inside the school, specifically, a restricted area.
Where did you get these anyway?"

Zola snatched her phone back from Katya. "That's none of
your business."

"Hmm. Suit yourself."

Zola sighed. "Sorry. It's just," she paused. "Complicated."

Katya waved her hand. "Yeah, yeah, whatever. It's okay.
You're right, it's not my business. So, don't tell me. I don't want to
get caught up in whatever scheme that you're concocting. In fact,
I'm going to pretend that this conversation never happened. Just
be careful, okay?

"Thanks. I will."

"No problem. By the way, have you seen Mary? She seems
pretty upset."

Zola frowned. "No, I haven't. What's wrong?"

"I don't really know. Apparently, she's been having some weird
dreams, at least that's what Alyssa said. But she threw away her
previous blueprints and started making something else for her de-
gree project. No one knows what it is."

Zola frowned. "Weird. Well, I'm off."

Katya nodded. Zola shivered as she walked away. First Astra
getting really good at something she was bad at, virtually overnight, and now Mary's dreams. It could just be a coincidence, but
she had a feeling that something had changed. Zola was so lost in
thought; she didn't realize where she was going until it was too

late.

"Oomph." Zola ran straight into Elena. "Sorry," Zola half-whispered, helping Elena off the ground.

Elena laughed. "It's okay, it's okay."

Zola nodded, reaching down and picking up the blueprints Elena dropped. "Still, sorry. What are you building?"

Elena grabbed the blueprints out of Zola's hand. "Nothing that's of your concern right now. You'll see it when you see it."

Zola raised her hands defensively. "Okay, sorry." She walked away and soon started thinking about the coordinates. Somewhere in the school. Somewhere in a restricted area. There was no way that it wasn't important. Someone really wanted to hide something, unless, whatever was there was put there before the area became unavailable for students.

She wanted to figure out what was going on quickly. She couldn't just sit around and wait. But that was exactly what she did that night, since she had to wait until Astra fell asleep. Unfortunately, both of them were night owls. Astra tended to read until the early hours of the morning, which left Zola burrowed underneath her covers, pretending to sleep.

Finally, Astra fell asleep around one a.m., and Zola was ready to go. She slipped out of bed quietly, tiptoeing towards the door, careful not to breathe too loudly. She was so focused on getting out of the room quickly that she didn't see Astra's eyes open as she closed the door.

Out in the hallway, Zola checked her phone, just to make sure that the coordinates were correct. Then she set off. Katya had marked a place in the middle of the school, somewhere on the lower levels. It was a random spot for sure, but perfect if you wanted to hide something. Not only were the staff not allowed in that area, but it was also supposedly under construction. Anyone on staff wouldn't bother looking down there anyway, for fear of getting hurt, or worse, getting trapped down there.

Luckily, Zola wasn't afraid of that. Or, so she told herself as she made her way downstairs. For a place with restricted access, the lock was relatively easy to pick, and the door to the lowest floors swung open into suffocating darkness.

Zola switched on her phone's flashlight and carefully descended into the darkness, trying to avoid any fallen beams or faulty floorboards. Surprisingly, it was in pretty good shape, as if whoever was supposed to be working down there finished, and no one ever said anything about it.

According to her phone, she was close to the coordinates, and Zola spun to look for anything that seemed suspicious, like boxes or a safe. She wondered if they would even go far enough as to hide weapons down here.

But when she arrived, there was no important secret, box, or treasure. It was just a grey concrete wall, dusty and cracked. And the important hidden thing wasn't behind it. It was on it. Written in some sort of red paint were the words: '*Find me at the lowest point, where no one ever goes. Use the stolen key from the Dean's office. Don't you dare get caught. —J.*'

Zola reached forward and touched the wall, tracing the words. They seemed old, but not that old, and had an odd, almost rotten smell to it. It was only then that Zola realized the paint could be blood. She pulled her hand back, frantically wiping it on her shirt. She needed to wash her hands, or at least get some hand sanitizer. Zola took a picture of the wall all the same.

Then she ran up the stairs and back through the door, making sure to lock it behind her. She took the steps up to the dorms two at a time, hundreds of possible scenarios ran through her head about those words and what they could mean.

She slipped back into her room carefully and ran to the bathroom. Zola ran her hands under the water and scrubbed them until her hands were peeling and her palms were flushed. She slid into bed and pulled her covers all the way up over her head. She just lay there for a moment, eyes closed.

Zola tucked her phone underneath her pillow and rolled towards the wall. She didn't want anyone to know what she had done. She also wanted to know exactly where that message led her. Zola fell into a restless sleep that night. She had no idea what she had just found. However, she didn't know that she wasn't the only person to find it.

13

— J

Elena sat near the back of the room, half-listening to what the professor was saying. She sketched her machine blueprints in her notebook quietly, hoping that no one would notice her aversion to the rest of the class. After bumping into Zola yesterday, she no longer carried her blueprints unless they were in containers. She couldn't afford to let people see her things. This wasn't like a normal school. No matter if you were friends, people were known to steal and plagiarize work with no regard to the other person.

The school, of course, had no rules against it. If you were stupid enough to let someone else see your work, you deserved to lose the credit. She thought it was a horrible situation, but there was nothing she could do about it. No one gets on the bad side of the Dean, not unless they want to get expelled. They watched that happen over a runaway robot a few days ago. Even though she and Zola weren't even in the same major, she could sell her work to someone else. Call her paranoid, but she wasn't stupid.

Elena thought Zola wouldn't do something like that. Still, she wasn't going to take that chance.

Zola on the other hand was still wondering why Elena was acting so weird. She didn't expect the girl to be so uptight about her work considering they were friends. But she was also wondering about the words on the wall, about how Astra was acting, and who she could trust to help her out. If anyone, it would be Katya. After all, the older girl had helped her figure out the coordinates without any questions.

Katya was shy, so much so that she rarely talked to anyone. There wasn't really a chance that she would spill to someone else, but Katya was also a little on the scared side. She didn't always defend herself. Zola sighed. On the other hand, Astra was very much like her. Smart, cunning, maybe even a little manipulative. She would figure the riddle out fast. But Katya was safer, so Katya, it was.

Zola waited until after lunch. The others still sat at the same table, under the same tree, avoiding the same people. It was like clockwork. They were oh so predictable. She didn't like being predictable. As they went inside, Zola pulled Katya behind one of the pillars, watching the others as they continued down the hall, chattering and bantering about the other students and tests they had to take. With finals coming up in just two weeks, and only the summer semester and one year after that to prove their importance to the school, they had to work fast.

After they left, Zola turned to Katya, who stared at her curiously. "What?"

"Hang on, hang on. I need your help with something." Zola pulled out her phone. "Do you have any idea what this might mean? Like is it a riddle, or just a very random note?"

Katya took the phone and frowned. "*Find me at the lowest point, where no one ever goes. Use the stolen key from the Dean's office. Don't you dare get caught, J.*' Who's J? Where'd you get this?"

"I may or may not have gone into the restricted area…" Zola trailed off.

Katya glared at her. "Seriously? Do you know what could have happened if you got caught?! Are you stupid?"

Zola was taken aback by her outburst. "No, I was just curious. I really didn't mean any harm."

"Well, don't be. Being curious gets you in trouble. Well, at least in that way."

"Okay, okay, fine. Be that way. I just wanted your help."

Katya pursed her lips. "Okay."

"Hmm?"

"I'll help you. But whatever, or whoever, you find, I won't take the fall for it. I don't want to get expelled. Don't expect me to cover for you. And I can't promise to keep it a secret, but I'll do my best."

Zola smiled. "Thank you!" She threw her arms around Katya, who stumbled back slightly in confusion. "Ahem." She looked down. "I promise you won't regret it. Tell me what you find okay?"

"I will. Just text the photo to me and I'll see what I can do. Now shoo."

"Thanks again Kat, you're a lifesaver!" She turned and ran towards her room.

Katya watched Zola run down the hallway. Her heart was in her throat. She remembered the visit she got last night, strange though it was—Astra knocking on her door in the middle of the night and dragging her into the hallway. The warning to not trust someone named Destiny Duke, should Katya ever run into her. Most importantly, Astra told her not to stick her nose in places where it didn't belong. She remembered the look on Astra's face when she told her that Zola was going to get in trouble.

Katya wasn't sure how Astra had even found out about her helping Zola, but even her suspicions wouldn't keep her from listening. Astra had told her that what Zola had found was priceless, no matter how insignificant it seemed. She just had to find a way to convince her otherwise. Apparently, Zola was going down a dangerous path, and Astra had asked that she do her best to keep her from it.

Katya had agreed. If anything, she was going to send Zola on a wild goose chase. Or maybe she would tell her the truth. Either way, she wanted to consult Astra first. It wasn't hard to find her. Astra was in one of the computer labs, typing up some codes for her major project.

"Hey, Astra," Katya said. She dropped her bag on the floor and slid into the cubicle across from Astra.

"How's your telescope coming?" Katya found out pretty soon

that Astra didn't care for greetings, she liked to jump straight into the conversation. That didn't stop Katya from greeting her every time.

"Pretty good, why?"

"You need to hurry. Aiken is already almost finished, Mary and Elena have finished their blueprints and started building, Nasra is writing some form of a research paper, Alyssa is testing medicine and Zola is working on her codes, and I'm pretty sure Henry is creating a supercomputer."

Katya raised an eyebrow. "Wow. They told you?"

"Of course not, I found out myself. They don't really talk to me. Besides, I don't need them being suspicious of how I know what I know, or what I'm going to do with that information."

Katya took a deep breath and opened a new document. "I'm not even going to question it at this point. You know I do think you're crazy, right?"

"Yes, I do. That's a pretty good choice, I don't think you'd want to know anyways. What did Zola want?"

Katya hesitated. "She sent me this photo of where she was last night."

Astra hummed. "Is it important?"

Katya held out her phone. "Decide that for yourself."

Astra took the phone from Katya and stared at it. "Wow." Monotone.

Katya stared at her "You knew she found it, didn't you?"

Her silence was enough confirmation.

"Of course you knew. You're Astra, you know almost everything."

Astra snorted. "That's not true." She passed the phone back. "What are you going to do?"

"What do you mean?"

Astra turned back to the computer and resumed typing. "What are you going to tell her? That's between you and Zola, it's not my problem to fix. She didn't ask for my help, you did, and I'm telling you to figure it out on your own."

"Didn't you say not to let Zola go down the wrong path?"

"I did, and I meant to keep her out of trouble. If you want to help her, go ahead, it's not my problem. Just be careful." Astra closed out the program she was running and pulled the jump drive out of its port. "I'm not responsible for babysitting you guys, and I certainly am not your mother. I'm just here for advice if you want it. This"—she gestured vaguely to Katya and the phone—"is not something I need to deal with. I'm not going to deal with it."

"Wha— Astra!"

"Look Katya, you're an adult. Do what you want. Again, she asked for your help, not mine. Now if you excuse me, I have to go work on something that is actually my problem." Astra stood up and left the lab, slamming the door shut behind her.

Katya sat there in shock. "Well then."

14

Dreams

Katya sighed. A few hours after her interaction with Astra, Katya had returned to her dorm and stayed there. Elena and Nasra had returned to the room, but she ignored them. She had a decision to make, and it wasn't an easy one. She had tried to work on homework, to no avail. No matter what she tried to focus on, Katya's thoughts always drifted back to what Zola told her, and Astra's warning.

She wanted to help both of them. Did she really have to choose which one to prioritize in the matter? Was keeping Zola safe more important than helping Zola decipher the clue? Katya glanced down at the photo on her phone. She couldn't bear to lose the trust that Zola had placed in her. She'd figure it out, no matter how long it took. And she'd tell Zola the truth.

A few floors down, Mary was struggling to hold all the art supplies that she had dragged into the study room. She felt awkward and sweaty, tired from the night before. She hadn't been able to fall asleep until one in the morning, and when she finally did, her dreams had been filled with random shots of blueprints to a machine she hadn't even thought of building before a few weeks ago.

They were like supercharged batteries she realized when she started sketching them, and they were much smaller than any other thing she had worked on. Technically, she didn't need to build it. She only really needed to work on the prints and then join in the group project at the end of the year. But she really wanted to. Mary noticed there were flaws in the prints. She labeled all the parts that needed fixing, where roads of wires and little bridges of metal would help stabilize power sources.

She was very proud of her work, and even though she was slightly confused about where she even got the ideas, it didn't matter. She was sure it would work somehow. She had begun a scaled-down model, hoping that somehow it would help her perfect the prints so she could begin proper building next year.

Her phone lit up, indicating that Alyssa was calling. Mary answered it, continuing to mess with the pieces on the table. "What's up, Alyssa?"

"You're coming to dinner with the rest of us."

"I'm working on my project."

"Mary, it wasn't a question. We only have so much time before finals and even though we're all staying through the summer, it'll be nice to catch a break. So, what do ya say?"

"What are we going to get? Can we get noodles? I like noodles."

"I'm sure we can work something out."

Mary smiled. "Okay. Give me like 10 minutes." She looked down at the model. Mary bit her tongue as she carefully moved the last of the *first floor pieces,* as she called them, into place and set it on the table to dry. Mary rolled the prints up, slipping them into a plastic tube, and screwed the top on tight. She dumped the tube in her backpack, swung it over her shoulder, and kicked the chair into place.

She grabbed the model gingerly, cupping her hands so that she covered all sides. She then headed straight to her dorm, nearly running into Nasra as she did so. They both automatically nodded to each other, chattering apologies as they entered their respective rooms. Mary could hear Elena next door as she screamed something about not knowing where her phone was. On the other side of the opposite wall, Zola nagged at Astra, reminding her to grab a jacket.

They had all moved dorm rooms the second semester and would move again for summer housing. Mary wasn't sure whether or not it was a good thing, the seven of them in side-by-side rooms. At least it was better than Aiken and Henry, who were now on the top floor and had to either get up early or sprint to get to their morning classes on time.

Either way, they had gotten used to sticking together. It wasn't like they really had a choice. But then again, it didn't matter if they were outcasts or not. They had learned to trust each other, for the most part.

Alyssa burst into the room. "Mary!"

"Hang on, hang on!" She transferred the model into a small case and slid it underneath her bed. "Okay, now we can go." Mary glanced back, just to make sure the case holding her model was fully covered, then the two girls left the room. "So, where are we going?"

"Some Italian restaurant, I don't know. It's Astra's pick to-night. And speaking of which…" Alyssa trailed off.

Astra came up behind them. "Catch!"

Astra tossed a water bottle at Mary, who fumbled, but managed to catch it. She opened it. "Thanks," she mumbled.

Astra nodded.

Mary took a sip and stared at Astra. "So, Alyssa said you're picking tonight. Where are we going?"

Astra grinned. "It's this small Italian place, a bunch of pastas and soups, really nice, and honestly it's one of my favorite restaurants. I found it during finals last semester. I think you'll love it."

"I've never seen you this excited, and to be fairly honest, I'm not feeling it," Elena quipped.

Astra rolled her eyes. "Okay, just because you're Miss Grumpy-Pants, doesn't mean that I can't love food."

Mary jumped in between the two of them. "What's it like? You know, the atmosphere."

"Well, it's small. There's an indoor place of course, warm lighting. It kinda feels like home. The outside seating area is made of white brick, covered in vines, very pretty. You can see the sunset from out there."

"That sounds pretty."

"The food is great."

Mary nodded, smiling. "I sure hope so."

"Oh, you don't have to hope." Astra winked and ran to catch up with Henry to carry on whatever sort of conversation they were having. Mary stuck by Alyssa as they walked downtown. Her mind drifted back to the model in her room, and how much she needed this project to work. She was so worried in fact, that she barely paid attention to the chatter over dinner, though she did shake herself out of her thoughts long enough to tell Astra that her food choice was a good one. She skipped dessert as well, which didn't slip Alyssa's watchful gaze.

As they walked back, Alyssa stared at her. She was worried for Mary, especially since she wasn't her usual bubbly self, but she didn't say anything. She didn't want to. Alyssa wasn't good with talking about feelings, that was Mary's job in their friendship. Especially since they were with other people, she didn't want to worry them. It wouldn't be right to ask her tonight. She'd ask Mary what was wrong tomorrow. Though, at this rate, she might put it off forever.

When they got back to the dorms. Alyssa pulled out her notebook and a vial. She had skipped the study day to tweak her serum just a little. She hadn't expected it to work so well. Alyssa took a deep breath and drank it all in one gulp, then slipped under the covers. Elena's thoughts were loud on the other side of the wall. Across the room, Mary's dreams were once again filled with shifting plans, and visions of what her project could be.

15

Ginkgo

Nasra looked down at her phone. The stupid device wouldn't stop buzzing. When she gave Morgan and Castor her number, they added her to their group chat. Unfortunately, they texted non-stop about things such as homework, food, and pranks they wanted to play. Nasra wanted to chuck her phone across the room.

Henry raised an eyebrow at her. Nasra just rolled her eyes. *'They won't shut up,'* she mouthed. Henry nodded, smiling. He nudged Zola and whispered something in the girl's ear. She grinned and pulled out a piece of paper, scribbling furiously. Astra leaned over and wrote something on the page too.

Henry passed it to Nasra, who frowned. What could they possibly want to say? She unfolded the piece of paper. She recognized Zola's handwriting immediately. *'If you want to, you should invite them to lunch with us, we don't talk to many people.'* She wasn't opposed to it. Nasra tilted the paper to read Astra's note. *'Meet me after class please, I need your help with something.'*

Nasra looked up. She gave them both a thumbs up then turned her attention back to the front of the room, where the professor was still droning on. There were still twenty minutes left on the clock. She dropped her head down on the desk and groaned. She hated this class. It was going to be a long twenty minutes.

Eventually, the professor let them out, with a reminder to do the reading and take advantage of the school-wide study day for finals. Nasra sighed. Finals week. Starting Monday, all bets were off. The library would be open basically all day, students would go for hours without sleep, sometimes passing out in the hallways. Last semester was a pain. She could only imagine what it would be like for those who were graduating this year. They would be in even more of a mess.

Nasra stood in the hallway and let people pass her. She spotted Zola making her way over to her. Nasra pressed herself against the wall so that she wouldn't get trampled by the crowd.

Zola ran up and grabbed Nasra's hand. "You invited them, right?"

"Yeah, I did. Or I will."

"Great! I look forward to lunch then." She smiled and ran off. Nasra raised an eyebrow and turned around, almost running into Astra. "Woah! Hi, Astra."

Astra smiled. "Hi, Nasra."

"What's up?"

"Well, you see, I kinda need your help."

"Yeah, the note said that. What do you need?"

Astra sighed. "I uh, actually need you to go grab something from the lab for me."

Nasra frowned. "You can't go get it yourself?"

"That's the thing. I might have been kicked out of class earlier, but I forgot something, and I'm too embarrassed to go get it my-self."

Nasra looked at her in disbelief. "Really?"

Astra nodded. "Yep."

"Wow." Nasra huffed. "Well, I guess I can go."

Astra looked up. "Really?"

"Of course, you're my friend!"

Astra grinned. "Thank you so much!"

Nasra smiled back. "No problem."

The two girls headed towards the classroom in question, As-tra leading the way. She stopped outside the door and glanced in. "Good, there's not many people in here." She nodded her head at the door. "Go first?"

Nasra laughed. "Sure. I didn't know that the Astra Aracelli was afraid of anything."

"Oh, you know, just the normal things. Crowds, embarrassment, the weight of knowing everything that I'm not supposed to—"

"Wow. Well, I mean, it makes you seem a little more human. You know, cause you act like a robot?" Nasra opened the door. Astra rolled her eyes and stepped inside. A few people turned at the sound but went right back to work. Nasra waved at Alyssa who was near the back, then spotted Astra's bag on one of the tables.

She walked over and grabbed it and turned around to see Astra standing behind Alyssa looking through the fridge full of chemicals. She pulled a vial out and slipped it into her pocket. She nodded towards the door and the two left.

"What'd you grab?"

"Huh? Oh, just some Ginkgo extract." She tapped her pocket. "I thought I might as well get it while I was in here. Thanks for coming with me by the way. It wasn't as awkward with you here."

"Sure, no problem." Nasra frowned. "I have to ask, what's Ginkgo?"

"Oh! Otherwise known as the Maidenhair tree, this stuff is supposed to help with brain health and memory. You can get pills, but I did an extract, it's easier to consume."

"Huh. Weird, I would not trust that."

Astra shrugged. "Wouldn't hurt to try. See you at lunch?"

"Yeah." Astra disappeared, and Nasra was left to wander the hallways, lost in thought.

Astra raced towards her dorm room. She was almost packed, due to the fact that as soon as the semester was over, they'd be moved to summer housing. But she had the few things she needed out on her bed, and she wanted to make sure everything was in order.

She didn't really have any qualms about what she was doing. Astra only wanted the results. She recreated the serum pretty easily one night, and when she tested it, it worked. It was so easy to steal the recipe out of Alyssa's bag, to slip it back in before she was noticed. It was so easy to tamper with.

It's not like she was hurting the other girl. In fact, she was making her stronger. She was only worried that she would get caught. That was one mistake she couldn't afford to make. Astra shuddered. She remembered the last time that happened. It wasn't a good memory, and it was a terrible experience. There was a lesson learned there. Failure is not to be tolerated.

Astra made her way back to her dorm room, clutching the vial tightly. It hadn't taken her long to figure out the correct amount of the ginkgo extract to slip into Alyssa's serum, or to edit the surveillance footage so no one could see her tamper with it. Every single batch that Alyssa made, she spiked. And it had gone so much better than planned, even sneaking around behind Alyssa's, Mary's, and Zola's backs went well. She had to plan around their schedules. Everything had fallen into place so quickly. Except for Delilah. She hadn't expected that.

Astra angrily kicked her door open. She'd take care of Delilah later, that wasn't the goal right now. Astra kicked the door shut and moved over to her desk. On her bed were Alyssa's test vials. Alyssa always left them underneath her bed. Mary left her models underneath her own bed as well. Astra scoffed. They needed to find better hiding spots; both were so predictable. She carefully measured the liquid and poured it into each vial, depositing them back in their proper place in the dorm next door. It was so easy. All she had to do was figure out the right time to set the next part of her plan in motion.

It was up to Katya now.

She knew Katya would make the right choice, her urge to help others surpassing everything except for her love of the stars. Astra pulled out her phone and checked the tiny cameras she had placed in several of the labs, and as she expected, there was Katya, trying to figure out the clue.

Astra smirked. "Check," she whispered. "Your turn." She

turned her phone off and ran out the door. The next piece of the puzzle could wait. She had plenty of time to modify, and even create new steps in her plan. For now, she just had to get through lunch, and not get caught.

16

Destiny

Zola huffed. "I'll look forward to lunch then," she mocked herself. "Anyone who's anyone could probably tell how fake that was!" She stormed back towards the dorm. It was a weird reaction, but she wasn't sure if Nasra was going to pick up on it or not. The older girl was smart enough, but she didn't always pay attention. Zola smiled.

Luckily for her, the obliviousness of other students was just what she needed in order to work without looking suspicious. Zola hummed as she looked for her notebook. She needed to focus on figuring out what the clue in the restricted area was.

If anything, it was probably just a cruel game played on whoever was brave enough to go down there. It might have been someone's old project, though the graffiti was too fresh. She hoped that maybe it really meant something, and she wasn't going crazy over the fact that she just wanted to solve the mystery. What was going on behind the scenes didn't matter at the moment, because even if in the end it was unsatisfying, Zola wanted to know. She had to know.

After giving the clue to Katya, Zola took to deciphering it herself. It wasn't that she didn't trust Katya, but rather that she wanted it to go faster. Two minds were better than one, and if they were working together they could cut the process in half. Of course, with finals starting the next day, she couldn't really do much. She had worked on it a lot so far. After having spent the previous day researching, Zola found that the clue hadn't shown up anywhere on the internet, so it couldn't have been a reference to any popular horror media.

"Find me at the lowest point, where no one ever goes. Use the stolen key from the Dean's office. Don't you dare get caught, J,"

Zola repeated under her breath. "Why is this so hard?"

Later, when she tried to go to bed, Zola couldn't stop thinking about the supposed paint, which she had decided wasn't actually paint at all. While she had made the list of all the J names at the school, she had thought long and hard about it. Judging by the smell, how dried it was, and just the general look of it, she had come to the conclusion that the *'paint'* she found was in fact blood. It was old but looked like it had been refreshed recently, as in, within a few months, suggesting that the person who had done it was still at the school.

She had already disregarded several people, including staff. The thing was, who would write in their own blood, and if it wasn't their blood, would she and Katya be dealing with a murderer? It made her on edge. The J could be anything: a first name, middle name, last name, nickname, a character in a book, anything.

What scared her the most about that revelation was the fact that Willow's last name was James. One of the reasons why she thought it would be a good idea to invite the group to lunch. She doubted that Willow was the J who left a message on the wall in blood, but she wasn't about to disregard it simply because she didn't seem like the type.

Zola sighed. She tossed her notebook onto her bed and flopped backward. She was an idiot, wasn't she? Even though she wanted to believe that the message was something interesting, exciting, maybe even a horrible secret, it was childish. She shouldn't expect much. It might just be a prank. But who writes a prank in blood?

Zola heard a knock on the door, and she quickly sat up. She opened it to find Nasra standing outside. "Oh. Hi Nasra."

"Can I come in?"

"Uh yeah, sure." Zola moved aside and let Nasra pass her. She grabbed a chair and sat down. Zola sat down on her bed. "So, what's up?"

Nasra held up a notebook and clicked her pen rapidly. "Well,

I need to ask you a few questions, given that you're very knowl-
edgeable on the subject."

Zola raised an eyebrow. "Are you using me to study?"

"No! Not at all! Well, maybe a little bit. It's more for research
purposes than anything. A research paper actually."

"Hmm." Zola stared at her then shrugged. "Okay. What do you
want to know?"

Nasra brightened. "Okay, um, I didn't actually expect to get
this far, heh." She fidgeted and laughed awkwardly. "Um, so you
know how people have compared the human brain to a supercomputer?"

"Yeah, why?"

"Well, I need your opinion on this. What if you could control the human brain like a computer? And what if you didn't stop
there, what if you could control DNA?"

During the entire conversation, no matter how interesting it
was, Zola couldn't stop thinking about her list, and the upcom-
ing promise of lunch with the other students. Every so often, she
would zone out, ignoring Nasra's rant and getting caught up in her
thoughts. Eventually, Nasra would notice and ask her a question,
pulling Zola back into the moment, and leaving her scrambling to
answer.

Finally, Nasra closed her notebook and stared at Zola. "Alright, what's on your mind?"

Zola laughed. She was suspicious of the other students, and
she had every right to be. After all, they acted as if they knew everything, and at the same time, knew nothing. It was strange. But
it was better to act as if there was nothing wrong and figure it out
on her own than to voice her suspicions and be proven right, possibly ending up dead. Well, that was a little extreme, but nothing
was truly extreme with her. Zola didn't really trust anyone outside
of her family. Not yet.

She hesitated. "I'm just worried, and a little curious about the things I've discovered at this school. What I know could be dangerous, or it could be nothing at all. I just think I might be spending too much time obsessing over it."

Nasra smiled. "Isn't that how it is here? You and I both know that something's wrong, but we go along with it, just like the other students. We watch lifeless bodies get grown in a lab, ignore the student volunteers getting worked to the bone or they finally decide to throw themselves off the roof. The way they look at us, it's almost as if they were in our shoes, and want to help us, but can't." Nasra frowned and looked off into the distance. "I have no idea why."

"Wow. You're way more observant than you let on."

Nasra nodded. "Yep, and that's why I've survived on this campus." She checked her watch. "Ooh, we're going to be late for lunch, let's go." She grabbed her bag and ran out the door, and Zola followed quickly.

The two walked down to the campus grounds together in silence. They ignored the questions that they both wanted to ask but were too scared to speak aloud. Zola berated herself. Nasra would make a great ally if she managed to get her help, but on the other hand, she would make a formidable enemy.

Zola started picking at her nails as they neared the group already gathered on the front lawn, eating. She would get to know them all in time, but for now, she just had to watch and learn. This sort of picnic reminded Zola of when her brothers would sit her down on the floor of their shop after school. They would eat sandwiches together and compare grades. She didn't regret coming to Torsion, but she missed them more than anything. Zola side-eyed Nasra. She really wanted to ask how she had come to notice the little things in the other students, but before she knew it, they were noticed by the others and forced to sit down.

After the initial awkwardness in the first few minutes, they started to act more comfortable, and to outside eyes, it was going well. Mary and Alyssa started joking around. Morgan and Cassian got into some loud debate with Astra about aliens, Katya chiming in every few minutes to add some sort of hypothesis about UFOs. Nasra discussed the biology of plants versus humans with Castor while Eric ranted about engineering to Elena, who tried not to laugh.

Aiken and Henry talked about grades with William, who started calculating how everyone would do on their exams. Zola huffed. He was lucky. Since he was in accounting, he didn't have to do a major project. He did have to take extra tests, but he was a good test taker. *'Rude,'* she thought to herself. She wasn't sure about her own project.

She didn't have time to think about it as Nicole pulled chicken out of a cooler, and the boisterous conversation continued. Astra finally stopped arguing about aliens and started talking computers with Henry, leaving Katya to cover the rest of the conversation.

Zola found that she was actually having fun, and maybe her suspicions were just that, suspicions. Maybe nothing was actually wrong. Maybe it was all in her head. After all, they didn't display any signs of weird behavior, despite the fact that they were barely friends. They all seemed so nice and friendly, a little closed off, but that was to be expected. They didn't seem like they were a threat. Then again, no serial killer ever did at first.

Zola was pulled out of her thoughts by a jarringly shrill voice.

"Hey," Delilah said. Warning lights went off in Zola's head. She noticed that she wasn't the only person made uncomfortable by the sudden interruption. Zola watched as the others exchanged pointed glances and eventually everyone around her started making excuses and dispersing until just Zola and Astra were left sitting on the grass in silence.

Zola was the first to break it. "That was awkward," she commented.

Astra rolled her eyes. "I know! Do you think anyone actually likes Destiny?"

"Destiny?"

"Delilah, sorry." Astra looked away. "I'm a little tired."

"Wait, who's Destiny?"

"No one," Astra said hurriedly.

Zola narrowed her eyes. "Astra!"

"Nothing, bye!" The older girl ran off, leaving Zola in the courtyard confused.

'She has to be hiding something,' Zola thought. "It's Astra," she spoke aloud. "When is she not hiding something?"

The List

Zola headed towards the library. She had asked Katya to meet her there. After all, it would be the only time they would be able to work together before the whirlwind of last-minute assignments and tests. She hated finals last semester, and she knew that she would hate them even more this year. Ever since the awkward lunch last week, the group felt even more on edge. Well, minus Katya and Aiken, who seemed oblivious to the whole thing.

That's how she got Katya to come meet up with her in the first place. Katya was a smart girl, but with the amount of time she spent in her own head, or staring at the night sky, it was no wonder she didn't feel the tension. It had crossed Zola's mind that they might not ever bounce back, and that thought worried her. It was almost disappointing to think that she wouldn't have anyone to trust when she finished out the semester.

Luckily, she had the clue to look forward to deciphering, even though she would still be taking a summer class. For some odd reason, everyone else was taking two, but Zola was perfectly fine with just the one, even if it meant picking up an extra class during the Fall semester. Who really needs summer classes? Certainly not her. But having one was required. So, she was going to do it. She would be very salty and angry about it, but she would do it.

As expected, Katya was waiting for her, motioning to a study room she had reserved. She sat down awkwardly, avoiding Zola's eyes.

Zola frowned. "What's wrong?"

Katya continued to avoid Zola's gaze, muttering her answer underneath her breath.

"Come on Katya, just spit it out."

"I, uh, may have told someone about the photo."

"What?" Zola's eyes narrowed. She took a deep breath. "Who?"

"Astra!" Katya sighed. "I'm sorry, I know I told you I wouldn't. A couple of days after you asked for my help, I told Astra about the clue, and I felt really bad, but she was the one who told me to help you and now I don't know what to do."

Zola sighed and hit her head on the table. "Well, there goes my attempted secret."

"I'm really sorry!"

Zola sighed. "It's okay. As much as I hate to admit it, Astra was probably the best person you could have told. I just don't like sharing secrets with her because she never does the same." Zola stared off into the distance. "Just, make sure you don't tell anyone else. Don't worry, I'm not that mad at you, just kind of disappointed. But we may need her brain for this."

"You'll need a lot more than just my and Katya's brain if you want to figure it out."

Zola turned and saw Astra leaning against the doorway, Aiken peering over her shoulder.

She frowned. "How long were you two standing there?"

"Not long. I was summoned by the sound of despair and frustration."

"Sorry," Katya whispered.

Zola waved dismissively at Katya to get her to stop talking. "And? Do you think that we require your services?"

Astra straightened and moved into the room, folding her arms and glaring. "What do you think the answer to that question is?"

Zola huffed. "Fine! You and Aiken can help, just, don't let anyone else find out."

Astra clicked her tongue. "About that…" she trailed off, opening the door wide. "I may have gotten everyone to come."

Zola whirled around and glared at Katya. "Really?"

"I swear I didn't call them. I only called Astra."

"Yeah, don't blame Katya, this was entirely me."

Zola groaned. "Why?"

"Because you need us." Astra motioned to the others to come in and sit down before she closed the door behind them. "Everyone here is so distrustful of each other. But if there's anything that I am certain of, it's that we can only trust each other."

"Hmmm, yeah then what are you hiding?" Zola leaned on her hand and smiled innocently at Astra.

Mary opened a bag of popcorn and started sharing with Alyssa as Astra raised an eyebrow. "Hiding? I'm quite sure I don't know what you mean?"

"Well," Nasra commented.

"*'Well'* what?" Astra asked.

"You run away whenever something important is going on, for one," Aiken said.

Zola laughed. "And what about sneaking out of the dorm?"

"Your weird codes," Henry chimed in.

"Whoever Destiny Duke is," Katya added.

"Yeah, who is that?" Zola asked. "Because you mentioned a Destiny earlier."

Astra pursed her lips. "No comment."

"Astra!"

"Someone I wish I had left in my past. That's all you need to know."

Mary whistled. "Well that…" she trailed off.

"…does not answer the question at all." Alyssa finished. She sighed. "I guess that's as much about this Destiny we are ever going to get out of Astra, how about we take a look at this picture?"

Katya frowned. "Uh, is that all you care about?"

"Yep!" Mary stuffed more popcorn in her mouth.

"That and adventure. Sometimes frogs," Alyssa quipped.

Katya shrugged. "Okay then. Zola?"

"Right." She pulled her phone out of her pocket. "Here it is."

Nasra leaned in. "Wow."

"Wicked," Mary and Alyssa chorused.

"Is that blood?" Elena asked.

"Pretty sure," Zola said.

"Oh."

"Oh indeed," Astra whispered.

Zola turned to her. "What are your thoughts on this?"

"What are yours? This is your photo. Your fault for going into a restricted area," Astra said.

"This is partially my fault," Katya half-whispered.

"Shut up Katya, I never should have gotten you involved!" Zola sighed. "Sorry, Katya."

Katya looked down. "It's okay. Continue."

"The point is, none of you were supposed to know. But I guess, I think it was made by someone still here in the school. Most likely an older student, so I've already made a list of people I've encountered who have J names."

Astra held out her hand. "Hand it over."

Zola passed it to her. "Well?"

Astra flipped through it. "Why do you have Castor on here?"

"He's kinda creepy sometimes."

"He's actually pretty nice," Elena commented. The room fell silent. "What?"

"Okay, if Elena likes him, then he's definitely somewhat suspicious," Aiken said.

"Wow."

Astra rolled her eyes. "Moving on. Um, Julia Rayes?"

"In my statistics class, and she looks like a serial killer."

"Valid. Um, Jacob Daniels?"

"That's one of the upperclassmen who gives me spooky vibes."

"Huh. He's in my history class and I've never talked to him." She continued to flip through the pages. "Michelle James, Jaina Jaisi, Lia Jeon, Everett Jones, Jade Johnson, Jessica Michaels. Quite the list, but that's not everyone."

"It is a lot," Elena said. "You can't expect her to get a list of everyone in the school with a J in their name that quickly. Especially since we haven't included nicknames, or middle names."

"What are we going to do about it?" Henry questioned.

Zola sat there for a bit, quiet. "I don't know."

"We could stalk them," Katya mentioned.

"That's a bit out of character for you," Mary pointed out.

"It could still work though," Astra said. "I mean, Katya is quiet, we really don't know what she sees. But all of us could work on studying anyone who had a J in their name or goes by a J name."

"We won't have much time though." Alyssa chewed thoughtfully. "If it's an upperclassman, they'll be leaving soon."

"I guess we'll just have to hurry." Zola looked around the room. "We'll have to get a student list."

"I have one," Astra said.

"What." Zola stared at her. "Astra how— you know what, I don't want to know. Can you get us copies made of all people with J names?"

"I can do you one better." Astra pulled a folder out of her bag and set it on the table. "I already have one. This is a list of names, including headshots, of every upperclassman who has a J name or a J nickname."

"How did you know we were going to need this?"

"Because I know how you think." She smiled. "And I always come prepared."

18

Second Finals

To say that everyone hated final exams would be an understatement. They were the hardest tests to pass, the teachers were stressed, and the students drifted like zombies through the halls. They really needed coffee. Of course, they couldn't get it because the machine had broken within the first two hours of the day.

Astra sighed. She had run out of contact lenses, resorting to the silver-framed glasses that she used to wear. They fogged up from the steam of the strongest tea she could get ahold of. It restricted her sense of smell enough, so she didn't have to deal with the smell of sweat-soaked students crammed in small cubicles, mixed with old coffee grinds from runs to local convenience stores.

She banged her head on the table. She wanted it to end soon. Everyone did.

Mary once again got no sleep. While her dreams weren't overwhelmed with plans the past few days, she still lay awake thinking about them. She couldn't focus. Mary stared down at the copied notes one of her fellow classmates had lent her. Her eyes were blurry. She blinked a few times. *'The mitochondria is the powerhouse of the cell,'* her brain screamed. "Shut up," she whispered.

Mary glared at the paper. History. Who needed that anyway? It was her next test, the last one too, luckily. At least for the day. But she didn't have to take history anymore, not after this year. Next year she'd get to do more engineering classes, more tasks, more fun. No more General Studies. Not as much time with Alyssa. That's what they got for studying different majors.

Speaking of which, Alyssa was sitting next to her, dozing off ever so slightly, then jerking awake to go over her chemistry notes. Alyssa sighed, doodling in the corners of her notebook. She'd pass. It wasn't like she was bad at chemistry; she was bad at studying.

Alyssa scoffed, replacing her chemistry notes with algebra ones.

She really hated the fact that she needed math for science. Who cared about algebraic formulas, she could just use a calculator! But she needed to be precise, unfortunately, so she studied all the same. Being a Health Science major was probably a bad idea, though it made sense at the time. Her project didn't always work as expected. A couple of the trial runs had gone haywire before she had gotten her formula under control. But once it was done, it would help people. She knew it would. All she had to do was perfect it.

Katya exited her classroom. Finally, she was free of testing for the day. She did not look forward to tomorrow. It brought even more tests, tired students, and angry professors watching over your shoulder to make sure you didn't cheat. She never did, but the teachers always seemed to love staring at her. Katya wasn't particularly fond of calculus. She wasn't bad at it, in fact she was top of her class, but she didn't like the environment.

Katya shivered at the thought. She really hated the glares and suspicious glances thrown her way. She headed back to the dorms, ready to put notebooks away, and move once again. The dorms were always changing. That was the one thing that she wasn't always sure about. Summer housing meant new roommates, and she was slightly nervous about the outcome. Katya dumped her books on her desk, switching them out for the next days' notes. She just wanted to sleep.

Elena fiddled with her pens. She had the least amount of tests of the whole group, which was nice for her, but quite annoying to the others. She spent her time finalizing sketches and formulas, planning out metals she would need to use, and the proper dimensions of her work. She'd need to reserve a special major room next year, it wouldn't be hard, in fact, she would probably get assigned one, but just in case, she needed to let someone know.

Elena took a sip of her water. She had bumped into Astra in the hall earlier, and the girl had been kind enough to give her a spare water bottle. If Elena was more suspicious of her, perhaps she might not have taken it. But she was thirsty and tired, and Astra looked just as drained as Elena felt, so she assumed it wasn't poisoned. Logic outweighed her paranoia, and Elena was confident that if the girl wanted her dead, she would be. Elena glanced down at her paper, seeing where she could add or remove things. It was like the drink strengthened her mind and made everything clearer. She smiled. Almost done.

Zola typed faster, her fingers flying over the keyboard, doing her best not to look down. Looking down meant slowing down and she couldn't afford to lose those few precious seconds in between. Not in this test. She typed out her last few strands of code and clicked enter. She smiled at her display and raised her hand "Done!" she yelled.

Zola watched as her professor let the code play out. She could feel her heartbeat in her ears. The half-minute in which her code ran felt like eternity. Finally, he nodded. "Five minutes flat. Not bad. Pass."

Zola nodded and sprinted towards the door. She stopped to high-five Henry on the way out and wished him good luck. It was nice to have him nearby before their tests. They had discussed their potential class schedules for the summer and had laughed at the fact that the room had been double booked by their professors, causing them to have to share a testing room.

Once she was in the hallway, Zola breathed a sigh of relief. She had done it, and she was very proud of herself. That test was one of the most feared by computer majors. If you couldn't break through the professors' codes, you might be kicked out of the program. Zola took a deep breath to calm her racing heart. She was fast enough this time. Would she be fast enough next time?

Henry took a deep breath as Zola left the room, then turned to assess what was on his desk. He cracked his fingers, preparing to take on the last part of his test: assembling a computer. He was racing an upperclassman, which made him all the more desperate to prove himself. Henry wasn't a quitter. He was silent, yes, but he made up for it in skill. He practiced, out of sight, out of mind, for the most part.

The teacher gave the signal, and he sorted through the pieces to put it all together. The students watching screamed, cheering and cursing when one of them got behind. Finally, Henry finished, setting it down on the table. The teacher nodded.

"Ten minutes. Not bad. Beat your classmate. Pass."

Henry nodded. *'Perfect.'*

Aiken glared down at the paper. He and Nasra had the same class, and therefore the same test, one that they both had no problem with. However, it was the bonus section that Aiken was angry at, the pop quiz of components of human cells for him. He should have switched tests with Nasra, as he knew she had the plant questionnaire that he could have easily passed.

Neither of them were cheaters, so Aiken just grit his teeth as he tried to recall those few moments that Nasra rambled on about her research. He hadn't paid attention during that section in class, he was too busy working on his cross-germination. He did remember the few parts that Nasra had told him when she let him borrow her notes, but he didn't really know if he was remembering correctly or not. He glanced over at Nasra, who was glaring at her paper.

It seemed that she was in the same predicament.

Nasra didn't care about plants as much as she should have. She knew everything about them that was required for the main test, but not for the bonus. She berated herself silently. It didn't matter that plant science wasn't her focus, as a perfectionist, she wanted to do better.

Nasra sighed as she passed her test to the front. "I probably failed that section."

"It's a bonus, it doesn't count."

Nasra hummed. "Doesn't mean I didn't fail."

"Don't worry, you'll be fine." Aiken grabbed his backpack. "I mean, you've never gotten anything less than an A in this class, it won't kill you to not ace the bonus section."

"I suppose you're right."

"Of course I'm right." Aiken looked down at his phone and perked up. "Hey, they just fixed the coffee machine in the cafeteria!"

Nasra grinned and took off running.

"Wha— Hey! Nasra! Wait up!" Aiken chased after her. "Wait for me!"

19

Summer

It was a relief when finals ended. The short summer break before summer classes began was welcomed with open arms, at least by the ones who stayed. The halls felt empty, too empty, now that most of the students were gone. Really, only the first years who were required to take classes stayed, and those who didn't want to leave, or couldn't afford to go home.

"I'm so glad it's summer!" Nasra yelled, flopping backward on her bed. Elena raised an eyebrow, side-stepping to avoid Alyssa, who was balancing ten books and a pizza box. Mary grabbed the pizza from Alyssa as she dumped the books on her bed.

Elena wasn't particularly happy with having to change rooms or roommates, especially now that she was stuck in a four-bed dorm. Three extra people to worry about. She should have gotten a single dorm.

Next door, Katya shoved her bags underneath her bed, not wanting to unpack. She had requested to stay with only one other person, and luckily, she got Zola. Zola was a pretty good roommate, Katya found. She was very clean and organized, spent most of her time in the library, and best of all, Zola stayed up just as late as she did. Katya was happy about that; she never wanted her stargazing habits to be an inconvenience to other people.

While the girls were settling into their new dorms, the boys just returned their books. Aiken and Henry were the only ones who didn't switch dorms or arrangements. After throwing out his school schedule and clearing his desk of all study materials, Henry started tinkering with his computer's motherboard. It was the largest and most impractical thing Aiken had ever seen, but he didn't want to tell Henry that as he looked too happy.

"A whole week until the summer semester starts. A whole

week to not worry about studying, or teachers, or projects, so what do you want to do?"

Henry turned around. "You want to do something? Really?"

Aiken shrugged. "I mean yeah, why not? There's nothing to do here."

Henry laughed. "I might just sleep all day tomorrow. Where do you want to go?"

"Hmmm. I think there's an art museum in the area."

"Yeah, you go visit that."

"Maybe I will."

* * * * * * * * *

"This isn't fair." Zola sat on the floor picking her nails.

"What isn't?" Astra set her computer on the desk and tossed her bag onto the top shelf of the small closet.

"You get a single dorm."

"I asked for a single dorm."

"I should have asked for a single dorm."

"Well, maybe you should have thought about that earlier." Astra threw a water bottle at her. "Drink up, go on."

Zola caught it, and unscrewed the cap, gulping it down. She swallowed roughly and laughed. "Well, even if you are a weirdo, and literally one of the most annoying people I've ever met, you gotta admit, you make us have healthy habits."

Astra nodded. "You have to drink at least three bottles today based on your weight."

Zola frowned. "You know how much I weigh?"

"Not really, I just estimated."

"Oh." Zola got up off the floor. "Well I better head back to my dorm, I have unpacking to do. You coming to dinner?"

"Nope. Got more important things."

"I'm gonna pretend like I'm not insulted by that. Night!"

"Bye."

Zola left the room, and Astra locked the door behind her.

Astra picked up her phone, which had been buzzing with notifications for the past few minutes.

She unlocked it and checked her messages. *'I'll be visiting next month, okay?'* She snorted. *'It's about time,'* she responded. Astra flopped down on her bed. They had the whole summer ahead of them, and so long as the person hadn't graduated, Astra intended to find them. *'Who is J? And what will we find if we find them? When we find them?'*

She glared at the ceiling. Better not to think about it. Astra grabbed her journal and began writing down a to-do list and the day's events. She wouldn't say that she would miss Zola, she would see her in a lot of her future classes, but there was something weird about having a room to herself. Astra shook her head. She didn't need to think about that. She had a lot of work to do, and having another person in her dorm would only make things more complicated.

Especially if it was Zola.

* * * * * * * * * *

Zola stomped back towards her dorm and threw the door open, startling Katya, who fell off her bed.

"Warn me next time," she grumbled, pulling herself back up.

"Yeah, yeah, yeah, sorry." Zola plopped down on her bed. "Any ideas for what we're doing before school starts again?"

Katya stared at her for a second. "Maybe you should sleep, seeing as you're so grumpy," Katya said. "And I want to get food. If you're feeling nicer, maybe we could try to figure out what that clue means later."

Zola rolled her eyes. "Whatever you all want, I just want to do something."

Katya pulled her phone out. "Well, I've half figured this out."

Zola frowned and hopped on the bed next to her. "Hmm?"

"The lowest point, it means the lowest point in the school. I have no idea where that is, but that's what I think. I also narrowed down on the handwriting. I wouldn't go as far as to say it is definitely a boy's handwriting, but I ruled out most of the girls in the school, and a lot of the boys in our grade. I would say that it's probably an upperclassman if it's a female's handwriting. But I have eight people now."

"Interesting. Who?"

"Daia Jansen, Castor Allen—his middle name is Jackson apparently—Jo Barrera, Yoanna Joffre, James Kawle, Jenny Ross, Julia Allaire and Justin Juarez."

Zola squinted at Katya's phone. "I thought Elena ruled Castor out."

"I haven't checked his writing so I can't know for sure, and to be honest, I don't always trust Elena."

"Fair enough. Well, let me know when you figure it out." Zola hopped off the bed.

"What, no 'thank you?'"

Zola stopped. "Thank you for your help Katya, you're amazing."

"That sounded sarcastic."

"I swear it wasn't!" Zola was out of the room before Katya could get another word out.

"Hmph. I do all the work around here, don't I?"

Katya plugged her phone in and pulled a piece of pizza out of the box that Alyssa had dropped off a couple of hours earlier. There was a knock on the door.

"You can't get the door yourself?" Katya grumbled as she got up. "Oh, hi Henry. What do you need?"

Henry smiled awkwardly. "Hi. Aiken told me to pick something up from you, he's taking astronomy as an elective this semester, but he's on the phone with his mother so he couldn't come get it himself."

Katya pursed her lips. "Yeah, I have a couple of star charts I said I would lend him. Let me find them. Oh." Katya picked the pizza box up and passed it to him. "You two can have what's left of this, Zola probably isn't going to eat it."

"Oh yeah, I passed her on the way over. Don't know what she's doing. Thanks."

"No problem. Here they are!" Katya emerged from behind the door and dumped the charts on top of the pizza box. "Is that all you need? I still have some work to do."

"Work?"

"Yep, my favor for Zola."

Henry raised an eyebrow. "So, you're still gonna go after whatever it is that Zola wants you to find?"

"Of course! It's interesting. Though, I do need to narrow down my list more."

"Can I see it?"

"See what?"

Henry rolled his eyes. "This list."

"Oh." Katya looked taken aback. "Uh yeah, it's on my phone. Here."

"Hmmm." Henry scrolled through the list. "Interesting."

"What?"

"It's not Castor, Jenny, Daia, Yoanna, or James."

"You know that for a fact?"

"Of course. I've gotten all of their phone numbers. Except for Castor. I swiped that from Elena. She is right though." Henry passed the phone back to Katya. "Maybe don't be so suspicious of people just because they have a suspicious face. Elena is more trustworthy than you probably think. The point is, I've seen their handwriting, and it doesn't match."

Katya shrugged and tucked her phone into her back pocket. "I'll keep that in mind. How do you get people's numbers anyway?"

"Because unlike you, I actually talk to people."

Katya scoffed. "I don't need people to live."

Henry laughed. "Maybe you don't. But you do need to figure that out. Now, I better get going, and if you're going to actually keep researching this, you should probably go to sleep."

"Go to sleep," Katya mocked. "Fine."

"Goodnight Katya." Henry waved and disappeared down the corridor.

Katya rolled her eyes and retreated back into her room. Though her list was shorter now, it wouldn't make her work any less difficult. Katya set a soft alarm on her phone, placing it right by her ear. She'd wake up in a few hours to look at the stars, but for now, it wouldn't hurt to sleep just a little.

20

The Lowest Point

The next day, Katya woke with a start. She checked her phone to find that not only was it noon, but she had several missed calls and messages. The others had gone out for lunch and decided not to wake her. It was a good idea, given her midnight stargazing. She hadn't actually fallen asleep until around four a.m.

Katya slid out of bed, dragging as she got dressed. She grabbed a granola bar and her purse on her way out of the dorm. Today, all she could think about was her promise to Zola to help her figure out the clue. *'The lowest point, the lowest point. What could that mean?'* Katya headed towards the closest computer lab, stopping at a vending machine to get a bottle of coffee.

It was her first time in the room alone. The computer labs were usually packed, it was typically difficult to even find a computer open to use, that's why there were so many computer labs scattered across the school. Katya turned one of the computers on and sat down, humming softly under her breath. She wasn't exactly sure what she was looking for, but she was sure she'd know it when she saw it.

Katya started off by typing the university name into the search engine. It wasn't hard to find articles and videos on Torsion University and the application process. Most of these websites were familiar to her, as she used many of them back when she applied. The more she scrolled through articles about Torsion, the more she felt like she was going nowhere. She almost exited the browser when an old, abandoned science blog caught her eye.

It wouldn't hurt to read it. Katya skimmed it briefly, noting the older tech schools and festivals that the author of the blog wrote about. She was surprised to find that Torsion University had its own section. The last article published about the school was in the year 2000, titled *'Torsion University's 15th Anniversary Showcase.'*

Katya raised an eyebrow. "First of all, that is a terrible title. Second of all, come on, this is your last post about Torsion? People really never keep up with writing their blogs anymore, do they?" she questioned aloud.

She clicked the link all the same. The post was shorter than she expected, filled mostly with background information on the school and the students' accomplishments, as well as photos of the projects presented in the showcase. "Hmm, okay, here's something that we all didn't know," Katya said sarcastically. " *'Torsion University is known worldwide for its work in technology. It attracts people from all over the world, as freshmen, transfer, graduate, and international students. Torsion primarily works with computers and biology, and it's ground-breaking 2000 showcase, which featured a computer that could react and adapt to emotions shown to it.'* Now that last part is interesting though," she quipped to the empty room.

Katya clicked on the photo at the bottom of the page, a small group of students standing in front of a computer displaying a smiley face on its screen. Katya's eyes widened. Because there was one person in the photo that was too familiar to ignore. "Cassian?" Katya exited out of the browser immediately and slumped into her chair. This was something that she couldn't ignore.

Katya ran multiple scenarios in her head. There were only two possible explanations that she could think of: either it wasn't Cassian, or Cassian Brooks was not who they thought he was. And if the latter was true, then he must have had a part in the codes and clue that Zola had found. She knew Cassian wasn't the one who wrote on the wall, he couldn't have been. It wasn't his writing; it wasn't his name. But whatever the case, he had to have been involved. Which meant that the only way to get an answer for his appearance in a 20-plus year-old photo was to figure the clue out.

"The lowest point, the lowest point," she muttered. "Of course! Why didn't I think of this before?" Katya pulled up the college website, searching for the map of the school. Sure enough, the restricted area that Zola had found the clue in was the lowest known level of the school. Katya took a deep breath. She texted Zola to let her know where she was going. If anything happened, and Katya shuddered at the thought, she wanted them to be able to find her.

Katya left the computer lab and headed towards the stairs. There was only one thing that Katya couldn't wrap her head around. If the restricted area was the lowest point in the school, how come Zola hadn't seen anything in the area? Katya arrived at the entrance to the restricted area and hesitated. Then she took a deep breath and descended into the darkness.

Katya turned on her phone flashlight, and pointed it into the hallway, searching for the clue that Zola had found earlier. She spotted it at the bottom of the staircase. Chills ran down Katya's back. She was terrified that something was going to jump out at her. But there was nothing in the darkness. Katya turned around in a circle. There didn't seem to be anything down there but a wall.

It wasn't until she headed back towards the staircase that she noticed the door behind it. She tried to open it, and unsurprisingly, it was locked. She groaned. If there was anything that she had learned from her brother that stuck with her, it was how to bypass locks, and it was a useful skill, but it required a few things.

Katya reached into her purse and pulled out a small multitool. It was a gift from Astra, and she was very grateful to have it at this moment. She opened it and selected a small screwdriver. It was the closest in size to the lock screws, and in a few minutes, she had unscrewed the handle and entered the hallway behind it.

She screwed the handle back on, then turned towards the soft white light coming from the end of the hallway. She trembled, flipping her multitool to a small knife. Her phone buzzed.

'We're almost there,' Zola had texted.

'Hurry,' she replied. Katya noticed a window to the side of the door and crouched low, not wanting anyone to see her as she got closer. There was no one in the room when she looked through. Katya touched the doorknob tentatively. Nothing shocked her or burned her, and no alarm went off. She turned the handle. The door swung open easily and she walked inside.

Katya gasped. The room wasn't just any room. It was a lab. Tubes lined the walls, several of them, some were so tall they touched the ceiling, others were half their size, or even smaller. The room was pure white, sterile, clean, containing nothing other than medical instruments and a couple of computers and tablets. Her phone buzzed again.

'We're at the stairs, we're coming down, are you okay?'

Katya gave a sigh of relief. *'Yes.'* She heard footsteps down the hall as the others rushed into the room.

"Katya!" Nasra ran towards her and hugged her. "We thought you were dead or something."

"Yeah!" Mary glared at Katya over Nasra's shoulder. "You're very lucky we were already on our way back."

Alyssa fell into the closest chair. "My lungs hurt," she complained.

"You're out of shape," Aiken commented.

Nasra released Katya from the hug only to grab her by the shoulders. "Are you sure you're okay?"

"I'm fine, thanks for asking."

Nasra nodded and let go, turning around to stare at the room.

Zola did the same as she walked in. "You found it," she said.

"Yeah, I did. But guys, I have to tell you someth—" Katya's voice was drowned out in the chaos as the others began to explore the room. She sighed and looked down. "I just wanted to tell you that I thought I saw Cassian Brooks in a photo from 2000," she whispered.

They didn't hear her in their race to search the lab and the connected rooms. Katya was secretly grateful for that, because maybe, just maybe, she had hallucinated it.

However, Astra still heard her. Astra frowned as she started to dig through the hundreds of files in the cabinet labeled *'Acquired Projects.'*

'Cassian Brooks, huh?' she thought. *'I'll have to look into that. Now, where are they? Davis, Dixon, Duncan, aha! Duke. Here it is.'* Astra pulled a couple of files out of the cabinet and snuck them into her bag.

"We'd better hurry up and leave. We can explore later. What if someone comes?" Astra rushed them out of the room.

Later in her dorm, Astra sat on her bed, flipping through the stolen files. Most of the files didn't have much information in them, just tests, records of meetings, and half-finished blueprints. She didn't care much for those. She did care, however, about the sentence in the second paragraph, on the fourth page of the third file. It made her blood boil, a cruel joke from a cruel man, referencing the game they were forever locked in.

'PROJECT CHECKMATE: SUBJECT ZERO — Duke, Destiny: reprogrammed.'

Headless

Life after the discovery of the lab wasn't the same. Once they determined that it was safe, they made regular trips down in order to look through the rooms. There was a lot down there, and they wanted to be careful, but as always, curiosity outweighed any worries. That day, Aiken wished he had thought of the consequences.

He had gone to visit the lab by himself, in the hope of finding some biology research, or maybe some interesting plants. What he found was a door in the corner, behind one of the many tubes. There were at least 15 more of them in the room behind, and something else sitting on one of the tables, and he wished he could burn the picture from behind his eyes.

He hadn't screamed, well, at least not loudly. He also hadn't told anyone, for fear of bringing it to life. All he could remember was staring into the blank, lifeless eyes of a head that resembled Willow James, and it was too perfect, too close to her likeness to be a coincidence. Wires were sticking out of her neck and ears, and as soon as he saw it, Aiken had gotten out of there as quickly as possible.

It finally hit him as he reached his dorm, and he immediately threw up in the toilet as soon as he got back to the dorms. He had sat on the bathroom floor for an hour, until Henry finally knocked on the door.

"Aiken, get out of there, I need to use the bathroom too!"

He got up, brushed his teeth, and opened the door. Henry hurriedly rushed past him and pushed Aiken out of the bathroom, muttering something in Korean as he closed the door. Aiken trudged towards his bed and flopped down on it. Unfortunately for him, he didn't sleep that night.

The next morning, Aiken decided to skip breakfast, instead

opting to pace up and down the hallways of the school. Every so often, a few stray students passed him, carrying books and boxes that he knew contained supplies for the start of summer classes on Monday. Aiken avoided them, keeping his head down. That was a bad idea, as he soon ran headfirst into something. Or rather, someone, who dropped her papers on the floor on impact.

"Watch where you're going! Seriously."

Aiken looked up into familiar brown eyes, not blank as he last remembered, but very much alive, and slightly angry. "I, you—" he stuttered.

"Come on, spit it out!" Willow glared at him in irritation.

"I'm sorry?"

"Sorry?"

Aiken panicked. "Sorry that I ran into you, bye!" Aiken ran past her, darting down another hallway so he couldn't hear what she said next. Aiken stopped on the third floor and flopped down on the steps. He had a flashback to Willow's head on the table and winced. How could she be in two places at once? How could her head be on that table when she was right in front of him just a few seconds ago? Aiken was pretty sure that Willow was human, she couldn't be anything else, right? He shook his head and took off towards the dorms. He needed to stop thinking too much.

There was no way that was even possible. Willow James was very much human, and as a student at the school, she could have made that robotic head, or someone else could have, for fun, or as a project. There was no other logical explanation. He didn't want to entertain the other ideas that entered his head.

Aiken nearly hit Henry in the face with the door when he entered the room.

"Woah there buddy, what's the rush?" Henry asked.

"Oh, nothing." Aiken fell backwards onto his bed. "Hey, what are you doing here, shouldn't you be down there having breakfast?"

"Already ate," Henry said dismissively. "I was thinking about the lab, and—"

Aiken groaned and buried his face into his pillow "Oh, don't talk about the lab," he said, voice muffled.

Henry frowned. "Why?"

"I don't want to think about that right now."

Henry rolled his eyes. "It's not that deep, and besides, we've barely scratched the surface of what's in there, but classes are going to start soon which means we can't spend as much time there anymore."

"Good," Aiken muttered.

"What?"

"Nothing, focus on whatever you're doing."

* * * * * * * *

Astra paced back and forth in her room. Everything that had happened, all that she had found in the lab, finally came crashing down on her. Destiny Duke. A friend. A traitor. Astra laughed; she was so stupid. It was as if she hadn't gone along with the plan, hadn't agreed to go to Torsion, to apply. Her being here was supposed to fix what they lost. She wasn't sure it'd be enough anymore. With Destiny here, that meant there could be any number of people like her, and anyone could be a killer. From what Katya said, Astra was already sure that Cassian was one of them. Anyone could be an enemy. She was no longer doing grunt work, and if she slipped up even a bit, well, she didn't want to think of that.

'Trust no one.' The last words she remembered when her brother handed her a plane ticket. *'Stick to the plan.'* The plan had to change. Astra returned to the dorm. She opened her text messages, scrolling until she found the person she was looking for.

'We need to talk in person, hurry up.'

Astra closed her phone and put it in her back pocket. She wasn't happy with her current situation. Not only did she have to follow through with her original plan, but she had to deal with Destiny as well, which would really slow her down. If there was one personality trait that Destiny had, it was that she was cunning. No matter what you threw at her, she could solve it.

It was a great skill to have on your side, which meant it was terrible to be on the opposing team. Astra facepalmed. It was her fault after all, that Destiny was taken. She wasn't as careful when she was younger and let Destiny slip through her fingers. It was one of those life lessons that her guardians didn't punish her for. She got a lecture instead, and more training time. It was better than nothing, that was for sure.

Even though Destiny was reprogrammed, and there was no guarantee that she'd even recognize Astra, she didn't want to take any chances. There was no point in risking her entire operation, so she'd have to play it safe from now on. She knew how to act like she was being watched, it was a part she had played many times. But Astra hated that role. It meant she had to tiptoe, and sneak around, let lying become her second nature. That was the odd thing about her family: They were always honest with each other but hid behind a mask the second they stepped outside the door.

She was never told the real reason why, but she was content to not ask questions, and to simply blend in with the walls. Yet another useful life skill. Astra picked through a box of old computer parts and started tinkering with them, trying to distract herself. She still needed to work on her project.

It was something like a virtual beacon, a technological anchor in a sea of information. For the school, it wouldn't be too impressive. It was like saving your spot in a book. But it would get her enough points to graduate, as far as she knew, no one had done anything with the dark web. Something about the kids in the school made Astra think that they were either too stuck up, or too scared to go off the internet grid.

Astra looked down at the mess of wires and gears in her hands. She could make this kind of processing unit in her sleep. She tossed it into the basket of parts and kicked it underneath her bed. She sat down. Her mind once again drifted to Destiny as she got up and got ready for bed. This was going to be very difficult.

Astra slipped underneath her covers, trying to relax. Her mind was still racing, calculating, adjusting. She'd have to go through the rest of the files in that lab soon. She'd need to find and then stick close to Torsion's androids. Astra flipped to face the wall. And whatever she did, she couldn't let the others know.

22

Mourning

The next few weeks went by pretty smoothly. The group still went down to the lab every once in a while, until they started noticing changes to the lab, things being moved, missing files, weird smells. After that, the visits were sparse. Astra went down there the most despite the dangers. Though, most of the time, the others didn't even notice she was gone. She spent hours poring over the files until she finally found what she wanted.

After that, Astra didn't make any more trips to the lab. Instead, she stayed in the library, tutoring some other students in math and working on her project. There were days that Zola and Henry joined her. They worked together in silence, though they occasionally traded notes. Then, Astra got a phone call, and two visits to the dean later, she got permission to leave the school for a while.

No one had time to question where Astra had gone. Summer finals were just three weeks away, and per usual, the school got busier. Of course, summer courses were a lot less crowded since most already completed their required summer semester, but it didn't make anyone less stressed. Zola found out that summer class final preparation started way earlier than regular classes, which was most likely a product of the fact that they were shorter.

Zola thought that the group would study together, but to her surprise, everyone just started doing their own thing. Henry no longer joined her in the study room on Wednesday nights, and Zola found herself missing Astra. She was worried too. Astra didn't seem like the kind of person to just get up and leave, especially not right before finals. She hoped that Astra would be back in time for the tests.

The last three weeks of the summer semester went by in a flash, and then they were free, for a week. Astra had returned halfway through finals week and didn't speak to anyone until she had done make ups for all her tests. Zola followed her around for a few days, trying to get answers out of Astra as to where she had been, but failed.

It wasn't until Zola ended up in Astra's dorm the night before the fall semester started that she found out.

"You're so quiet," Zola complained. "All you do is mope about, and you don't work with us, you haven't gone out to lunch with us, the semester starts tomorrow, and you still haven't done anything fun. What's the point of having a week off if you won't even take off? I thought that maybe, at least you would take a break, but no, you work on your own."

Astra sighed. "Everyone has different ways of mourning Zola."

Zola frowned. "Mourning?"

Astra nodded and sat down on her bed, crossing her feet. "My mother died years ago. The call I got a few weeks ago was to let me know that my father had finally passed away." Astra looked down. "He was supposed to be on a business trip, and instead he went somewhere else to die. He was in critical condition, some illness that they couldn't cure him of."

Zola stared at her sympathetically. "I'm really sorry for your loss Astra."

Astra looked up. "Don't be. Sorry won't bring him back. I just wish there was a safe way for him to spend his last moments with us."

"Safe?"

Astra half-smiled. "You could say that the sickness he had was contagious. He didn't want to hurt anyone. My father was a good man, at least, that's how I see him. It really depends on whose side you're on."

Zola cocked her head. "What?"

"Everyone who's ever had a parent who was a soldier knows that when it comes to war, there is no good or evil, just people fighting to survive. We all fight for the same cause Zola. No one wants to die, but for their family? You'd do anything. I would do anything."

Zola stared at her. "You know, this is the first time that I've ever heard you say anything about your family."

"Well, they're not really my parents, and none of my siblings are truly related to me. We're a bunch of street kids, and they gave us a home." Astra looked her in the eyes. "I've grown up since then. As a kid, I used to think that there was nothing as stupid as following your heart. Better people than me have been killed for just following orders." She looked down. "The more you lose, the more you realize what you have to cling to Zola. In this life, nothing matters more than how you live."

"Wow."

"What?"

Zola pursed her lips. "It's just— you talk like you've seen way too much for someone your age."

Astra snorted. "I guess you could put it that way. Though, my family did put a lot of emphasis on education. We had to be the perfect kids. We were taught how to live on our own, just in case something happened to them. I mean, we were free to come and go as we pleased, we were never officially their children, but they looked out for us. It's nice to know that you always have somewhere to go back to."

Zola nodded. "I bet it is."

Astra sat on her bed staring off into the distance for a long time after Zola left. She hadn't spoken to anyone about her family before. It was ingrained in her, ever since the first incident. Astra remembered her mother braiding her hair and making her recite the list of rules.

"You do not speak about your home, anything you say can and will be used against you. People get put in harm's way if you talk. You are always polite, you speak when spoken to, you stay in the shadows. It's best to observe instead of interacting," she said soft-ly. Years of training had drilled that lesson into her head.

"I miss you," Astra whispered to the empty air.

Just another reason to finish up quickly. The sooner she got done, the sooner she could go home and pay tribute to her guardians. Her parents, she corrected herself. They raised her for a time, and she didn't have anyone else. Astra closed her eyes tightly, trying to ignore the memories that welled up in her mind. This was the only way she knew how to repay them. She just hoped she wouldn't let them down.

Astra got up and began to clean, straightening up her dorm and trying to make it look presentable. Of course, she had time to prepare, and who cared if her room was a mess, they knew her all too well to complain. Astra didn't mind trusting other people, so long as they proved themselves to her. But on this type of mission, she couldn't. Feelings only got in the way. Her phone buzzed, revealing yet another disappointment. Astra sat down and read the text message.

'Won't be able to make it for a few more months, but you can handle yourself, right? We'll talk when I get there, be careful Little Star.'

Astra sighed. She could put off organizing her room even more, now that she wouldn't be having people in here. She guessed the questions and the help could wait, but there was only so much time until she would take matters into her own hands. She deleted the conversation. There was no use in people reading her messages and finding out.

Astra pulled her journal out of her bag, opening it to the checklist she had created when she first arrived at the school. *'Get into Torsion, check. Don't be suspicious to teachers, check. Figure out what Leroy Parkes was hiding, check. Befriend the others, check.'* Astra looked down at the bottom lines, the last pieces of the puzzle. *'Eliminate the Glitch, request backup (first time for every-*

thing).' Astra snapped the book shut. *'Fine, I'll do it myself. I'll eliminate the Glitch.'*

23

Building

The first few days of the fall semester started normally. The group quickly began to get back into their routine of hanging out, almost as if they didn't ignore each other during summer finals. It was the first semester that they didn't change dorms. After a long fight with the school board, they were allowed to stay where they were. Alyssa suspected that they were simply tired of having to deal with them.

The first three weeks of the semester for second years were reserved for working on projects. No assignments were due, just show up to class, take a quiz or two, listen in on the lecture and then the afternoon was free.

Henry was the one who was most excited. He strode down the hall carrying a large box, eager to get back to work. Unfortunately, he was still missing some of the materials he needed for his project. The science department ordered them a couple of days ago, so he assumed they would arrive soon. Henry got one of the bigger rooms to work in, which was lucky considering the size of his computer. His project might not be one of the best, but it would certainly be one of the biggest.

Henry fumbled with his student ID for a minute, then swiped it at the panel and pushed the door open. He set the box on the table, pulled his notebooks out and set them aside, then dumped the box on the table. He had grabbed a bunch of wires and several other motherboards from old computers. He had started to remake them a few days ago, a process that required welding the smaller motherboards together into one big one and then rewiring.

That main motherboard was sitting in a thick protective glass case, surrounded by the steel cage he was working on. He had made a second one as a backup in case the original one did break and had installed it yesterday. The cage would serve as a sort of box to hold the inner workings of the computer, and then he would build the screen above it. The problem was, he didn't entirely know how to power it yet.

The thing would drain hundreds of batteries just to stay on for a few minutes, and Henry wasn't entirely sure if he wanted to have it run off electricity, lest it take out all the power in the school. But it was a start. He'd figure out something, even if it wasn't right now.

Henry attached the new wires and plugs, doing his best to add to the contraption. Until the bigger parts came in, the thing couldn't do much, which was disappointing but unavoidable. Henry finished up the last of the wiring for the base and ticked it off on his list.

He'd have to get some steel poles and panels to make up the protective outer container and line the inside with fans and holes for ventilation so the computer wouldn't overheat. Finally, after determining that he couldn't do anything else, Henry left the room, making sure it was properly locked before heading back to the dorms.

Aiken was sitting cross-legged on his bed reading when Henry came in.

"What's up?" he asked.

"I got most of my wiring done, that's about it. You?"

Aiken turned the page of his book. "I'm working on the research paper now. My plant is done."

Henry laughed.

Aiken closed the book. "That sounded condescending."

"It's not, I swear. It's just different."

"Of course it's different, we're in different programs," Aiken snapped.

"You know what I mean." Henry sat down. "For us computer science majors, we just build things. I've talked to Katya, Elena, and Mary, and they basically do the same thing, except Mary also has to turn in her blueprints. Elena just uses hers for notes or something. But you, Nasra, and Alyssa are the oddballs. You have those papers to write."

Aiken nodded. "Odd way of putting it, but yes, we do have to write papers. It's a summary of all our research, the hypothesis, trial and error stage, and our results. We have to present both because we have to prove how we did it, unlike you guys. You just have to build stuff."

Henry snorted. "Build stuff."

"Tell me I'm wrong, I dare you."

"No, you're right. It's just funny."

Aiken raised an eyebrow and picked his book up again. "At least I have it easy. Alyssa's trial and error stage is twelve pages long. And poor Nasra. Her introduction, thesis, and hypothesis alone is longer than my entire paper."

Henry whistled. "Wow. To have motivation like they do? I would kill for that."

"First of all, you wouldn't hurt a fly. Secondly, you barely get up in the morning. How are you going to find the motivation to kill someone to get motivation?"

Henry frowned. "It's an expression for goodness sake!"

Aiken rolled his eyes. "Unfortunately, I'm not as fluent in English as you are, so please refrain from expressing yourself using idioms."

"Tch. You literally— never mind."

"Just because I know how to use big words, doesn't mean I know everything about this language."

"Yeah, yeah, yeah, whatever." Henry looked down at his phone. "So, how long until you're done with your project?"

"Again, I just have to finish the essay, so however long it takes me to edit."

"Lucky."

"Maybe you should have chosen an easier major."

"And work on something other than computer science? No way! You know, the sole reason I got into computers was because my older brother broke our shared one and my mother couldn't be bothered to buy a new one, so I just fixed it. Bam! New hobby."

"That's an interesting backstory."

"What about you? How'd you get here?"

Aiken closed his book for the second time and placed it on his nightstand. "My grandmother was a botanist, she taught me everything I know about plants. Eventually, I got to the point where we started making a game out of it, trying to identify every single plant in our area. I got her notes when she died. I was finishing elementary school at that time. I decided to study in order to go to university so I could follow in her footsteps. Mother always told me that learning English would be the best for me, so I did. I didn't get very far when I was younger though."

"You seem to be just fine now."

"That's now. Mother sent me to visit a cousin in England for a summer. I had to speak English there the whole time. Then I went back home for my last year, I kept studying, but I didn't speak it, and forgot how to pronounce things. Then I did a crash course in pronunciation right before I came here, and I still feel uncomfortable speaking sometimes."

"You sound good."

Aiken stared pointedly at him. "Henry. We're both international students. Of course it sounds good, anything is good to someone who doesn't have English as their first language."

Henry shrugged. "Yeah, I guess you're right."

"How'd you learn?"

"Learn what?"

"English?"

"Oh, it's required, I took it from elementary school all the way up until I graduated high school. My parents do business overseas, so they placed high emphasis on speaking second and third languages. You should meet my sister. She's the oldest, and she speaks five."

"Five languages?"

Henry nodded. "Yep! She's super successful, and so is my brother, and we're all competitive, so here I am."

"You're the youngest then?"

"Yeah, but I don't mind as much anymore."

"Is it fun, having siblings?"

"Depends on where you're from. My siblings and I are very respectful of each other, so I would say we're close. Now, other people might say that having siblings is the worst thing in the world. Why?"

"I'm an only child. I never had any siblings, I was raised by my mom and grandma, so that was it for most of my social interaction up until I started high school. I kind of wish I had a brother."

Henry smiled.

"What?"

"I just had a great idea."

"What?"

"You're my little brother now. Don't question it."

"What?!"

"Come on, I've always wanted a younger brother, I didn't like being the youngest."

Aiken rolled his eyes. "You're so weird."

Henry laughed. "Yeah, wait until you meet my family. I'm the least chaotic."

"I highly doubt that."

"Doubt all you want. If you ever get to meet my family, you'll see for yourself."

Aiken chuckled. "It's a deal. Then you can meet my mom and she'll make you bread and rant about bees."

"Bees?"

"Yes, bees. You cannot escape the bee lecture."

"Bee lecture?!"

Aiken nodded aggressively. "I was already scared of bees. Now I hate honey."

"Is this a contest now? Who has the weirdest family? I kind of want your mom to meet my mom, simply because my mother, the serious businesswoman that she is, has this odd hobby of weaving. She made our clothes for a whole two years when I was in middle school. Even though we could have just bought them. But hey, at least I know how to embroider."

Aiken snorted. "That was the funniest thing I've ever heard in my life."

"I'm serious!"

"I know! That's what makes it funny!"

Henry rolled his eyes. "Yeah, okay." He checked his watch. "Oh no!"

"What?"

"I'm late for class, I gotta go, but when I get back, you have to promise to explain the bee lecture."

"Only if you tell me about how you learned to embroider."

"Deal." Henry raced out the door.

"Good luck!" Aiken called after him. He shook his head and laughed softly. "Embroidery… That's actually a pretty cool skill." He shrugged and picked up his book again, settling back down to read.

24

Nasra Takes a Break (Sort Of)

Elena hit her head against a beam and fell down. "Ugh!" She touched the side of her head and hissed slightly at the pain. That was going to leave a bruise. She needed to be more careful. Elena had been assigned to one of the smaller project rooms, meaning that she had to build in a way that made it difficult to get in and out of the room. Currently, she was building the skeleton, a waist high cylinder looking thing, silver, messy, and slightly sharp. She stepped around it, trying to give it as much space as possible. A few days ago, she had ripped one of her shirts on a spike and she had no desire to repeat that.

There was a knock on the door. Elena frowned and opened it to see Nasra standing outside holding a box. She lifted it slightly, smiling. "Got the parts you asked for."

Elena moved, trying to open the door wider. "Come in, if you can. It's a little difficult."

"That sounded like a threat, was that a threat?"

"Could be. Careful!"

Nasra laughed as she maneuvered into the room. "Wow, you really have absolutely no space in here. What are you even building?"

"Ah, ah, ah, you're not getting me to tell."

"Well, it was worth the try."

"Not really. Move please." Elena scooted past Nasra to grab a screwdriver, clambering onto the ledge behind her project and adding in more screws to hold the thing together.

Nasra frowned. "Seems complicated. Aren't you scared you're going to fall?" she asked.

Elena grunted. "Sometimes, but I just out-logic myself. I'm not going to fall too hard if I do fall, and I take the necessary precautions. There aren't any sharp objects underneath me, and I wear long sleeves. However, the sharp parts are on the other side. I need to sand them down, or cover them, but I haven't gotten around to it yet."

Nasra shrugged. "Well, good luck I guess. I'm going to the cafeteria, want to take a break and come with me?"

Elena sighed. "Nothing against you, but no thanks. I have a lot of work to do."

"Are you sure?"

"Yep."

"Do you want me to bring you something back?"

"No thanks, but thanks for the offer."

Nasra hesitated. "Alright, but let me know if you need anything, okay? Good luck!"

"Bye!"

Nasra left the room and headed towards the cafeteria. She didn't expect to do much today. She still had a few pages left of the second section of her paper, but she could wait until tomorrow to do them. Nasra wasn't in any particular rush today. In fact, she didn't plan on doing anything.

Nasra Dabiri considered herself to be organized. She scheduled herself, though as of late, she had learned that rest was important. So, for the entire day, she wouldn't work on her project, or on any of her other assignments. She did help the others though, besides bringing Elena her parts, Nasra had helped Katya move her telescope, quizzed Astra on chemical formulas, and worked with Alyssa while she tested her serum.

All in all, she would consider it a successful day, especially since she now had time to read the book that Mary recommended to her. Nasra tucked herself into a corner of the cafeteria and pulled out her book. She read while she ate, careful not to get any food on the pages. One of the life lessons she received from her mother was that you never ruin something lent to you. Always return it in the same or better condition than it was.

Katya seemed to have the same idea; it was one thing they agreed on. Any time they lent each other Tupperware, they were always returned with food in them. At this point, Nasra wasn't sure that she was ever going to get out of the cycle.

Speaking of Katya, Nasra spotted her out of the corner of her eye and waved her over. "How are you doing Kat?" she asked.

"Pretty good." Katya set her bag down on the floor by her feet.

"I've done a lot of work recently, and I think I'm on the right track. But you had a good idea, setting aside a rest day. I mean, technically"—she put air quotes around the word—"I haven't actually rested all that much, but I slept in, and that was certainly interesting. What about you?"

"I haven't touched any of my work, but I helped most of you with yours, so I'm not sure if that cancels out or not."

Katya shrugged. "I wouldn't know. But I'm sure you could go back to your dorm and sleep if you wanted. I know for a fact that Mary is still in the study room, and Alyssa is pretty quiet even if she is up there."

Nasra nodded. "Yeah, but I kinda feel bad for leaving Elena all by herself. She told me not to, but I still want to bring her food."

"Then do it. I don't see the problem here."

Nasra stabbed at her food with her fork. "I don't know, what if I'm intruding?"

Katya frowned. "Would you really be though?"

Nasra put her fork down and sighed. "I guess? I don't know."

Katya shrugged. "If you're not sure, you don't have to do it. I'm sure she'll be okay if you do it or not."

Nasra nodded. "Yeah, you're right. I guess I just wanted to do something nice for her."

Katya smiled. "Nasra, you do nice things for everyone. Look at all you've done for everyone this morning alone! It's okay, you don't have to worry so much."

"I know, I know. I guess, this is one of the few chances I have to be nice to people, I feel like I can actually do stuff, you know? I'm useful for once. I spent most of my life indoors, my friends were doing stuff for me. I want to be able to pay that forward."

"That's very admirable Nasra, but you need to remember that you can't do everything. It's okay to not please everyone. Besides, you said that she told you she didn't need it. Even if you're worrying about her, she made a choice to continue working. You can always check in later, right?"

"Yeah." Nasra got up. "Thanks for having lunch with me."

"Of course!" Katya grabbed her bag. "Do you want me to walk you to your dorm?"

"Oh, are you sure? I don't want to be an inconvenience."

Katya nodded. "Oh, don't worry, I want to. I don't have anything else to do anyway."

"Okay, sure."

The two set off towards the dorms.

"So…" Katya pursed her lips. "Do you have any plans for the weekend?"

"Probably just catching up on all the work that I didn't do today. Why?"

"Well, I'm going to be going into town for the first time to go get some food, and also some parts that are coming in for my telescope and I wanted to know if you wanted to come with me?"

Nasra nodded. "Sure, why not. I need to get some more paper and mail some letters anyway."

Katya smiled as the two came to a stop in front of Nasra's dorm door. "Perfect, I'll let you know what time I'm going. Well, we're here."

"Thanks for walking me, I'll see you around, okay?"

"See you!"

Nasra waved until Katya was out of sight before going into her room. She pulled her book out of her bag and flopped down on her bed. She might have to stay up all night to finish it, but it sure would be worth it.

25

Stolen

Aiken sat in the middle of the empty study hall, typing furiously. Once he got started on an idea, it was hard to stop. This caused him to spend hours at the computer writing, focused solely on what was in front of him.

The people that surrounded him earlier had long since left the room and gone to bed, but Aiken just couldn't leave. He wasn't even tired, though he was sure that he would be in the morning. Today's section was on the results of his growth serum. Ever since he figured out how to do it, he had grown hundreds of plants, all of their effects stronger as a result of his serum.

He spent an hour alone simply writing about how his flowers could be used to heal scars, reduce pain, keep a person awake longer or send them to sleep instantly, and help with headaches. His current work was a cross between peppermint and aloe vera, something that he hoped would be able to be used for a fast-acting burn cream.

He had questioned Alyssa about it that morning. He wasn't good with medicines, but she had agreed to be his lab rat after burning herself while making breakfast. It worked so well that Alyssa joked about stealing it and using it for her project. After that, Aiken worked alone. Even if it was just a joke, he wasn't going to take any chances.

Aiken knew one thing about himself. He was an Earth Science major, specializing in botany. He grew plants, he most definitely did not work in health science. But, if there was anything that his research could be used to help with, he wouldn't have anything against it. Well, only after he graduated and published his research.

As the night wore on, Aiken's eyes began to grow heavy. He struggled to stay awake and continue writing. He was lucky it was the weekend. He wasn't sure if he would survive having to wake up early and go to class. It was only after he started repeating himself and misspelling words that Aiken decided to go back to the dorm.

He packed up and left, trying to make as little noise as possible. The hall monitors were a lot more gracious to students leaving the library at late hours, but the ones in the dorms were not as kind. Aiken managed to sneak past them and make it into his room safely. Unfortunately, he tripped over Henry's backpack and fell flat on his face in the entryway.

Henry woke up just to laugh at him and promptly fell back to sleep. Aiken groaned. He almost wanted to fall asleep on the floor, but he dragged himself around the room to get ready for bed. Then, he didn't go to sleep, instead subjecting himself to another hour of editing. He almost broke his computer by dropping it on the floor when he dozed off for the first time.

It was around four a.m. when Aiken decided to test his plants on himself. He had made a couple of pills for testing. They were powdered forms of some of his plants, some containing copious amounts of melatonin, the others made of caffeine. Aiken was pretty sure that he would stay awake way longer if he took the caffeine pill tonight. With Henry asleep, he couldn't prevent him from trying the medicine. He had already suffered through Henry's rant about him possibly having a heart attack or dying from the amount of concentrated caffeine. He didn't want to go through that again.

Aiken stared at the small red pill in his hand. He had taken some of Henry's advice and lowered the dosage. Aiken took a deep breath, dry swallowed it, then went back to work. After a few minutes, he could feel burning in his chest before his head cleared and was able to focus on his task. Suffice to say, Aiken didn't sleep at all that night. In fact, he didn't sleep for the next three nights.

* * * * * * * *

Elena tapped her fingers on the counter absentmindedly. She rarely ever left her project room for anything. But Nasra had asked her so nicely to help her bring boxes into the dorm, that she just couldn't refuse. After Elena had helped her, Nasra invited her to stay and made lunch. Elena had to admit that her cooking was way better than whatever the cafeteria had to offer.

She stayed even later when Nasra started talking about baking and how some interests are passed down genetically. Elena started rambling about her uncle who liked cars and had her work with him on his cars which was how she chose engineering as her major.

"I just really like working with machines. They're fascinating, and I think you would relate well to the computer science majors because they give machines brains, and you work on human brains."

It was three p.m. when Elena finally left the dorm to get back to work on her project. She took the stairs two at a time, eager to make up for lost time. Elena got to the room, opened the door and dropped her keys on the table. She glanced at the cylinder and froze. The plans that once sat next to her project were gone.

Elena panicked. She ran straight to the security office and got the tapes for the hallway. She skipped through the footage, heart racing. She stopped when she saw a familiar figure walk out from the direction of her work room.

She ran out of the room, headed towards the cafeteria. That's where they would be, they always were there. Elena ran faster, knocking a kid over as she burst into the room. She spotted the girl near the back and headed straight for her.

"It was you!" Elena pointed angrily at Zola.

"Me what? What did I do?"

"Don't even pretend like you don't know, you stole my plans!"

"What?"

"Yes you! The security cameras saw you in the area! They saw you exit the room!"

"You can't even get into the room without a key card, and until now, I didn't even know that was your room! Besides, did you actually see me exit that room?"

Elena paused "No," she said, unsure. "But that camera doesn't show the whole hallway, and you were the only person in the vicinity!"

"It wasn't me!"

"You're lying, it had to be you!"

"I promise you I didn't steal your plans!"

Elena slapped her in the face. Zola stumbled back, tears welling up in her eyes as she fell on the floor. She held her face gingerly. "Ow."

Elena clenched her fist. "Zola, did you or did you not steal my plans?"

Zola glared at her. "I swear, I didn't steal them, you have to believe me."

Elena looked into Zola's eyes. They were angry, but sincere, and she knew the other girl was telling the truth. "Fine. I believe you." She bent down and pulled Zola to her feet. "That doesn't mean I trust you, and I don't particularly like you right now. But if you didn't steal my plans, then who did?"

26

Found

"Thanks for your help," Elena said.

"Of course." Mary smiled at her.

The two stood in the courtyard right outside the library. Their majors overlapped in most places, they shared classes, and took similar tests. They never talked about their projects with one another, but they weren't above studying with each other. It wasn't the first time they had worked together. Most of the time however, they did it before class, using flashcards to quiz each other on terms.

Today was different, however. Elena was quieter, and when Mary asked her why, she was very cryptic in her answer. Finally, after about an hour of pestering her, Elena told her about her missing plans and how she suspected Zola was the problem.

"Why would Zola steal your plans? She doesn't seem like the kind of person to sell them to someone, and she most certainly doesn't need them."

"I didn't need to know her motives, I thought I had enough evidence, so I just reacted. She can be sneaky sometimes. I mean, I'm not stupid enough to only have one copy, but I don't want my work floating around somewhere where it could get plagiarized."

Mary nodded sympathetically. "I'm sure you'll find the culprit soon." She left shortly after to go get lunch, which left Elena to work on her own. Elena sighed. Zola would join her soon. Since their incident, Elena had reviewed the tape over and over and came to the conclusion that Zola wasn't responsible for the loss of her plans. However, that didn't make the job finding the person who did any easier.

Luckily, Zola had agreed to help, begrudgingly so. It helped that Elena had bought her food as an apology, and Mary had come with her.

"Good afternoon El, how are you?"

Elena started and turned around. She cleared her throat. "Uh, hi Zola. Sorry about the uh," she pointed at the pink still spread across Zola's cheek.

"It's fine. What's done is done, and while it still hurts, at least I can cover it up if I want to. It'll fade soon anyway." Zola left out the conversation with her older brothers, both of whom advised her to forgive Elena, and give her the benefit of the doubt, just this once.

"So," Elena looked at her feet. "Where do we start?"

"Well, I was hoping I could take a look at those security tapes you have."

"I've gone over them hundreds of times though."

"It doesn't hurt to have a second set of eyes."

"I suppose that's true. Come on."

Elena and Zola got access to one of the smaller study rooms where Elena proceeded to show Zola the area from multiple angles.

Zola paused the footage. "Can I get a look inside the room?"

"There aren't any cameras in there."

Zola frowned. "Why not?"

"So no one can hack the footage and spy on you while you're working."

"Huh. Well, I suppose that makes sense…" she trailed off. "That's strange."

"What's wrong?"

Zola pointed to one of the screens. "Look at that. The camera is pointed towards your room door here." She fast forwarded a few days. "But it's not pointed at your door here on the day the plans were stolen."

Elena sat back in her chair. "So, whoever did it was able to move the security cameras."

Zola nodded. "They could have had access, or they could have just hacked it. Either way, we're not going to be able to tell from here. And, even if we could find another camera, there's a chance that the person was able to get in another way." Zola paused and looked at Elena. "Do you know if there are any passageways in your workroom?"

Elena shook her head. "No, I checked when I went in there."

"What about near your room? There's a possibility that there's a passage near your workroom we didn't know about, and that a camera could have caught it."

"If that was their way in, why would they forget to move a camera?"

Zola grinned. "Everyone overlooks things. Hang on a second."

"What are you doing?"

"I am getting a hold of Astra to see if she can ask Morgan if her friend know of any passageways in the area."

"That seems pretty complicated."

"Oh don't worry, Astra's always ready to help."

Elena nodded. "Yeah, she is."

Zola pursed her lips. "One of her many good qualities. She may be weird, and secretive, and know too much, but she helps us, and that's all that really matters. She's the kind of person you do not want to have as an enemy— oh, good!"

"Did you find one?"

"Yeah, it's down the hall, and it opens up into the workroom across the hall apparently."

Elena pointed at the screen. "But it's out of the camera's range too."

"That room is. The entrance to it isn't. Move." Zola took over the computer and switched to one of the cameras a floor above. "Okay, so, see that wall right there? It swings open. There are multiple passageways connected there, so we're going to have to watch a lot of the footage. See, there's Morgan and Eric, late for class, I remember that."

Elena raised an eyebrow. "There's Astra, I didn't know she used the passageways."

"Oh, of course she does. How else did you think she was able to pop up out of nowhere all the time?"

"Fair enough."

Zola fast forwarded more. "A lot of people walk by this place so it's hard to tell who's going in and who's coming out."

Elena leaned forward suddenly and pointed. "Hey, stop, go back."

Zola frowned and rewound the tape. Her eyes widened. "Oh… is that?"

"Delilah?"

Zola's laughed in shock. "Wow, well," she shook her head. "That was unexpected."

"Why would Delilah Hayes, of all people, want to steal my project?"

"I'm not going to question her intentions. But, if you want to confront her about it, you're going to have to act quickly. She's not an easy person to find, not when she doesn't want to be found apparently."

Elena nodded. "But how am I going to confront her? You know the rules, if you were stupid enough to lose it, you deserve it."

"You can appeal to the school board since you have evidence. There have been a few cases. I looked it up." Zola grabbed her bag.

"Hey, where are you going?" Elena questioned.

"I have to work on my project too, you know," Zola replied. "Good luck!"

27

Theoretical Immortality

Zola sat on the floor of the computer lab and sighed, leaning her head on the leg of a nearby table. She hadn't wanted to use a computer, instead opting for loose-leaf paper to write out the basic codes she wanted to integrate. It was a bit confusing when she started out, but the program worked basically like a virus.

Once started, it would take over other programs, collecting data and instructions. Finally, it would send all of this information to whatever device it had been sent out from, allowing the user to control it. Zola liked to use her phone, and so far, everything she had tested it on had worked.

She was confident in it now. Even though it still needed a few tweaks, the base of the program was almost perfect. At this point, she was sure that anything could be taken over with this program. Zola wasn't sure what she wanted to use it on, but she knew that the program would be deadly in the wrong hands. You could load it onto anything, even robots, using them to take over other programs.

She didn't want to tell anyone, especially knowing how many people before her had tried to do exactly what she was doing now. People had started wars over less developed programs. Zola recalled her conversation with Nasra about her research from last year. Her eyes sparkled with satisfaction when she spoke.

'What if you could control DNA?' Nasra had asked. With this, she might be able to. Zola added in more notes, then stapled the pages together, carefully tucking them into the folder she had brought with her. She sighed, closing her eyes. She was tired, so she would run the codes later.

Zola's eyes snapped open when she heard the door to the lab open. She narrowed her eyes. "What are you doing here?"

Isaac raised an eyebrow. "I should be asking you the same question."

Zola huffed. She remembered meeting the kid, especially nearly attacking him, and she wasn't too keen on spending time with him. She didn't know how to apologize for her previous behavior, and she wasn't exactly sure that she wanted to be friends with him. Especially not with Delilah around. Speaking of which. "Where's your shadow?" Zola questioned.

"I'll have you know that she's not always with me, she just always needs my help with homework apparently." He pulled one of the chairs away from a computer and sat down, pulling up whatever it is he was working on. "Please stop glaring at me," he asked, not looking at her.

"Why?"

"Because to be quite honest, it's rather disturbing, and I'd rather not be murdered before I have the chance to present today."

"You like giving presentations." Her flat tone left the question in the air, more of a statement that he didn't have to answer, but he did.

"I like a lot of things, you wouldn't know." He turned to her and glared. "You don't know half as much as you think you know. You shouldn't base so much off of first impressions. I know we all got off on the wrong foot, but that's normal. Maybe try giving people a chance instead of hating them the moment you meet them."

"Rude," Zola muttered underneath her breath.

"I heard that."

Zola snickered. "You act so high and mighty kid, why are you like this?"

"First of all, we are practically the same age, you can't call me that. I'm about as much of a kid as you are. Secondly, I don't act high and mighty. That's just how you perceive me. I hold myself to a high standard, it's not my fault you see me as above you."

Zola stared, mouth opening and closing as she tried to come up with a witty comeback. She couldn't think of one. "Well. I—" her phone buzzed. Zola frowned and pulled it out. "Nasra wants me to come to the courtyard."

Isaac laughed. "Good excuse."

"I'm serious!"

"If you say so. If I remember correctly, Nasra is the older one that hangs around the scary girl right?"

Zola nearly choked on air laughing. "If by *'scary girl'* you mean Astra, then yeah, she hangs around Astra a lot. And if you know the computer majors, Henry also hangs out with her a lot. They work in the same department, as do I."

"Oh. I may or may not know who you're talking about. I think I've seen him before. I wonder if I should talk to him sometime."

Zola got to her feet. "You don't have to, it's not your business." She grabbed her bag and codes, slipping her phone into her back pocket. "I would say this encounter was nice, but I'd be lying. See you." Zola left the room, smirking as she saw Isaac's shocked and offended face in her peripheral vision.

She took the fast way to the courtyard, passing other students who glared at her, or smiled, depending on the person. Zola responded in kind, trying not to laugh. She would consider herself an okay person, but she wasn't entirely sure how people saw her. Maybe Isaac was right, people perceive you differently than how you see yourself.

She shook it off. "Nasra!" She spotted the older girl sitting at one of the tables in a corner. "Oh, hi, Cassian."

"Hi, Zola." He smiled.

Nasra looked at her. "Do you have it?"

Zola rummaged through her bag. "I don't get why you couldn't have just run up to the dorms yourself, you're lucky I carry these around." She passed Nasra a phone charger and battery pack. "Make sure to return it."

"I will, don't worry." Nasra turned to Cassian, rolling her eyes as Zola left. She plugged her phone into the charger.

"She's right, you know, you need to remember to bring those sorts of things with you."

"And why should I, I wasn't planning on staying out here."

Cassian raised an eyebrow. "Oh, so I was a surprise."

"Yeah you were a surprise, I was supposed to take a nap."

"Be grateful. I'm helping you with your research, you can't just insult me and expect me to still be nice."

"Cassian?"

He looked at her curiously. "What?"

"I don't think you can be anything but nice. You're just like that."

"Wow, okay, guess I'll go." He got up, grabbing his laptop.

"Wait no," Nasra laughed. "I was just kidding, you're a welcome surprise. Please stay, I still need your feedback."

Cassian laughed and sat back down. "Yeah, that's what I thought."

Nasra rolled her eyes. "Okay, so, I was thinking. You know how artificial intelligence exists, artificial adrenaline exists, artificial organs exist? Therefore, a full artificial human body might be able to be created. And not just what we do here, I'm saying, what if we could jumpstart their hearts? Get them to function like humans do?"

Cassian's eyes widened. "Woah, woah, woah, hold on a second. You're talking about growing a human in like, a lab? Like, outside of what we do here, fully functional and everything?"

"I mean, have you seen the tech we have available? It's possible."

"But is it ethical? You're going to grow a whole human for nine months and then what? Raise it? You'll need to map out the DNA of how it'll look, to be exactly right, make sure that it grows in an environment that will make it how you like it, but if you do it like that, it'll just be a puppet."

Nasra nodded. "More of, I was thinking, we could grow replicas of ourselves, as insurance when we die. But of course, as you were saying, that might prove to be difficult. Especially since you'd have to raise it with the proper ideals, again, make it essentially the exact same way as you were in DNA, and there's no way to guarantee it'll be just like you, and it won't have your memories or consciousness. But, what if we could transfer memories, a consciousness into the clone? That would be revolutionary!"

"But…" Cassian trailed off and sighed. "It's a lot to take in Nasra. I mean, sure, maybe you save a person's body, maybe this helps with cancer research, maybe it allows people with incurable medical issues to have a chance of living again. But think of all the bad stuff, I mean, if it works, in theory, you're creating immortality. A way to live forever, just by changing bodies. Think of how people's images will change Nasra. If a person gets dissatisfied with themselves, then what? They just change bodies? Leave their old one to just die?"

Nasra nodded. "I know, there's a lot of risks, but if the pros outweigh the cons, do you think it's possible?"

Cassian nodded. "Maybe. I mean, you could do it, the cloning part at least. I just think you'd need to think about it before releasing it to the public. Remember, all the good that you can do has the power to be corrupted. Besides, the technology needed to control a person's DNA or transfer one's thoughts doesn't even exist right now. But your research is a good start. I'm sure that what you're going to do with it will save thousands of lives, even if it's not in the way you envisioned it."

Nasra looked down. "I guess. I just really wanted to give this a shot."

Cassian looked at her sympathetically. "Hey, don't get discouraged, your essay will get you more than a passing grade. If it's not about grades, then try it I suppose, just keep in mind the responsibility of this project." He smiled. "And who knows, maybe someday you'll figure it out. If you've found a way to keep people in check, away from all the bad side effects, maybe you'll see it happen. Just stay hopeful Nasra, I'm sure you'll make the right decision."

28

Priorities

Alyssa curled up in one of the many chairs in the corner of the library. She had been working on her project for the entire morning, even skipping breakfast to finish writing the research paper that went along with it. Alyssa wasn't done testing it yet. However, she had begun to test its effect on some of the lab rats. She had discovered that they were pretty mean creatures, and even more so when you had the chance to listen to them.

She hadn't really liked talking with them. However, it was still an accomplishment. She did have a lot more to do though, such as lowering the strength of the serum. She wanted to be able to focus on one animal at a time. She didn't have a fun experience earlier when she had to listen to the sounds of hundreds of animals all talking at once.

Today, she was writing a list of things she still had to do today. Number one, dilute the serum to dull the effects of it, number two, study for her test, and number three, which was in her opinion the most important, find a nicer lab animal to work with. Alyssa set her notebook to the side and picked up her textbook. She should have started studying for her statistics test hours ago, but she opted to take a walk around the grounds with Aiken. He had taught her about plants that could be used for her project, and in return she had helped him with flashcards for his quiz about modern medicine.

Alyssa wiggled in the chair, trying to find a comfortable way to sit. She had just opened to the chapter when her phone buzzed. Alyssa shut the book happily. So much for that. She checked her notifications to find a text message from Mary. She grinned. Unfortunately, now that their classes no longer overlapped, Alyssa rarely saw her best friend. Alyssa was always happy when they were able to meet for lunch or study together late at night. It reminded her that they were still friends, even if they rarely saw each other.

Alyssa took the stairs two at a time as she rushed towards the cafeteria. It wasn't hard to spot Mary sitting in their usual spot. Mary waved at her as Alyssa ran up.

"Hi," Mary greeted her cheerfully.

"Hey!" Alyssa plopped into the chair across from Mary. "So, what's up with you?"

Mary smiled and stabbed a tomato with her fork. "Not much really. I mean, my grades are pretty good right now, despite the struggle to turn in assignments on time." She put her fork down. "Do you know how hard it is to do everything? I'm always running around, doing assignments, working on my project, talking to people. I'm so tired!"

Alyssa frowned. "Just good?" She raised an eyebrow. "Huh. Well, at least your grades aren't suffering too much. Though, if you feel this overwhelmed, why don't you take a break from your social life?"

Mary looked aghast. "And miss out on gatherings that I finally feel comfortable in? Alyssa! You and I both know how hard it was for me to even look people in the eye, and now I actually have some friends. I want to keep up with them."

"You barely keep up with me," Alyssa muttered under her breath.

"What?"

"Nothing, I'm just worried about you. What if you focus too much on other people and not enough time on your schoolwork? I get it, you need to have friends so you can network and eventually get a good job to make lots of money and be comfortable in life. But you also need to graduate."

Mary waved her hand dismissively. "It's alright Alyssa, you don't need to worry too much, I've got this."

Alyssa looked apprehensive. "Are you sure? I don't want you

to get behind, because that leads to being overwhelmed, and if you're overwhelmed then you won't turn stuff in, and your grades will get lower which means you'd have to drop out."

Mary stared at her. "Are you done?"

Alyssa looked down. "Yeah."

Mary huffed. "I don't know why you worry so much, it's not like you're my mother. I can take care of myself, you know. You always come up with the worst possible scenario, and they never come to pass."

Alyssa sighed. "Mary, I care about you, you're my best friend. We went into this together, and I want to make sure you're on track. I don't want to continue without you, but I might have to if you don't get your act together."

"Do you think I can't manage my time well? Or that I'm somehow not as smart as you?"

"That's not what I'm saying at all! Can I not be worried about you?"

"No! Because it makes me feel like you don't trust me enough to handle myself! I am perfectly capable of doing all of this."

"And what if you're not? We both know you burn out easily. Don't act like you know everything."

Mary got up. "You know what, I don't have to deal with this." She grabbed her food and dumped it in the trash can. "I'm not hungry anymore. I hope you're happy."

"Mary—"

Mary ignored her and stomped away. As she walked, her anger faded, and she began to feel guilty for blowing up at Alyssa. Alyssa was just looking out for her, like she always did, and Mary had made a mess. Right now, she didn't want to face it. Mary put her phone on Do Not Disturb and chucked it in her backpack.

She might as well go to the library. She had to admit that Alyssa was right about her grades. Mary didn't let her grades be just *'good'* often. She always had great grades, straight As, sometimes even perfect scores across the board. Mary picked up some books and sat in a study room, going over her engineering notes and some old architecture books, eventually switching over to her project. After a few hours, her eyes became heavy. She yawned and thought about heading back to the dorms.

Mary hesitated. She needed to finish up her blueprints, there were still a bunch of blank spaces she didn't know how to fill. That, and she wasn't quite sure she was ready to face Alyssa yet. But staying in the study room to keep working on her project while she was sleep deprived would only make her ideas terrible and not well thought out.

In utter distress, Mary hit her head on the table. She didn't need to rush her project, she had time, the whole semester ahead of her. She didn't want to feel awkward in front of Alyssa, but she wasn't ready to admit she was in the wrong yet. Mary sighed and closed her books, collected her notes and put them away. She really needed to get food and then sleep for a while.

Once she grabbed food from the cafeteria, she trudged up the stairs towards her dorm. Thankfully, only Nasra was in there, and she barely acknowledged Mary when she walked in. Mary silently got ready for bed and buried herself under her covers. Maybe she'd feel better in the morning.

29

To Touch the Stars

Katya sighed. She was once again polishing her telescope. It was a normal thing for her to do, given that it calmed her, but she might be hurting the metal from the number of times that she cleaned it. It wasn't even nighttime, and yet she wanted to look at the stars. Honestly, who wouldn't? The stars were beautiful. Even if a person didn't understand them, pretty things were pretty things. People love pretty things.

In the same way, Katya loved telescopes. She loved small ones, and big ones, though she especially loved the ones that she could carry around. She liked working on them, and finding them in vintage shops, reading up on their inventions. If there was a world in which there were no telescopes, no way to see the sky up close, Katya was sure she would have invented one too.

She gently set the telescope back in its case. She needed to stop touching it and focus on the problem at hand: The fact that she was still lost in the overwhelming amount of work she had to do. She had taken over a bigger space to work on her project.

Ever since the fall semester started three weeks ago, she had been building the telescope. It was still just a shell of what it could be, but Katya wasn't a computer major. She didn't know how to bend the telescope to her will. However, it was big and beautiful, and if she could get some help, it'd be perfect.

Telescopes that size were usually in orbit, a part of satellites. It would need a computer to match it. And it wasn't even the kind of telescope you would find in an observatory somewhere, allowing people to see the stars in ways they hadn't thought possible. No, the telescope would reach further than even those, further than the satellites of which more successful people were so proud.

She wanted to be able to feel like she could reach the stars, even if she was sitting here on earth. And she would figure the specifics out eventually. Katya had replaced the lenses a few weeks ago. They were stronger now and with more adjustment, they might even be able to focus without coding or commands, just by the small knobs on the sides. Katya was still a bit scared that she might not reach her goals. That she would again be told *'that's not enough.'* That she would fail herself and not live up to the expectations given to her. "Stars don't put food on the table, Katya."

Well, if the stars didn't reach out to her, she'd reach out to them. She couldn't wait to meet them. Katya grabbed the case and left her dorm room, headed down to her assigned project space. The lenses were the only things that she could really work on in that room, given that when the telescope was operational, it would need a much larger space.

She had finally gotten that space and started building a few weeks ago, but there were still a lot of problems. She could only control the telescope slowly by focusing the lenses herself. She'd need to hook it up to some sort of program that would do it with just a few commands. But she could worry about that later.

Katya swiped her student ID and pulled the door open, gingerly moving the case into the room. She didn't dare drop it. The case was durable, but she couldn't risk jostling the telescope inside. It was a smaller model of the real thing, but it was just as precious. Katya moved it to the table and opened the case. Next to it, she placed the prints and instructions she was working on. The shell of the larger telescope was already done. It was the lenses that needed changing. They hadn't been focusing right as of late, even though it could see as far as she wanted it to.

She could see across the lawn just fine, to the dorms, to the town, and beyond, a couple miles. She stared into the telescope, looking out over the curve of the earth that dissolved into the blue sky. Unfortunately, the telescope wasn't of much use on a planet, given that it couldn't see over the curve of the earth. However, at this range, she could see the landing sites on the moon, something that no other telescope had been able to capture. Her telescope was strong enough to capture tiny images, though not even she could see the flags, only shadows.

Besides that, the galaxy was too big to see out of it, but, with some more adjustment, she might be able to get the telescope to see 100,000 light-years away, just 20,000 light-years away from the edge of the Milky Way's bright center. It would be a hard goal to reach, something that no one else on the planet had ever done. She had the guts to do it, and she knew she had the brains, but would she be able to handle it if she failed?

Questions like these had often filled her head. Not being able to reach the stars was a constant fear. What if she wasn't good enough? What if her goals were unattainable? What if, what if, what if? She needed to stop worrying about the what-ifs and start focusing on the hows.

How could she work towards her goal? How could she fix the focusing problem with the lenses, what material might magnify them, and make the images clearer? She was already using optical glass; she'd need something better if she wanted to even get close. She was raised to problem solve, not to spend life worrying about failure.

Katya picked up her prints and headed to the library. There was more research to be done, more things to be thought of, more work. Everything was always just a little out of her reach. She couldn't waste time looking at the stars, longing and dreaming of them. If she wanted them, she'd have to work for it. It would take a lot of time to figure out how to do it on her own. She didn't have help, she certainly didn't have the experience, but she had an idea, and she wanted to bring it to life.

Katya reached the library and immediately started looking at books on glasses. She jotted down notes on glasses and magnification, reading glasses, far-sightedness, and sight correction. If you could correct eyesight in humans, maybe you could correct it in telescopes. She'd have to treat her lenses as if they were eyes and there was something wrong with them.

With eyes, if light bent the wrong way, it would cause your vision to be blurry. Maybe she could adjust the telescope lenses to work as a makeshift eye. If she managed to correct it, that telescope would reach further than what most people thought possible. If she didn't, well she didn't want to think about that anymore. It was okay to be afraid of failure, but not to let it overcome her. Katya checked out a few more books. She was getting a little more confident now. Maybe it wasn't going to be as hard as she thought.

30

You Believe in Happy Endings?

Astra sat on her bed, legs crossed, chewing on the back of her pen. She was once again annoyed by her current circumstances. Destiny was proving to be a bigger problem than she previously expected, and she was nowhere close to figuring out who the *'J'* was. Zola had stopped looking for now, and to be honesty, Astra didn't know if she even cared about finding out.

However, Astra wasn't done. If she had an ally in the school, she wanted to know who it was. It didn't do her any good if she was smart. They were smarter. And she didn't like that. Astra looked down at her notebook. *'Eliminate the Glitch.'* Those words still resonated with her. The only problem she still had left before she could bring Leroy Parkes to his knees.

He deserved it for the kind of trouble he caused. Astra sighed, snapping the notebook shut. Leroy Parkes had no goodness in him, no compassion. Where there would be a heart, Astra imagined that he had nothing. Whether he was born that way, or someone did something to him, she didn't care. Because Leroy Parkes was the kind of monster that fairytales warn you about. Those who are consumed by greed and care nothing about others. The only thing that they have to offer is selfishness and they make business transactions with the accursed.

Astra wanted to rip out his throat. Nevertheless, there was no use in dreaming of her problems. She actually had to get up and fix them. But catching Destiny in the act would prove tricky, especially now that she no longer used that name. Astra stood up and threw her notebook in her bag. She left the room, skipping down the hallway. Students moved out of her way as she went.

She rounded a corner and nearly ran into Katya. "Astra! You startled me! What's with the"—she gestured vaguely at Astra—

"skipping? Did something good happen?"

Astra shook her head. "Nope. Just trying to get the blood flowing and hopefully, something good will actually happen later."

"Huh." Katya stared at her. "Are you going to come hang out with us later? We're all getting lunch."

Astra smiled grimly. "Sorry, I can't. I'm a bit behind on my project, so I need to work on it."

Katya made a face. "That sucks. Well, good luck!" She walked past Astra, back towards the dorms.

Astra shook her head. "Thanks." She waved goodbye, soon losing Katya's small frame among the rest of the students. Astra continued skipping down the hallway, lost in thought. Getting the others to get rid of Destiny would be hard without proof, proof that only they could find out for themselves. She wasn't allowed to mess with that side of life, she didn't have the means, nor did she have the time.

Besides, it would be way too suspicious for her to just find research. No doubt that to them, she was already shifty enough. She couldn't just give everyone the answers that they needed. Someone else would have to do that. It would be better to do it on their own, but she could give them a little nudge in the right direction. Not now of course, not yet. She just needed to figure out the right moment to do so.

Right now, she needed to work on her own project. Astra arrived at one of the computer labs and swiped her student ID. Out of the entire group, she needed a room the least, but it was a quiet space, and she could hide things in here that she didn't want other people to notice.

Astra flung her bag down on the table. She took out her notebook, turned on the computer, and got to work. A few hours passed, and she was still working on codes, adding lines, commands, and signals in. It had to be perfect. No room for mistakes. If she was off by even the slightest distance, it would be missed. And she couldn't afford that.

She sighed, resting her head on her arms. She wished she had time to hang out with the others, she knew they were having fun today as planned. But she didn't have the time, and she couldn't let her guard down. Not when she was so close to finishing her job.

Astra took a deep breath. She drank some water, then returned to her codes, fingers flying over the keyboard. As she calculated the coordinates, she broke a pencil. Astra groaned. This was a lot harder than it needed to be. She was making it harder by being stressed, wasn't she? She wasn't used to feeling so much at once, it had been practically forever since she was this over-whelmed by her emotions. Astra's phone buzzed, pulling her out of her thoughts. She looked down at the screen. *'Meet me on the roof?'* Secretly, she was thankful for the break, but of course, she didn't feel like telling anyone.

She was probably just tired. She'd work on it in the morning, and all of these weird feelings would go away. Everything would work out fine. Astra saved the code, uploading it to an external drive that she wore as a necklace. No use in losing it, no use in be-ing caught right now. She picked up her notebook and scribbled down the same thing she'd been writing for the past few weeks. *'Eliminate the Glitch. Finish the code. Get rid of Parkes. Take over the school, take over his projects. Don't get caught.'*

She sighed. That was always the most important thing, don't get caught. On the streets, in her childhood, here at the school, don't get caught. Don't be yourself, because being you gets you killed. And you're not of much use if you're dead. She rolled her eyes and headed for the stairs.

When she reached the top, she spotted Morgan sitting near the edge of the building, staring out over the gardens.

"You called?" She plopped down next to her.

"Technically, I texted, but I'll take that."

"Why?"

"Why what?"

"Why'd you ask me to come up here?"

"Why not? I mean, even you need a break from life."

"How dare you, I do just fine."

"Fine doesn't always mean good, Astra."

"That's true." Astra smiled. "Thanks."

"For what?"

"Texting me. It's nice up here."

"I know. It reminds me of home, especially strawberries." Morgan handed her a small plastic container. "My mom makes these all the time. She's an artist you know?"

"Oh?" Astra opened the box. It contained a few small pancakes in the shapes of strawberries, and some chocolate. "Huh."

Morgan sighed. "Yep. She really loved those. Told me every single time I made them that it was good for me to have friends."

Astra raised an eyebrow. "Really?"

Morgan looked at her. "Yep. She probably would have liked to meet you. She loved meeting new people."

"Hmm. It might have been nice to meet her."

Morgan grinned. "Did you know that she fell in love on a rooftop like this? There's a nice one, with a garden in my hometown. I wonder what it feels like."

"I don't know. I've never been in love, and it's not something that's pressing right now. Love isn't something I've been taught."

Morgan looked at her. "Surely you must have some kind of love, right? I mean don't you love your friends?"

"I suppose, but not in the way you see it. I mean, love is an illusion. My kind of love is respect. Because love, no matter how much people say it's beautiful, it gives you a weak spot." Astra looked her straight in the eyes.

"And when you live like I've lived, you don't have time for love, you can't have that weakness. All the love I've ever gotten was a reminder to keep working hard, to keep doing what I'm told.

When you are who I am, you'll find that love is just a fairytale to keep people compliant. That's all it's ever done for me. Not everyone gets a happy ending."

Morgan frowned. "That's a sad view."

Astra looked back towards the gardens. "I like sad views, they put life into perspective. Not all stories have happy endings Morgan, especially not mine."

Morgan hummed. "Well, I like being an optimist. We all need a little bit of hope."

Astra snickered.

"What?"

"Oh, nothing." Astra sighed. "It's just that, you're a good friend Morgan, but sometimes you think too highly of people who don't deserve it."

"How so?"

"You believe in love, which is good for you, and maybe if you met me in a different life I would have agreed with you. But you didn't and I'm sorry you didn't. What's strange is that you also believe in me. You befriended me, you *trust* me. And you shouldn't."

31

Trials

Alyssa trudged down the hallway, lost in thought. Since her argument with Mary, she had been confused. Was Mary still angry at her? Had she been too harsh? Alyssa rolled her eyes. It was useless to think negative thoughts, but she didn't want to be away from her best friend. She didn't like to fight. It wasn't like they had never fought before, but those childish arguments had all but disappeared, except for the occasional friendly banter and debates.

This time was different. Finals had come and gone, the spring semester had started, and they had even gotten to spring break, yet Mary was still distant. Mary spent months avoiding Alyssa's gaze when they were in the same room and ignoring her entirely whenever she could. Alyssa couldn't help but feel as if this time she had gone too far.

As she walked, she found herself near the lab staircase. Alyssa shivered. The lab was creepy. She wanted to forget ever being in there, she wanted to forget the all too familiar feeling of being watched. But at the same time, she was curious. What was down there that they hadn't explored? If they hadn't left so abruptly, would there have been something terrible? A secret longing to be uncovered? She hesitated.

It would be stupid to walk down there with no one else around. She grasped her backpack strap. The thing was heavy enough to knock someone off their feet. Enough time for her to run, get back up the stairs and out into the open, to find help if she needed it. Alyssa switched on her phone flashlight. She was curious, right now that outweighed the logical part of her brain that told her to turn away from the stairs and run. Yet she would also do anything to get her mind off of her spat with Mary. So, against her better judgment, she descended into the darkness.

The lab door was still unlocked when she reached it. Alyssa opened it carefully, trying not to make any noise. She stepped inside, heart beating fast, relaxing when she realized no one was there. She made her way through the tables. There were new things in the room, wires, papers, and plans that had not been there before. Alyssa picked some up, rifling through files and trying to figure out what the new objects went to.

"What are you building?" she wondered aloud. It was too quiet in the lab. She didn't like it. Alyssa moved towards one of the side doors that she knew they still hadn't explored. She tentatively pushed it open and peeked her head around it. It was dimly lit and full of filing cabinets. Alyssa stepped inside, not bothering to close the door behind her.

She walked among the walls of cabinets, marveling at them. "I gotta give it to him, this guy is really organized." She laughed. "Huh." Alyssa noticed a drawer slightly ajar. "That's not foreboding at all." She pulled it open. Files. "Of course." She picked the first one up and opened it.

"Trial One. Day 1: The prototypes have had their first human interaction. Day 6: The prototypes seem to be adjusting well. Day 15: Prototype Nine has failed. Day 20: Prototype Five has failed. Day 30: Trial completed. Prototype Eight seems to be the most adjusted. Prototype One has shut down. Calibrate, and try again. Overall: failure."

Alyssa raised an eyebrow. "Okay, Mr. Science Man. You seem to be having some fun. What sort of experiment were you doing?" She closed the file and put it back, flipping through the others. "Trial Two: Overall, failure. Trial Three, failure, Trial Four, failure, Trial Five, failure, Trial Six, mild success, that's still a fail though." She snickered. "Mild success. What does that even mean? Okay, Trial Seven, fail, Trial Eight, fail, Trial Nine, fail, Trial Ten, fail, so on and so forth." She got to the last one and paused. "Trial Twenty-Three in progress? What do you mean, in progress?"

Alyssa pulled the file out. She almost didn't want to open it, in fact, she could have put the file back, picked up her backpack, and went back to her dorm room. Except she didn't. She was curious, so she opened the file, and what she found made her heart sink into her stomach.

"Trial Twenty-Three: Start Date: August 14th, end date to be determined. Prototypes will be meeting a new batch of students, so far only Prototypes Three, Five, and Nine, seem to be having problems." She frowned. She shuffled the pages, allowing a small photograph to drift out of the file and fall to the floor. She picked it up. Staring up at her were Nicole, Cassian, Willow, William, Eric, Castor, Morgan, David, and Isaac.

Her friends, labeled by number, stood in a line, expressionless. They were wearing white clothes, matching the white walls of a room that could only be the lab she was standing in. Next to them were open white pods. There was no doubt that they belonged in those pods. Alyssa's heart fell into her stomach. She dropped the photo again. Alyssa put the file away and closed the door, then stared down at the photo on the ground. "What the—?" She didn't want to pick it up.

"How?" She gingerly knelt, reaching out and poking the photo. She jumped back. She picked it up with her nails. This wasn't just a photo of her friends, this was a photo of Parkes' experiments, and if they were something of his, they were dangerous and not to be trusted. Which meant she had to tread carefully, choose wisely who to talk to on their account. "Who can I tell about this?"

* * * * * * * * *

"This certainly complicates things." Astra stared back at Alyssa, making the other girl fidget. "Not just for them, but for me."

"What does it mean?"

Astra looked down at the photo. "What do you think?"

"Oh, they're robots aren't they; I knew something was off!"

"Androids to be specific, but yes."

"How are you so calm? We just found out that our friends aren't even human!"

"To be fair, I figured it out before you did. It's you finding this out that complicates it for me."

"You knew? You knew but you didn't tell anyone?" Alyssa stared at her incredulously. "How could you!? You can't just keep that kind of information from us!"

"It was for your own good. I didn't want to worry anyone, and besides," Astra dropped the photo into Alyssa's hand, "It wasn't the most pressing matter at the time."

Astra strode down the hallway.

"It wasn't the most— Astra! What could possibly be more important than this?" She hurried to keep up, jumping in front of the girl, who simply folded her arms and glared. "What are we going to do?"

Astra huffed. "We can't do anything. That's the problem. They're androids. Programs, like most of the things in this school. An experiment. And we're the control group."

"Wow, such a great observation. What are we going to tell the others?"

"Absolutely nothing. I have some other problems to take care of, such as my project and Dest- Delilah."

"What does Delilah have to do with anything, she hasn't done anything to you except be annoying."

"You're wrong about that."

"Okay, so I'm wrong about the girl who annoys you. It's not like you are behind on your project. The only person who is really done is Zola."

Astra frowned. "Zola's done with her project?"

"Mostly. She's in the testing stage now, but last I heard she was pretty confident."

"Huh." Astra stopped and smiled at Alyssa. "I have several other things to worry about besides our friends being made of wires and metal rather than flesh and blood. So why don't you focus on being less suspicious, instead of sticking your nose where it doesn't belong." Astra turned on her heel and left Alyssa standing in the hallway.

"I still need to know what to do," she called out.

"Figure it out on your own, you're a smart girl, you can do this!"

Alyssa scoffed. "Hmph. Maybe I will!" She turned towards the dorms. It was time to get some answers.

32

Androids

"I'm sorry, they're what?" Henry exclaimed.

Alyssa nodded violently.

Henry threw his hands in the air. "That's it. No one is safe anymore. Our friends are robots—"

"—androids," Alyssa corrected.

"Androids. Everything is a government conspiracy! What if they're spying on us right now?"

"Calm down Henry. We don't know that they're dangerous," Elena said.

"They probably are," Aiken said, in a monotone voice.

"Calm down, Aiken, we need to stop overreacting," Elena snapped.

Zola raised her hand. "Okay, so let me get this straight. Our friends are robots—"

"Androids!" Alyssa said, annoyed.

"Sorry okay, androids, created by our Dean, who's been experimenting on them, and us. Astra already knew this, and she doesn't think it's a problem." Zola stared at Alyssa. "Don't you think that's suspicious?"

"To be fair, Astra is always suspicious, but I think it's safe to say that whatever she thinks is more important than androids in the school and us being a part of an experiment is more important." Alyssa sighed. "Even if I don't agree with her keeping things from us, it's her life, and who knows, maybe she's actually protecting us."

Aiken shivered. "I'm scared to know what is more important to Astra than this news."

"How about the fact that our friends aren't the only androids in the school?"

Aiken jumped. "Astra! You came out of nowhere."

She ignored him. "Here's a little secret I've been keeping. Delilah Hayes is an android, a stolen one, and I think that she's the original one that the prototypes are based on."

"You're serious?" Henry stared at her. "Great."

Zola waved her hand. "Wait a minute, can we go back to the '*Delilah is a stolen android*' part? Also, where have you been?"

"Wouldn't you like to know?"

"Wow."

"So." Nasra cocked her head. "What's the problem, and how do we fix it?"

"Well, for one, someone has to figure out why the androids were created in the first place," Zola said.

"I vote you, Katya and Alyssa," Aiken shouted.

"Why us?" Katya asked.

"You're the ones who got us in this mess, you better get us out of it. It would've been fine if we didn't know, but no, you just had to go and snoop around," Aiken said.

"I'm okay with it," Alyssa said.

"Good." Astra clapped her hands. "Now that that's settled, Henry, Zola, come with me." She turned and left, leaving the two to look at each other frowning before following after.

"What?" Henry asked, taking long strides to match hers.

"Is this about that important problem you have?" Zola questioned.

"Yep."

"Okay, and what do you want us to do about it?"

Astra smiled at Henry. "You'll see. Zola, I need you to cause a distraction, get rid of the teachers."

Zola pursed her lips. "Really?"

"It's important, I promise."

"Fine." Zola ran off.

Astra grabbed Henry's hand. "Come on." She pulled the boy

down the hallway to a small door at the end. She looked him in the eye. "I don't need you asking questions. When I tell you, you step in that room, and you shoot, and you shoot to kill, don't you dare hesitate, okay?"

"Woah, woah, woah, woah, wait. What?"

"Don't question me, okay? I have enough of that going on. Just take this." She handed him a small pistol. "Shoot when I tell you, okay?"

Henry closed his eyes, took a deep breath, and nodded. *'Think happy thoughts, think happy thoughts. If you don't do this you might end up with a bullet in your head.'* He opened his eyes. "Okay."

"Good. Follow me." Astra opened the door. A girl was sitting on one of the two beds in the room, reading a newspaper.

"Destiny!"

She got up quickly, and surprisingly, with a smile on her face.

Henry frowned. "Delilah?"

She ignored him. "Hello, Astra."

Astra smiled. "Did you really think I wouldn't recognize you?"

Delilah walked around the room, circling Astra, and eventually, turning her back to Henry. "I wished you had forgotten me. Though, if I remember correctly, you don't forget a lot of things do you."

Astra smiled. "I don't. Besides, how could I forget? I created you. Henry?"

"You created her?" Henry asked.

Astra glared at him. "Henry!"

"I know!" Henry raised the gun and placed it against the back of Delilah's head.

She froze. "You would shut me off with a bullet? Shame on you."

"Well, there's only shame to me if I don't kill you. Shoot."

Henry hesitated and winced. "I can't kill her," Henry lowered the gun. "I'm sorry."

Delilah laughed. "Coward."

Astra just raised an eyebrow. "I can. Get out of the way." Astra pushed Delilah to the side and grabbed the gun from Henry. She shot Delilah three times in the head. Delilah fell backward onto the ground, face frozen in shock. Astra stepped over her body and ripped the control panel out of the back of her neck. She turned to Henry, who stared at her in shock. "She's not even really alive. I don't know what your problem is."

Astra pat Henry on the back and opened the door and stepped into the hall. "Well, you tried. Close enough."

Henry stared at Delilah's smoking body; feet frozen to the floor in shock. "What. Did. You. Do."

"She was programed to protect her master and destroy threats at all costs. She's extremely dangerous, and we're lucky she wasn't set on us sooner." Astra looked down at her phone. "It's a long story, but I think that she has a little more autonomy than she was intended to have. Zola, come in here!"

Zola hesitantly opened the door. "I heard gunshots, what's going on?"

Henry took a deep breath, trying to lower his heart rate. "Not much. You missed a very awkward *'I didn't actually shoot Delilah'* part. Astra did, I couldn't kill her. Android or not, she looks too human."

Zola stared down at the android on the floor, surprised to find she didn't even feel sorry for her. "Okay then. I'm not going to ask any questions."

"Yeah."

Astra smiled. "Well, I have to go. Dispose of the body, will you?" She disappeared into the hallway without waiting for an answer.

Zola and Henry just looked at each other. There was a long silence before Zola spoke. "Now what?"

* * * * * * * *

Astra headed towards the front doors where her next mission was waiting. Now that Delilah was taken care of, she didn't need to worry too much, but there was still a lot left to be done. She felt a pang of what could have been guilt in her stomach, but she pushed it aside. Yes, she was sorry that she had to shut Destiny off. Maybe, if she had waited, she could have reprogrammed her. But chances were that whatever made Destiny work, all Astra's codes and programs, had been completely erased by Parkes. Yet another reason to get rid of him.

Astra sighed. It was a good idea for her to hand the android off to Henry and Zola because at least she wouldn't know where they put her. It would be too much of a temptation to just keep Destiny, simply because she had made her. Not Destiny. That wasn't her creation anymore. Astra knew that the sooner she started, the easier it would be to continue. But it wasn't very easy at all to start referring to Destiny as simply *'Project 52'*. Destiny was more than just a project to her. She was a friend. Granted, a friend that she built, but a friend all the same.

Astra shook her head and checked her phone. Mary's tracker was blinking in the same spot, finally. Astra rolled her eyes and headed for the front of the building. She had long since started tracking the others, but today she would try something entirely different. And if it worked, well, Astra didn't want to think too far ahead. But if it did, she would finally be going home. She ran down the hallway and stopped right before the front doors. She slowed her breathing down, so it wouldn't show that she hurried, then, she opened the door. It didn't take long for Astra to spot the younger girl sitting on the steps. She took a deep breath. *'Showtime.'*

"Hey Mary, how are you feeling?" Astra sat down next to Mary on the steps to the gardens, the sun cast shadows across the ground in the evening light.

Mary looked up at her. "Okay, I guess. Tired."

Astra shrugged. "Water?" She held out the bottle to Mary. "It's flavored."

Mary took it. "Sure, why not?"

Astra sighed. Her heart was beating very fast. She didn't know why she was so nervous. She didn't even have to be, because she didn't keep any evidence of this plan around. No one would know anything. Mary didn't have any reason to be suspicious of it. Astra pulled her phone out of her pocket and fiddled with it. Mary glanced at it.

"Codes?"

Astra nodded. "I've been working on my project." She looked down, adding a string of commands that Mary didn't understand.

Mary shrugged and downed almost half the bottle of water before setting it down on the steps beside her. "I don't know why this is so hard." She turned to Astra. "Don't you ever feel like the world is against you?"

Astra glanced at her. "Sometimes. But you have Alyssa, so why are you so sad?"

Mary looked down. "That's the thing about growing up with your best friend. You share everything, all the time, I mean, she knows me better than I know myself. But for once I just want someone who can tell me something straight, who doesn't know me. I want to have a friend that isn't always so nosy."

"So, you aren't that good of friends with Alyssa then?"

"No, I am! We're like sisters. But even sisters get annoyed with each other sometimes."

Astra looked down. "Yeah, they do. Is it something to do with your project?" She glanced back at Mary to see her reaction, bated breath, hoping. *'Work,'* she thought.

"Yeah, my project. Stupid thing. Supercharged batteries, just what I would come up with. Can't do anything right."

Astra breathed a sigh of relief. *'Good.'* She hummed. "Maybe you shouldn't do just batteries?"

"What?"

"Yeah. Maybe something, like a supercomputer, which will help in some form of government thing. It could be powered by your batteries."

Astra could almost see the wheels in Mary's head moving, her brain supplying images as Astra's words echoed in her head. "You don't even have to build it; you just have to draw it." Astra typed faster, filling in the spaces she needed.

"Yeah. Yeah! I could do that!"

Astra smiled. "Even if it doesn't work, it's worth the try, right?"

Mary nodded. "Yep! In fact, I'll start right now." She stood up. "That would work, thanks so much Astra, you're a lifesaver."

Astra's eyes widened. "Wha— okay. Good luck!"

Mary smiled. "Thanks! And thanks again for the advice!" She turned and ran into the school.

Astra dropped her head into her lap. The hardest parts were over. Plans were changing, she had to change too. She couldn't do anything but her best. It wasn't allowed. At least she could be kind to the girls, and at least Destiny was off for good. She sighed. *Almost. Just a bit longer.*

Her phone buzzed, and Astra groaned, rubbing her eyes before picking her phone up. She glanced at the new messages. *'I'm almost here,'* it read. *'Expect to see me tomorrow.'* Astra half-smiled. "Finally, some good news."

33

Xavier

Astra stood in the hallway, facing the doors. She tapped her foot on the floor impatiently. She was tense and anxious, and for what? It didn't really make any sense. This was her best friend, her brother. There wasn't any point in being nervous. She called for backup, she called for him. She didn't need to worry.

Astra had been preparing for this for days, and yet she still felt sick to her stomach. Maybe it was the length of time it had been since she'd seen him last. Maybe it was the fact that she was a little behind schedule. Maybe it was the boy in question that she had a problem with. Or maybe it was all just in her head. Whatever it was, she had to ignore it.

Her heart rate rose as she waited. As the minutes passed, Astra's mind wandered. It wasn't the first time that she had waited. He kept her waiting most of the time. He was never in a rush anywhere, and yet always hurrying people. Astra rolled her eyes. Xavier Zhang. The picture-perfect poster child. A prime example of her failures in her youth. She had grown up with him, in a way, and yet the boy had never been her equal. She was smarter, stronger, and yet, placed beneath him, and she had never known why.

She hadn't been bitter about it. It wasn't his fault, but Astra tended to be left behind. All good for her though, she spent hours tinkering in the basement with her father and not much else. She stayed out of sight and out of mind for the guests that came and went. Out of all her siblings, though she was certainly just as powerful as them, she was the most overlooked. She liked it when it benefited her, surveillance, keeping to the shadows, but hated it within her own home. Because what if this was just another repeat of her parent's orders?

'Stay home Astra, you will cause trouble. People will ask ques-

tions.' That was the case most times, and she never knew what caused them to change their minds.

Astra was pulled out of her thoughts by her phone vibrating. *'I'm here, come outside.'* She took a deep breath, pushing her feelings to the side. *'It's time.'* Astra opened the door and hurried down the steps. She spotted him across the courtyard and sprinted towards him. "Xavier!"

He smiled. "Astra, how have you been?" He ruffled her hair affectionately.

Astra's heart rate slowed. He seemed normal. Even better than normal. She smiled. "Quite well, and you?"

"Eh. Our older friends and siblings have a habit of being uptight and angry, especially now that we are closer to our goal. We are rather stressed right now."

Astra's smile dropped, and she beckoned him to follow her out onto the grounds. "Angry? They should be happy, especially now that the glitch has been eliminated. They should be grateful to have gotten this far."

Xavier hummed. "Project 52 was the least of our problems. You need to hurry up."

Astra huffed. "I am hurrying! Do you even know how hard it is to carry on like this? I'm doing everything I can to work towards our goal, have a bit of patience."

"You're a smart girl Astra. You can do better."

"They are just as smart as I am, Xavier. I am walking on eggshells around people that I thought I could run circles around, simply because I didn't realize that they can match and sometimes surpass my intellect. "

Xavier raised an eyebrow. "Really?"

"Never get too cocky, underestimating your opponent is never wise. Especially since I now consider these people my friends."

"Friends? You befriended your targets?"

"Targets? Xavier, what are you talking about? Parkes and Destiny, they were the targets. The others had nothing to do with it, in fact, they are elements that made my job easier. You forget that we were taught to use everything that was around us in order to succeed. I'm just doing what I'm told."

"They would turn against you if they found out what you do and who you are."

"Stop being so cynical. There's no harm in friends."

"You can't afford to have friends." Xavier stopped. "Listen here, Astra. You are here to get revenge on a person who stole our ideas, who waged war on the stars, enabling a problem that we have to fix. That you have to fix. There is no room for error!"

Astra frowned. "I haven't made a mistake."

"You called for backup."

"That was because I needed help. There's no harm in that."

"Your main target has fled the school thanks to your choice to deactivate Project 52."

"I'll find him."

"Your friends are mistakes."

Astra stared at him. "I thought you of all people would understand."

He sighed. "You thought wrong." Xavier turned, hiding the pained expression on his face, and resumed walking. "This isn't the Dukes' house Astra; this isn't our childhood. You have a job to finish. People only get in the way."

Astra hesitated, before following. She huffed. "What would you have me do?"

Xavier grimaced. "You know."

"You want me to kill him?"

"Of course. This was your purpose here after all."

Astra scoffed. "It might take longer than expected, after all—"

"He fled the school, I know. We've been trying to accommodate that. Since you're so adamant about working with the students here, do the others suspect anything?"

"Nothing other than wondering what he was doing."

"So, you aren't their concern?"

"I might have been originally, but at the moment, no."

"Good. We don't have time for any more interruptions."

Astra made a face. "You mean you don't have time for interruptions."

"Astra, there's a lot going on right now, I don't need your attitude."

"It would be helpful if you just told me instead of being cryptic."

"It's not my place. I can't."

"Can't?" Astra stopped. "Or won't?"

"You've already proven to be a weak link Astra, I can't afford to tell you, especially if you get compromised."

Astra's mouth opened in shock. "Me? I'm the weak link? You sent me here to die then? Father's gone, so I get to go next?"

"I didn't say that—"

"Then what am I supposed to think? What happened to you?"

Xavier stared at her. "Nothing has happened to me, it's you who's changed. You used to be so good at staying in the shadows, following orders, never deviating from the book, and now look at you. You put this whole operation at risk. "

Astra folded her arms. "Maybe. Maybe we all changed. A year is a long time to be cut off from all contact, Xavier. It's barely a dent in the time I've spent waiting. But don't worry, I'll complete my job. Just don't expect me to return when I do. I won't do anything else for you. No chance of messing up there, huh?"

"Astra."

"It's not your decision, Xavier. You don't get a choice."

"There are lives at stake Astra—"

"And I'm one of them!" She narrowed her eyes. "Leave, Xavier."

"You asked for my help, I'm here to give it."

"I don't want it anymore. I'll find someone, or something else, and if I die, so be it! All you're doing is criticizing my every move, and I just wanted someone who would listen."

Xavier took a step back. "Huh. You really are angry, aren't you?"

"Maybe."

"It's dangerous."

"So be it."

"Astra."

Astra ignored him and turned around, marching back towards the school. She was seething. They sent her on this job because they thought she was weak. If she failed it wouldn't hurt them. Of course. She was ever the peacemaker, wasn't she? She was expendable. She'd do whatever she was told because she still craved approval.

"Astra?"

She looked up. "Oh. It's you."

Zola laughed awkwardly. "Who else would it be?"

"I don't know. I just wasn't expecting someone. I'm busy, I just found out that Dean Parkes has left the school. I have to find him."

Zola frowned. "He left? Why?"

"I assumed because I just shot one of his androids."

Zola made a face. "Yeah, about that. When are you going to explain how you knew?"

"About the androids? In time," Astra said, monotone.

"Okay then. Who was that guy by the way?"

"What?"

"The one you were talking to."

Astra blinked. "Oh. Um, just an old friend."

Zola snickered. "I'm surprised you have old friends."

Astra half-smiled. "The more you know."

"Hey, let me defend myself here. When I first met you? Man, I was not prepared to get along with you, I thought you were going to kill me or something. Though, I suppose, if I can get past your weird exterior, I'm sure other people can too."

Astra fake laughed. "Thanks, I guess. I mean, I wouldn't say we're really friends, more like acquaintances, we happened to be in the same place at the same time. Enough about that. What are you doing out here anyway? Shouldn't you be working on your project, or fighting Elena or something?"

Zola smiled sarcastically. "Ah-ha-ha, very funny. I don't plan on making that a regular occurrence."

"I know, I know. It's just kind of funny. I wonder why out of all people she thought it was you."

"Because I was in the area? Except I literally just walked past the door, I didn't go in it or anything."

"Yeah. And since we know Destiny switched the cameras, it's not your fault, etcetera, etcetera."

"Yep." Zola elbowed Astra in the side. "But hey, at least my brothers are visiting tomorrow, and then we can worry about finding Dean Parkes."

"I'll worry about finding him, you just spend time with your family. It's good for you."

"Come one, spend some time with us! I think you'd like them."

Astra raised an eyebrow. "That's like saying you think I'd like to swim with sharks. Thanks, but no thanks. Besides, if you're taking a day off, there's no way that I will. I need to work on locating Parkes, you know that."

Zola shrugged. "Suit yourself. I'll catch you later Astra." She ran off, leaving Astra alone with her thoughts.

34

Brothers

Zola sprinted down the hallway. She didn't have time to think about Astra acting strange, her brothers would be here soon, and she had to worry about them. They would arrive early tomorrow, and she wanted everything to be perfect. She wanted them to be proud of her, even though they were probably already as proud of her as they could be.

It was their idea for her to apply, and she missed them more than anything in the world. After all, they were the only family she had left. Zola didn't like to think about that though. She only wanted to think about the fact that she would get to see them for the first time in a little over a year.

She headed to the cafeteria, bought a coffee and some chips, then went to her dorm. She crunched on her chips and tried to think of things they could do while they were here. She would show them her project of course. They'd walk around the town, and hopefully, she wouldn't cry when they left.

They could only stay a day, and that's what she regretted. Only a day. But she'd be with them as soon as the next semester ended, so she would just have to wait. She had gone a year without them, she could wait four months to see them. She was just glad they could visit.

Zola spent the rest of the day planning and worrying. No matter what, she couldn't shake the feeling that something bad was going to happen, though she chalked it all up to nerves. She wasn't exactly sure why she was scared of seeing them, or even if it was just the fact that she wanted to impress them. She didn't need to, they were always proud, no matter what she did, but that didn't change the fact that she wanted to.

The next morning, Zola woke up early. She spent an hour messing with her hair, trying to figure out if she wanted to do something with it, before just settling with her natural deep brown curls. That's how her brothers did it when she was younger. Granted, they were impatient, and didn't really spend time doing her hair as a child, leaving her to teach herself how to do it on her own. It was a good skill to learn, but it took hours, hours that she didn't have.

Katya left while she was in the bathroom, but she had also left a list of things that she wanted Zola to put away, and to be honest with herself, Zola was afraid of getting lectured if she didn't. She scrambled around her room getting dressed and trying to make her part of the room look presentable. After making sure that she had done everything on Katya's list, Zola checked her phone. She was surprised. Time had gone by quickly, and they would arrive in approximately ten minutes. Zola hopped a little to put on her boots and raced down the steps towards the front door.

She fidgeted on the front steps as she waited, playing with her hair and the strings of her hoodie. She paced around the courtyard, wondering. What if they got in a car accident? What if they took a wrong turn? What if they forgot, or had missed their flight? She was the worrier of the family, wasn't she? Zola took a deep breath and tried not to get lost in the questions of what could have gone wrong.

Her fears were eased when a blue car pulled into the courtyard. Zola recognized Jamal's bright orange hair, still colored because of a dare she had made him do before she left for school. She smiled as she ran up to them. She pulled on the car door, barely letting the boy out before she tackled him in a hug.

"I see you kept your promise and still look like a pumpkin."

He smiled. "Of course, gotta keep it till you finish school! You look happy."

"I do think I am happy."

"I sure hope so," said the other boy. He walked around the other side of the car smiling.

"Kyan!" Zola hugged him. As the oldest of the three, Kyan was the one who paid for Zola's college, well, the half that she wasn't able to.

"Zola! Are you liking it here?" Kyan asked.

"Of course! There's so much I want to show you guys, come on!"

She didn't leave them time to argue, instead, she pulled them into the school and dragged them down several corridors to her study room. She unlocked the door and flicked the lights on.

Kyan whistled. "Looks like you've been busy. Why do you have so many papers everywhere?"

"Product of sleepless nights and too much coffee."

Jamal picked up some of the pages. "I have no idea what these are, but I'm going to pretend like I do."

Zola grabbed them out of his hand. "Trashed codes, I don't need them anymore. I've already finished my codes, and they work pretty well, but for now, I'm just refining them."

"Ah yes." Jamal slung his arm around Zola's shoulders. "Our smart little sister who never turns in anything less than perfection."

Zola poked him in the side. "Of course, what kind of lazy person do you take me for?"

"Well—"

Zola threw his arm off her shoulder. "Don't you dare disrespect me, I'm amazing."

"Your confidence is stunning for someone who doesn't even dress properly unless she's forced to."

"Bold words for someone within tickling range."

"Wait a minute, think before you do that." Jamal backed up and Zola chased him around the room laughing while Kyan just surveyed the chaos. Zola giggled. She tackled Jamal and tickled him relentlessly until Kyan pulled her off of him.

"Alright, that's enough of that. Zola, you promised us food, and I intend to eat."

Zola tsked and brushed imaginary dust off her pants. "You and your stomach. Do you ever stop eating?"

"Not really. You're paying by the way."

"What?"

Kyan left the room before she had a chance to argue.

Jamal snickered. "I mean, if he pays for your tuition, the least you can do is buy him food."

Zola shrugged. "Fair enough, but you don't, so you have to buy your own."

"Hey! That's not fair!"

Zola laughed as she left the room, leaving Jamal to run to catch up to her and Kyan.

Jamal glared at her. "Are you really gonna make me pay for my own food?"

Zola shrugged. "I don't know, am I?"

"You little—" he huffed. "You should pay, after all, you're the smart one, you're gonna be making all the money."

"Hmm, okay, but only if you buy dessert."

"It's a deal." They shook hands.

Zola smiled. "Now hurry up, I know exactly where to go."

They spent the rest of the day in town, exchanging jokes, and talking about the newest developments in their lives. Zola knew the day wasn't going to last, but she clung to each passing moment. She talked about her codes, and listened as the boys talked about how well their shop was doing.

"All this time, you two have been making sandwiches for other people, and you still eat out?"

"What, you don't get tired of your own cooking?" Kyan asked. "Sometimes we want other people to do it for us, but I'm not gonna act like they can do better, when I know my sandwich making skills are amazing."

Zola snickered. "Yeah they are."

The sun was just beginning to set as they walked back towards the university. Zola glanced up at the sky, still pink and orange, and she sighed. "I don't want you to go. It's really pretty here, the sunsets, and the sunrises. Maybe you could stay another day? Or another week, or maybe just don't leave at all!"

Jamal hugged her. "We don't want to go either. But we'll always be a phone call or a text away, you know that. Besides, who would run the shop if we stayed?"

Zola smiled, hugging him tightly. She turned to Kyan and hugged him too. "I'm gonna miss you you know."

"I know."

She took a deep breath and stepped back, wiping her eyes. "I'm gonna miss you both a lot."

Jamal laughed. "Tch. Look at you, pretending like you know how to cry. You need to save your tears for if one of us dies, this ain't a *'goodbye forever'* kid, we'll see you again soon."

She snickered. "Yeah, yeah, yeah, whatever. You better visit me again soon or I'm gonna fight!"

Zola watched them get into the car, she wished that she was going with them. As they drove off, she waved until they were out of sight. Her hand dropped to her side. She missed them already. Zola never realized just how lonely she was until now. She wanted to run after the car and beg them to stay.

"Zola!"

She turned at the shout. "What?" She frowned. "Hey, what's wrong, why do you look like the world's about to end?"

Katya stopped, leaning on her knees, before standing up, clutching her chest. She panted, trying to catch her breath. "Ow, my chest burns, can't breathe. Ugh."

"What's wrong Katya?"

She looked Zola in the eyes. "Aiken's gone."

Missing

"What do you mean, he's gone?" The two stood in the hallway outside of Nasra's dorm room. Nasra stared back at them in shock.

"We mean, he is literally gone. His things are still here, but there's no sign of him, which is weird cause he never goes anywhere without his phone or a flashlight, and he would have told someone that he left because he worries too much." Katya sighed. "I hope he's okay."

"So, he got kidnapped?"

"We don't know that he got kidnapped," Zola said. "Though it does kinda look like it right now."

"If he did get kidnapped, the poor thing would be terrified. I'm hoping that I'm wrong, but it's not like him to just disappear." Nasra sat down on the floor. "Who would have taken him anyways?"

"Who do you think?" Zola flicked Nasra in the forehead. "Come on. There's only one person with any reason to literally kidnap Aiken, and that's Dean Parkes."

"He left though? There's no way he could have come back, kidnapped Aiken, and left without us noticing."

Katya cocked her head. "Actually no, this school is built over a maze of tunnels, so, there are many ways he could have gotten in, secondly, everyone was either concerned about killing off Delilah, doing their projects, or preoccupied with the android problem to really pay attention."

Nasra raised an eyebrow. "You know this, how?"

"I pay attention to blueprints!"

"Isn't that like, Mary's job though?" Nasra asked.

"Yeah, but if I didn't pay attention to what goes on at this school, we would have never found the lab. Besides, I did a lot of research, so did Alyssa, though she didn't really question what the tunnels were used for.”

Nasra frowned. “If we never found the lab, we never would have found out about the androids, meaning that Delilah would have never been shut off and Aiken would have never been taken, so technically, this is your fault.”

“Nasra, I swear—”

“What? What are you going to do about it?”

“Girls calm down.” Zola glared at them. “We need to go tell everyone else, and figure out when Aiken was taken, and what Dean Parkes wants with him. Also—” she sighed. “Astra, Elena and I knew about the tunnel too, it wasn’t just Katya, Alyssa probably knows about them too, given how much research she’s done on the place. We just never told anyone. You know that we didn’t really trust each other in the beginning.”

Katya’s eyes widened. “Oh!”

“What, Kat?” Zola stared at her in concern.

“I just realized something! What if Parkes kills him? I mean, an eye for an eye. Parkes is probably really angry, and considering he’s a madman who created the androids and we just killed one of them, I wouldn’t put it past him.”

Nasra pat Katya awkwardly on the shoulder. “Don’t worry, I don’t think he’s gonna kill him, if he wanted to take out someone in exchange for Delilah, he’d probably get someone like Zola, or Astra. He probably wants to use Aiken as bait, which, given the situation, is working. What I want to know is, how did he even find out that Delilah was shut off in the first place?” Nasra asked. “We weren’t exactly vocal about the fact that we got rid of another student.”

Zola shrugged. “Who knows? He has a way of finding out things, plus, he’s smarter than we give him credit for. I mean, look at what he’s built! Look what he’s hidden! The guy made an empire out of other people’s ideas, and yet he probably knows things we couldn’t even dream of knowing.”

Katya huffed. "Stop making Parkes out to be such a great man. He's annoying and has always been slightly suspicious to me."

"Ignoring Parkes' strengths is the thing that got us into this mess. We can acknowledge that he's a genius without liking him, Katya," Zola retorted.

"I guess. So, now what? Are we just going to look for him? Or are we just going to stand here and discuss what we could or should have done?" Katya stared pointedly at them.

Zola groaned. "Alright, let's go get the others."

* * * * * * * *

Astra facepalmed. "You all really let Dean Parkes take Aiken? Seriously? No one was with our most vulnerable, and scared, friend? No one? Not even Henry?"

Henry shuffled his feet, looking away. "Sorry, I thought he went back to the dorms."

"So, you're telling me that Aiken is gone, and we have no idea what Parkes is going to do with him, or even if he's still alive. What are we going to do now?" Astra sighed.

"Suffer," Mary said.

Astra rolled her eyes. "We don't have weeks. We barely have days. Parkes doesn't negotiate. We have to find him now."

Henry groaned. "This is all my fault."

Astra facepalmed again. "No, it's not. We all shoulder the responsibility of not putting some sort of system in place to watch out for each other. Right now, our priority is finding Aiken and Parkes."

Elena cracked her knuckles. "I say we find him and get rid of him."

Astra raised an eyebrow. "I appreciate your, um, enthusiasm, but we have to figure out how to find him first. Does anyone know what time Aiken went missing?"

Katya frowned. "All I remember is I went up to the dorms to go ask Aiken if he wanted to get lunch with us and he wasn't there, but his phone was on top of his dresser, and again, he never goes anywhere without that thing."

Henry waved his hand. "Wait a minute. We went through this whole panic mode based on the fact that Aiken doesn't have his phone on him? Maybe he just forgot it, forgot to tell us he was going somewhere and went out. It's possible."

Katya laughed. "For Aiken? Way out of character."

Zola shrugged. "I don't know. All of us have secrets. He might not be the scaredy-cat we know him as."

"But why would he just break his cover like that if he was trying to trick us?" Nasra asked. "I don't know, it just doesn't seem right."

Elena nodded. "She's right. Aiken isn't that kind of person. If he's smart enough to trick us, he's smart enough to stay in character. He definitely went somewhere against his will if he had to leave his phone."

Astra snapped her fingers. "El. There are cameras outside the dorms, can we check them?"

"I mean, yeah, but we'd have to convince a security guard."

"No time, just knock him out."

Elena shrugged. "Fair enough. I have a lot of pent-up anger anyway."

"Is this just what we're doing now?" Nasra asked.

"What? Committing a crime that might get us kicked out of school?" Henry laughed. "I guess so."

Astra pat Henry on the shoulder. "We already committed a crime by deactivating Delilah, this is just a rescue mission. So what if we have to knock someone out? Parkes has Aiken. This is war."

"Hey. We don't know it's really Parkes who took him, that's just an assumption—"

"It was him." Astra stared the Henry straight in the eyes as she cut him off. "There's no doubt that he was behind this, and if I know anything about our beloved Dean, it's that no matter what

he's planning on doing, he won't waste time, and neither should
we, now let's go!"

36

Help

Aiken slowly opened his eyes, trying to adjust to the dim lighting. He yawned, then froze, remembering what had happened. He had been sitting in his dorm room, waiting for Henry to return so he could do his biochemistry flashcards. He remembered smoke filling the room, falling off the bed, and hitting his head against the bedside table. That was it. Aiken winced, his head felt warm and sticky, aching when he moved.

He went to touch the area, only to find that his hands were tied. Aiken's heart dropped to his stomach. He started to panic, trying to pull his hands out of the ties and get out of the ropes. He couldn't. His wrists burned where the skin rubbed against the rough material, and he had no doubt that if he kept trying, his wrists would start bleeding.

Aiken took a deep breath. He could try to break the chair, or he could try to move around and find something sharp to cut the ropes with. He studied the room around him. It was still too hard to see anything. *'I guess I'll have to break the chair.'*

He slowly started rocking the chair back and forth, lifting the legs off the ground until he managed to fall over. He rolled to the side, breathing hard. One of the legs had split in half, but that chair was still intact. He sighed. "Does that only happen in movies?"

"Probably." The gravelly voice, combined with the room suddenly being flooded with light, made him freeze. Dean Parkes barked a laugh at his reaction. "Did you sleep well?" His feet stopped in front of Aiken, and he bent down to put the chair back into place, Aiken still tied to it.

"I wouldn't know."

"Hmm. Well, do you at least know why you're here?"

Aiken winced. "You're mad about something?"

"That's right!" he yelled, voice echoing off the walls. "And do you know why I'm mad?"

Aiken nodded. "Delilah. We got rid of her."

"Yes." Parkes moved around Aiken's chair, laughing. He picked the chair up and smiled, a crazed smile that didn't reach his eyes. Aiken gulped. "Luckily, she can be replaced, even if she was the original model. Besides"—he paused and picked up a scalpel—"I have everything I need right here."

* * * * * * * *

Astra stared down at the map Katya had handed her. "These are all the tunnels underneath the school?"

"Yep."

"Huh." She set them aside and opened a program on Parkes' computer. The two had broken into his office to find cameras and found the maps as well.

Katya frowned. "If Parkes took him out of the room, how come he never actually came out?"

"It's safe to assume that there must be passageways in and out of the rooms."

Katya nodded. "In that case, we better start searching."

Astra hummed. "Yes. In that case, we should. You go."

Katya frowned. "You're not coming?"

"I have other business. I'll meet up with you."

"What's more important than saving Aiken's life?"

Astra's eyes sparkled when she spoke, but her words were less than friendly. "In a game of chess, there must be sacrifice, Katya. You don't show your hand during poker, do you? Besides, I can look for a map of the passages under Aiken and Henry's room."

"Are you comparing Aiken to a chess piece?"

"We're all pawns in the grand scheme of life Katya, sometimes we don't get to pick a side."

Katya huffed. "You're impossible." She left the room.

Astra turned back to the screen. It was almost over; she could almost breathe easy. Unfortunately, Parkes would see her coming from a mile away. She had no doubt that Destiny would have told Parkes she was there, though she had no idea why he would let her live. She was stupid enough to think that Destiny wouldn't recognize her. Astra couldn't get him now, it was the others who needed to find Aiken, and when they did…

Astra clenched her fist and looked down at her phone. Aiken's tracker was still blinking in the same spot. She raised her head. They'd find him. Of course, she didn't want to make it easy, Parkes would suspect that. After all, he knew that she valued the boy as a friend. She recalled Xavier's words. *'You don't have time for friends!'* He was right. She needed to work on removing Parkes and everyone around him from the equation. It didn't matter if she lost anyone, did it? She could have told them. But that meant that she would have to reveal the tracker, and she couldn't afford that.

If she told them about his tracker, they'd find out about their trackers, about the things she had forced them to do, the things she had planned. And if they knew, her whole plan would come down on her head. It wasn't Astra's time to fall, it was Leroy Parkes'. Victory would be sweet. Astra opened a new program. If she couldn't be there to rescue Aiken herself, she would have to nudge them in the right direction, no matter how hard it would be.

* * * * * * * * *

Mary dug her fingers into the floorboards. Behind her, Katya tapped aggressively on the walls, while Zola checked the tiles on the ceiling. Henry sighed, dropping onto Aiken's bed. "This is no use, and totally my fault. I should have been with him. Now he's gone, and probably dead!" He dropped his head into his hands. Katya pat his shoulder awkwardly.

"It's gonna be okay Henry. We'll find him."

Mary frowned. She stared at the wall curiously. She stopped and kicked the vent next to Henry's bed. It made a loud echoing BANG! Mary jumped back. She dropped to her knees and felt along the wall, dug her fingernails in, then pulled. Part of the wall swung out like a hatch.

Zola smiled. "Nice!"

Henry jumped to his feet. "How'd you find that?"

Mary frowned. "I—I don't know."

Henry laughed. "It doesn't even matter, come on guys let's go!"

"Wait!" Katya grabbed his arm. "We don't know where that leads, and we certainly shouldn't go without telling the others, or figuring out what we're getting into."

"First of all, that vent is filled with gas," Zola noted. "I bet Nasra would know what it was. Secondly, we need some sort of weapon, a knife, or a handgun-"

"A thick book," Mary suggested.

Zola shrugged. "Maybe. Whatever the case may be, Katya's right. We can't just run headfirst into this."

Henry sighed. "Fine. Katya, will you go get Astra and grab the tunnel maps? I'll go grab Nasra, Alyssa, and Elena, we'll meet back here in what, ten minutes?"

Zola nodded. "Okay. Is that good?"

Various noises of approval came from the group.

Katya sighed. "I can try to find Astra, she was pretty angry earlier when I asked her to come down, maybe she'll be done by now. I just hope we're not too late."

37

Search and Rescue

Astra groaned in frustration. Mary was supposed to go straight in, they were all supposed to go there straight away. Unfortunately, she couldn't do everything. She'd have to leave the office. She couldn't go with them. She still had things to do. She clambered out of the window of Dean Parkes' office. Just in time too, Katya slammed the door open just as she moved out of the view of the window. She clambered to the top and threw herself over the roof railing.

Katya stood in the now empty room. She peeked her head out the window and behind the door. She wouldn't be surprised if the girl had left or hid, but still, it was good to check. "Astra?" No answer. "Astra!" Katya frowned. "Huh. I wonder where she went." She shook her head. She didn't have time to wait for Astra to come back. Katya started rifling through drawers, trying to find where Astra had put the maps.

Katya spotted a small drawer underneath the desk, and she grabbed it. Sure enough, inside lay several blueprints of the tunnels underneath the school. She pulled them out and noticed the prints of the dorms, specifically Aiken and Henry's room was on top. At least Astra had done something useful with her time. Katya scanned the map. There were only a few tunnels, only a few places they could go, where Parkes could hide if he truly wanted to. Katya folded it up and ran out of the room. She hoped she would bump into Astra, but unfortunately, if the girl had something she deemed more important, then there was nothing anyone could do to stop her.

Katya arrived at the boys' dorm slightly out of breath. She passed the blueprints to Mary wordlessly as she bent over to relieve the burning in her chest. "Astra wasn't there, so we'll have to go without her," she said softly.

Henry facepalmed. "Seriously? Every time we actually need her, she goes missing. What goes on in her head?"

Elena shrugged. "Probably something dark. That doesn't matter right now, because we have to worry about Aiken. Katya, how many tunnels are there?"

Katya frowned. "About four? Should we split up?"

Elena nodded. "Henry, will you take tunnel one? Katya, Nasra, I think you should go together, do tunnel two? Alyssa and Zola, do you mind going and taking tunnel three? Mary and I can take tunnel four."

They nodded and murmured agreements. Elena smiled. "Alright then. Henry, be my guest."

He hesitated. Then, he crawled inside the space in the wall. It was dark, and he turned on his flashlight to see. He had never thought that he'd be the one to be scared, but now he was grateful for the knife in his pocket, and he just hoped they'd arrive in time.

One by one, the others followed, jumped out of the pipe, and took a tunnel. Elena held her breath as she walked, trying to be as quiet as possible.

Behind her, Mary swiveled her head in every direction. She had a distinct feeling that someone was watching them. She ran to keep up with Elena.

Elena looked down at her phone, at the photo of the maps that Katya had given them. Mary peered over her shoulder.

"What are you looking for?"

"I want to see how far we have left to go." She turned. "This way. There's supposedly a room over here."

Mary shivered. "I know we have to rescue Aiken, but are you sure this is a good idea?"

"What do you mean, of course, it's a good idea!"

"Well, we don't have any backup, Henry is out on his own, and doesn't have anyone to help in case he's the one to find Aiken, and

Astra is nowhere to be found." Mary gasped. "What if Astra got kidnapped too?"

Elena scoffed. "No, Astra's definitely not kidnapped. The worst that would happen is that Parkes would kill her on sight. She's not exactly the kind of person to go quietly, and she's responsible for the deactivation of Delilah."

Mary clenched her eyes shut and tried to rid her brain of the image of Astra, lifeless on the floor at Parkes' feet. "That made it so much worse!"

Elena shushed her. "Hey," she whispered. "Do you see that?"

Mary strained her eyes. "Oh." There was a faint light up ahead.

Elena smirked. "I think we found him."

Mary groaned. "Yay, but also no, we aren't enough, we have to wait for the others."

"No time." Elena grabbed Mary's hand and pulled her towards the light. She crouched behind the door, then, once she confirmed it was safe, the two ducked inside.

The dim lighting was barely enough to see, but Elena managed to spot a table in the middle of the room. She whacked Mary's arm. "Hey. See that table? I think Aiken might be on it."

Elena had no time to react as Mary's worries disappeared. She ran towards the table. "Aiken!" She shook him. He didn't respond. "Help me!" She loosened the straps on his ankles and wrists, then paused at the feeling of cool metal. She felt sick to her stomach. In the place of Aiken's left hand was a metal one. "He took your hand," she whispered.

"I was planning on taking much more than that. Like a leg, or an eye."

Mary whirled around. Parkes was standing behind her, wearing gloves. He was holding an array of surgical knives, all of which Mary could see were sharp. She gulped. He glared at her as he set the tray on the table beside Aiken.

"You know, I was only planning on repurposing one of you,

but who knows?" He grinned. "I might just use both of you."

"Not today!" Elena came up behind him and whacked Parkes with a metal tray, stunning him momentarily.

He stumbled backwards and onto the floor.

"Mary, Elena! Are you two okay?"

Mary looked up. "Astra? What are you doing here, how did you even find us?"

Astra cocked her head. "What do you mean? I just decided to come down here and saw—" she paused as her eyes landed on Aiken. "Is he dead?"

"Aiken?" Mary asked. "Oh." She rubbed her face with her hands. "I don't want to think about it."

"Okay, why does Aiken have a metal hand?" Astra asked

"How should I know. I just got here." Mary turned away.

Elena nodded. "Yeah, I saw that, poor Aiken." She winced. "What are we going to do about him?" She pointed at Parkes, still motionless on the floor.

Astra shrugged. She walked over to him. "Turn him over the cops most likely." She turned back to Elena and Mary.

"Astra looked out!" Mary yelled.

Astra turned to see Parkes standing unsteadily behind her. He locked eyes with her and for a second, she could've sworn there was a bit of recognition in them. Then, he bolted. Astra almost ran after him, but the sound of clattering metal on the ground caught her attention.

Elena and Mary were gripping the side of Aiken's bed, careful not to touch him.

"He's moving," Elena said.

"Hey, you two. Back away, go back to your rooms. And grab Henry on your way out. Aiken is likely very traumatized and in shock. We don't need to crowd him when he gets up."

The two girls reluctantly let go of the bed.

"What if Parkes comes back?" Mary questioned.

"He won't. Even if he does, I'll be fine. Now go."

Elena and Mary left hesitantly, grumbling as they did so.

Astra waited until they were out of earshot before turning back to Aiken. His eyes fluttered slightly as he turned his head slightly to the side. She lifted his metal hand, and let it fall back on the table with a dull clank. "Wow. That really sucks."

She glanced towards the passage that Parkes had disappeared through. She wasn't going to worry about that. She'd find him. Astra looked away and down at Aiken. He was pale, most likely due to the loss of blood. The wounds would heal in time, but the scars would never go away. For a moment, she almost regretted letting Parkes take him. "I'm sorry that I didn't protect you," she whispered.

38

Guilt and Nostalgia

"So, now what?" Mary looked down at her hands. Somewhere in her mind, she was worried about Parkes roaming around. She tried not to think about it. Mary tried to focus on Aiken, but it just made her feel sick. She didn't know how to deal with the shock. "What do we do?" Her voice was dangerously low, almost a whisper. "With Parkes gone, the school is probably gonna close, and we might get sent home." She looked back up towards the others.

Tears threatened to spill down her cheeks, no matter how much she tried to hold them back. Alyssa pat her on the shoulder. She too felt the guilt of Aiken's situation, it didn't matter that it wasn't her fault. She was meant to swear an oath not to harm anyone when she became a doctor, and even though she didn't do it, even though she wasn't a doctor yet, she felt as if it was her fault.

Elena felt the worst. She had visited Aiken so she could talk to him. After, she went to her room and scrubbed her hands until they were red and bleeding. No matter what, she couldn't get the horrible feeling Aiken's now metal hand off her skin. She was jumpy. Part of her expected Parkes to jump out from somewhere and kill her.

The group had gathered in Astra's dorm, despite her protests. They wanted somewhere safe, and her room was as safe as anywhere else. Astra sat in the corner, not even trying to hide the fact that she didn't want them in there. She noticed Elena's dead stare and shifted uncomfortably. Astra glanced around the room. Everyone else was in similar states of worry and remorse.

She frowned. It was odd how guilty they felt for the Aiken. They sat there for a few minutes. No one answered Mary's question, in fact, they all just stared at the ground or the ceiling.

Aiken finally broke the silence and shrugged. "Don't look at me, I'm missing a hand!" He was sweating, and every so often a sharp pain would spike in his wrist where his hand was cut off. The painkillers wouldn't take away the phantom pains.

Henry awkwardly reached over and gave him a half hug. "Sorry," he murmured.

Nasra clicked her tongue. "I would grow you a new one, but it might take a while. Besides, it's kinda cool that you have a metal hand."

"I'm sorry, I didn't ask for the metal hand Nasra. If you can grow a hand for me, do it. I don't want to be a cyborg."

Nasra hummed. "It would be cool though."

"No."

"Alright, alright, suit yourself. You're taking it well though."

Aiken laughed hollowly. " So are you. I'll let you know how I feel later when I run out of adrenaline." He looked down. "I might need therapy, but this doesn't hurt as much as you think it should actually."

Nasra frowned. "If you say so, but if you ever feel like you need to sit out, let us know, okay? Now, since we're on the subject of robots and metal hands, what are we going to do about our android friends?"

Henry nodded solemnly. "Yeah. What happens to them? Like, are we going to reprogram them? Do we help them? Do they even know that they're androids?"

Alyssa gasped. "What if we have to shut them off? We can't do that; we'll miss them too much!"

"Well, what other choice do we have? It's not like they have any chance of being harmless. They have Delilah's protocol, they all do. There's really nothing we can do, right?" Zola said, turning to Astra.

Astra sighed. She hated the way they looked right now, so distraught and uncomfortable. She couldn't stand it, and there was only one was she knew how to fix it: pointing them in the right direction. She coughed. "Hey Nasra, weren't you working on growing human bodies? And Alyssa, your serum could transfer consciousness, right? If we use Zola's codes to upload their memories?"

Understanding dawned in Nasra's eyes. "We could grow them human bodies to use! So they wouldn't be androids anymore. We could give them a chance at a normal life!" Her shoulders slumped. "But wait, that would take years. And we'd have to grow them with the exact life experiences that they had before to cultivate their personalities to be the same. Not to mention, it takes a lot to raise a child, much less nine."

Aiken shrugged. "It won't necessarily take that much. I have a growth serum that I used to make my plant grow, and that's a pretty nice plant. It might work on human bodies, but I'm not entirely sure."

Everyone stared at him.

"You have a growth serum for a plant?" Nasra raised an eyebrow.

"Yep. How else would I know if my plants worked?"

"Why didn't you tell anyone before?"

"I didn't think it was relevant."

"You didn't think it was— ugh!" Nasra glared at him. "Aiken, I mean this in the nicest way possible: no one cares about your plants! Of course we can use your serum, that's perfect!"

Alyssa waved her hand. "I have a concern. My serum was only made to be used with animals. I have tested it on myself, but I'm scared that it might not work. It might not be strong enough where it's at right now."

Zola laughed. "Please. My codes can handle any potential problems, and if worse comes to worse, we'll have multiple backups of their memories. Whatever I can't do for the parameters, I'm sure Astra can figure out. We can totally do this."

Elena hesitated. "I'm worried."

Mary cocked her head. "Why?"

"Isn't this, like, inhumane? We have to ask them first, give them options. We can't just do it to them. Besides, what if we mess up? I can't have any more people die or get hurt because of me."

Mary nodded. "No, no she has a point. We have to ask permission first."

Astra sighed. "So, we're all in agreement? Gather the androids and give them the options of humanity or being shut off."

"Isn't it a little harsh to shut them off?" Henry questioned. "I mean, Parkes is missing. Can he turn them into Delilah clones remotely? Even if they do have that programming."

"That form of programming can be turned on without any sort of command," Astra said. "She was programmed to be a soldier, a weapon, and she will protect her master at any cost, should that protocol be turned on. If they do have it, which I'm sure they do, we'll have to edit that out when we upload their memories to their new bodies. And they're dangerous on their own. With no one to lead them, who will keep them in check? It's one or the other. No in between."

There were murmurs of agreement all around the room.

Astra clapped her hands. "Great! We've figured it out. Now get out of my room."

They scrambled to leave for their own dorms and projects. Astra scoffed. Apparently, none of them wanted to face her wrath. It was a good decision.

After they left, Astra leaned against the door and took a deep breath. "I've done it. Are you happy now?" She stared into the empty room. Were they happy? Were they glad she was gone? Did Xavier smile when he told them she wasn't coming back? Or were they sad? Were they at least proud? Did he even bother to tell them? Astra shook her head. She didn't have time to think of things like that.

She had to put the next phase of her plan in action. The others would have had her back at the Duke residence by now. They would have wanted her to sit down and be quiet until they needed her again. Astra smirked. *'Weakest link huh?'* She had been away from home for way too long. And it seemed that Xavier and the rest of the Dukes' had forgotten why she had come to live with them.

It wasn't her fault she was stranded. Well it was, but as the rules said, unless you ask for help, you don't need it. The rule had made sense at the time. It still did, but at the same time, it scared her. She had been left for years without people who understood her. If it wasn't for her training, she would have wrecked everything around her in anger. Though at this point, she wasn't entirely sure that being alive was much better. She was alone, away from the comfort of the world she grew up in. She had once thought that being dead was better than being stranded.

Astra took a deep breath. She didn't want to think like that anymore. After all, the halls of her home were calling her, and there was no use in dreaming when she was so close to reaching her goal. She pulled her notebook out of her bag. With Parkes and Destiny gone, she could focus. Yes, the androids would need some work. After all, she'd need some of their parts. She was confident in Zola's codes and Alyssa's serum being able to switch their consciousnesses, that is, if the androids agreed.

Astra flipped through the pages of her notebook until she reached the sketches of her current project. There were still a few things to consider. The memories of their old trials that the others would most likely want to upload into their brains. That might be a problem. However, if she could get there first, then there wouldn't be anything to worry about. Astra closed the book with a soft snap. Even if it was a problem, it wouldn't be too much of one.

She threw the book back into her bag and pulled out a hand. Light glinted off the metal that was showing underneath the skin of its pointer finger. It was kind of ironic. A hand for a hand, wasn't it? She remembered when Parkes received the hand, as an apology for an accident in the lab. Before he stole from them and ran.

She was lucky that he didn't remember her. Back then, she didn't look like herself. She was still blue and quiet, and tended to stay out of sight. He only met her once, in a corridor. She hadn't liked him then. If only they had listened to her. But she was a child, and they treated her like a child. They wouldn't be in this mess if they didn't. Astra set the hand on her desk. It would be both a trophy and a reminder. She might even send it to Xavier. Xavier. She almost missed him.

Almost.

Xavier would soon become just another memory, a relic of the past. Like all the other people she had ever met, ever killed, ever cared for. She remembered the first time they met, and she remembered the last time they talked. *'Weakest link.'* She curled her fist. If she didn't know any better, she'd think he was taunting her, that he wanted her to be angry. She sighed.

Astra walked towards the window and moved the curtain to stare up at the quickly darkening sky. She missed that too, being wide-eyed and curious. Yet, she had to focus on the present, not the time she lost. Her eyes glistened in the fading light. It hurt, the knowledge that she was so close to home, and yet so far away. Astra turned away and let the curtain fall. There was no time to dwell on the past when the future was just out of her grasp.

Unraveling

Nasra stood in the hall, facing the lab doors. She didn't want to go in. Unfortunately, the others had voted for her to be the one to break the news to the androids, something that she was not all too happy about. Her heart pounded as she stood outside the door. Then, she took a deep breath and pushed it open.

Cassian looked up when she walked in. He smiled. "Hi, Nasra. What's up? How are you?"

She didn't smile back. "There's not much going on. I'm okay, I guess. Where are the others?"

Cassian frowned at her curt answer. "Somewhere in the back rooms, why? Also, are we going to be able to leave soon? You didn't really give us any explanation for why we're here."

Nasra closed her eyes. She had voted against locking them up, but the decision was final. With what happened with Delilah, and Aiken's missing hand, they had to. The androids were locked up for four days while they discussed legal actions, and how to properly talk to the authorities if they were questioned about his disappearance. The students were notified immediately of his absence, though why he left remained a mystery to everyone except them.

Nasra didn't want to question how exactly the staff knew he was gone, though she suspected they probably got tipped off by Astra anonymously. Thankfully, it was all too easy to forget about Parkes when she had to deal with quarantining their android friends. They had been told that they had been exposed to a disease one of the bioengineering students had made. Judging by their reactions to that news, Nasra didn't think they knew exactly what they were.

She shook her head to pull herself out of her thoughts. "I have some news for you all, so can you gather everyone?"

He pursed his lips together. Nasra could tell he wanted to ask questions, and she knew she wasn't prepared for them. Thankfully, he didn't. "Yeah, sure." Cassian disappeared into the back, and Nasra breathed a sigh of relief. She didn't want to tell them. It was almost cruel that they had to go through this. They didn't ask to be made; they hadn't asked to be androids. She wanted, no, she needed them to accept being human.

The others came into the main room and plopped down into various chairs. They looked at Nasra curiously. She looked down at her feet.

Isaac spoke up. "Okay, so, what are we here for?"

Nasra fidgeted. "I have some, let's say, bad news."

"Bad news?" Isaac's voice seemed both angry and sad. Nasra flinched.

"Yeah." She almost whispered it. Nasra was suddenly hyper-aware of the dryness in her throat.

Morgan looked concerned. "What? Are we dying? Is someone else dying? Oh!" she gasped. "There's no cure, and we infected other people?" She whacked Eric. "See, this is why we can't play pranks on the teachers."

"Hey, if there's no cure and we're infected, why would she be here?" He turned to her. "We aren't dying, are we?"

"No, it's not that." Nasra finally met their eyes and swallowed the lump in her throat. "You guys, kinda aren't, human." She whispered the last part, eyes flickering back down to the floor that she wished would swallow her.

"We aren't what?" Nicole questioned.

"You aren't human," She said louder.

"I'm sorry?" The room exploded in questions and shouts that made Nasra want to curl up in a ball and disappear. Her head started to spin, and she wanted to cry.

"Hey! Quiet!" Cassian shushed the group. He turned to her and motioned for her to continue. "Nasra, what do you mean, we aren't human?"

She took a deep breath, tears threatening to spill over. "You just aren't human. You're androids, you were created by Dean Parkes for reasons we don't know, and we don't know why you don't know either. I'm sorry."

The looks on their faces were enough for Nasra to actually start crying, and she dropped her face into her hands as she sobbed. She was surprised when she was enveloped in a hug.

"It's not your fault," Morgan said, awkwardly patting her on the back. "Do you want to sit down?" Morgan guided Nasra to a chair, then sat down on the floor beside her, waiting for her tears to subside. Nicole brought her water, which Nasra frantically gulped down.

Once she had calmed down, the androids stared at her, until Willow finally spoke up. "So. We're androids. What does that have to do with anything? And since we're machines, we shouldn't have a disease, so why are we down here?"

Nasra wiped her face with the back of her hand. "You're right, you guys don't actually have a disease, well you do, just not in the way that you think. You can't actually get sick, I mean, you could probably get viruses, but not sick. And you're down here, well, because Astra thinks that Parkes might have programmed you with malevolent software, that's your"—she paused and put quotation marks around the word—"disease. And since he's dead," she added. She didn't want that to kick in, so she kept talking. "That's why you're here and not up there with us." Her voice shook, and she bit her tongue to keep from crying again.

"Oh." Willow frowned. "So, does that mean we're going to be down here forever? Are you going to try to find the programming?"

Nasra laughed, a shallow, choked laugh. "Actually no, and Cassian, you are not going to believe this. We found a way to basically grow your human bodies and upload your consciousness to them. We can make you human, restore your memories, give you a second chance, but only if you agree."

"Really?" David questioned.

Nasra nodded.

David looked at her solemnly. "Do we have any alternatives?"

Nasra shook her head. "There's only that. That or you get shut off permanently."

There was complete silence in the room.

"Permanently?" whispered Castor. "We become human or die? Does no one else think that it's even a little bit cool to be an android?" Cassian pat him on the back.

William sighed. "No. She has a point. If we do have programming like Nasra said, we're too dangerous to be left in these bodies. So, we need to make a choice. Become human or die. Well, as close to death as we can be."

"I want to be human," Nichole said. "I mean, I've always thought I was human. Do we get to work on it together? I'd want to have a say in how I exist as a human."

Nasra shrugged. "I'll have to consult everyone else, but I don't see why not."

Morgan, William, and Cassian also agreed right off the bat, while the others decided to think about it. Nasra took in the scene. She felt horrible and angry. Angry for them, angry that she had to be the one to tell them, angry at Parkes, angry at herself. She got up. She didn't want to be there anymore, not if she had to look at them and the looks on their faces. Everything they thought about themselves had changed, in seconds. She couldn't help but blame herself.

Cassian looked at Nasra sympathetically as she left. "Don't worry. I don't think any of them will actually choose to be shut off. They might just be a little worried about the changes and will still be taking in the fact that they're actually androids."

Nasra nodded. "I'm just worried. They have two days to decide. What if we do have to shut someone off?"

"Then you shut them off. It was good of you to give us a choice. Now we have to decide, and whatever they decide isn't on you, and won't be your fault."

Nasra half-smiled. "But I feel like it is. It doesn't matter that they're not human. They're worth a lot, you all mean a lot as friends to us. Shutting anyone down would be devastating."

Cassian nodded and gave her two thumbs up. "I trust you to do the right thing. Now go on, tell them our answers. I'll see you in two days."

Nasra nodded. "See you then."

She closed the door behind her and started crying again as she walked up the stairs. Two days. No matter what Cassian said, she was worried. She'd be worried until they made a decision. And she didn't know what she'd do if she had to shut any one of them off. She reached the top of the stairs and headed back towards the dorms.

She was surprised when she opened her door to find not only Elena and Katya, but also Mary, Alyssa, Astra, and Zola. "What's going on?"

Katya lifted a small box. "We wanted to make sure that you were okay when you came back so I made cupcakes for you. I know it's not much. How'd it go?"

Nasra sat down on the floor and accepted a cupcake from Katya. "Terribly. They looked so sad when I left. Some made the decision right away; they want to be human. Some are waiting. Two days."

Astra hummed. "Two days isn't long. We can get started as soon as they're ready."

Nasra glared at her. "It's not that easy. They want to be a part of the growing process."

"Hmm."

"What?" Nasra asked, curious.

"They can be allowed to be a part of the simulation process, but nothing else."

"What?" Nasra was indignant. "You can't do that!"

"Yes, I can. It's dangerous to even let them help." Astra sighed and leaned back against the wall. "We'll have to consult the boys, but if the androids are allowed to be a part of it, they can only be a part of the simulations and creating the DNA so that the clones look like them. That's it."

"So, we'll vote on it?" Mary asked.

"Yes, we'll vote."

Nasra tuned out the rest of the conversation, too upset to speak. She knew that if she even tried to resist Astra's decision, she would cry, so she threw the cupcake out and moved to her bed. She just wanted to sleep, but when she closed her eyes, all she could see was the looks on their faces. Sadness, and betrayal.

By the time the others left the room, and her roommates began to settle down, Nasra began to feel drowsy. Two days was still far away. And when she finally fell asleep, Nasra's dreams were filled with screams and the echoes of failure.

Decisions

Two days later, Nasra stood outside the doors again, accompanied by Alyssa, Zola, Aiken, and Astra. This time, Astra opened the door. She didn't bother to wait or hesitate outside as Nasra did. Nasra almost didn't walk in, but as Alyssa and Aiken passed her, she swallowed her fears and entered the room.

The androids were just sitting around. Isaac had gotten ahold of one of the lab computers and was doing who knows what on it. Willow and William were playing chess. Castor was writing, and Cassian was reading in the corner.

Aiken walked in and Eric did a double-take. "Hey, what happened to your hand?"

"It got chopped off," Aiken answered, monotone. "It's metal now. I've got a metal hand."

Eric made a face. "Ouch. But also kinda cool."

Astra rolled her eyes and cleared her throat. "Hey. Guys."

They looked up, stopping what they were doing to listen.

Astra surveyed them and met each of their eyes with her cold, dark ones. She pressed her lips together in a thin smile. "It's time."

One by one, the androids lined up and gave their answers. Nasra smiled at each one, her fears were eased as they all chose to be human. Well, all but one. Nasra's smile fell.

Astra raised an eyebrow at Isaac's answer. "Are you sure?"

He nodded. "There's just too much that would go wrong."

"You're willing to be turned off over the slight chance that your new body would be different? That we might have a problem uploading you to the new brain?"

He nodded. "I don't particularly like to admit this, but I am scared. I'd rather be shut off."

Astra shrugged. "Suit yourself." She reached up and opened

the panel on his head, feeling inside for a switch.

"Wait!" David yelled. "Wait."

Astra paused.

Nasra tensed up. She was nervous.

David stepped forward. "Are you absolutely positive? None of us really want to go on without you, it wouldn't be right."

Zola nodded. "Yeah. Wouldn't you rather be human?"

"Why? What if something goes wrong, and it hurts, or I die anyway? I may be a machine, but I was programmed to feel pain, and what if—"

"Maybe stop thinking about the what-ifs?" David asked. "Just a thought."

Isaac frowned.

Astra coughed. "Hurry up, will you?"

Zola whacked her arm. "Hey. This is a tough decision, don't rush it. And Isaac, it'll hurt if you don't do it either. You won't have the chance to keep living, or really live at all. You'll just be gone. What do you have to lose?"

He looked down at his feet. "Nothing really."

Astra scoffed and closed the panel. "I'll tell you what. Like the rest of the androids, grow your body, design it yourself, be a part of the process. And if you decide that you don't want to be uploaded to that body, then okay. We'll shut you off."

Isaac nodded. "Okay. So, now what."

Astra smiled. "I'll leave that up to Nasra."

Nasra laughed nervously, tapping her fingers on the back of the clipboard she had grabbed. "Um, yeah. So, I have all my research here. I will help you recreate the DNA needed to basically make a clone of yourself. With Aiken's help, we will then rapidly grow the bodies over the course of nine days, a month per day. This will ensure that they develop into the infant stage properly. Then, we'll inject them with another dose of the serum to grow them to adulthood, practically overnight, in special tanks. They will essentially be blank slates. Astra will be downloading your memories and saving them onto hard drives, and don't you have their older memories?"

"I do."

"She does. She'll save all your memories, and then, using the help of Alyssa, and Zola who will be guiding Alyssa using her codes, we will upload your consciousness to your new bodies. Any questions?"

There was silence.

"That seems pretty complicated," Castor quipped.

Cassian nodded. "I bet it makes more sense to them. But hey, I was right, your research would be put to good use. And now you are seeing it happen. But also, what are the odds that the technology you needed was being developed here?"

Nasra laughed. "I guess it was just a stroke of luck. Alright, now that you semi-know what's going on, we will be back tomorrow with the equipment. Henry is currently finishing up the codes that Zola and Astra started that we will be using to finalize the DNA structure of your human bodies. We're also testing out some other things. Is that it?"

"No." Astra stepped forward. "After you finish with your DNA structure, which we will be using simulations to make sure that the body looks exactly as intended, you will be going into the pods that Parkes has so graciously granted us."

Morgan frowned. "Pods?"

Astra nodded. "They're in one of the back rooms, we'll lock you in there to avoid any upload of malware while we wait for the bodies to grow. In ten or so days, we'll wake you up for the transfer."

"Oh." Willow pursed her lips. "So we don't actually get to see this all happen."

Astra shook her head. "Unfortunately, no. It's too much of a risk, and if anything happens to the memories you already have, we wouldn't be able to retrieve them, which is why I've decided to do them today. It's safer for everyone."

"But wouldn't our consciousnesses still be, you know, gone?" Castor questioned.

Zola shrugged. "Not necessarily. I mean, if you still have your memories, the old thoughts you had might stimulate the same way of thinking, but I don't study the brain so I'm not entirely sure. Nasra?"

"Don't look at me, I don't know. This has never been tested, and you're the machine expert."

Astra sighed. "It doesn't matter, it's just safe to have a backup. Zola, can you help?"

The two girls connected cables to the androids and proceeded to download all the information from them. Astra grabbed the computer and made sure that everything was saved to files under their names.

"I'll be going through this in order to make sure that there is no malware and will also be uploading your old memories. Zola will be working with Alyssa on testing the transfer, and I assume Nasra will be helping Henry. By the way, if Isaac decides he doesn't want his body, we just won't start its heart, we can give it to the biology department. So, good luck with that. I'll see you all tomorrow." She turned on her heel and left.

"Wow." Zola scoffed. "She really does not care."

Morgan frowned. "Don't say that. Maybe she does, and just isn't good at showing it. How would you know?"

Zola pursed her lips, choosing to ignore Morgan's comment. "Okay then. Anyways, as she said, we'll be back tomorrow. I hope you all are prepared; it's going to be a very, let's say, weird project."

Willow shrugged. "We were already experiments, what's one more?"

Eric laughed. "She's not wrong."

Zola shrugged. "Well, it's gonna be way different than what I think you're expecting."

Cassian smiled grimly. "Maybe, but we'll be prepared for it. Thank you, for giving us this opportunity. I'm glad at least someone cares enough about us to ask permission before doing something."

Nasra didn't think before she said it. "Then it's a good thing that we got rid of Parkes, and he won't do anything bad to you anymore." She winced. She shouldn't have said that.

If the androids thought anything of that statement, they didn't say anything. Nasra thought it was a good thing that that was not the weirdest news that they had received in the past few days because she wasn't prepared to elaborate. They all said their goodbyes and departed.

When they returned to their dorms, it was in silence. No one dared to voice the worries that all of them shared. Most held their breath and just hoped that the androids would make it. Some stayed up to work. It really didn't matter what they were doing, because no one slept that night.

Cloning

The next day, they all woke early to finalize the codes, plans, and serums. Aiken had worked throughout the entire night, not once taking a break. Henry, on the other hand, did take breaks and started watching videos at around three a.m. Eventually, he dozed off, drifting in and out of consciousness as he tried to get back to work.

Aiken had finally lowered the dosage to the proper strength when the sun started to peek through the curtains. "These children are gonna grow a month in a day," he whispered drowsily to the air. "That's so wild." He stumbled around the room, putting the vials into a case, and packing his laptop in his backpack. Henry laughed as Aiken nearly fell asleep on his feet in the hallway.

"Hey, come on man, this is one of the most important days in your academic career and you tried to use gloves as socks and are about to fall asleep. Why are you like this?"

"Did you stay up all night? I don't think so," Aiken muttered angrily. He set the case on the floor. "I have a terrible headache."

Astra marched over and thrust a cup of coffee into his hands. "You need to be awake."

Aiken just yawned in response. "Mmm, tired. Wanna go back to the dorm and sleep."

Astra flicked his forehead. "Not good enough, you can't fall asleep, you have to suffer like the rest of us."

Aiken nodded, taking a sip of his coffee. "I'll do my best. Ack, hot."

"Hmph. You better. If you fall asleep on the job, I will not be happy."

"I don't think that I'm here to make you happy, but whatever you say." He finger-gunned awkwardly and took another sip of his coffee. It burned his tongue and throat, but he felt a little better the more he drank. "Whatever is in this, thank you. You're a life-saver."

"I dissolved some headache medicine in there."

"Great." Aiken downed the rest of it in several large gulps.

Astra took the cup back from him. "How are you feeling now?"

"Better. Still tired though."

Astra surveyed him for a bit before walking away. Aiken grabbed his case and followed her down the hall. Henry was right, today was a big day. He'd see if his serum was truly capable of what he wanted it to do. Of course, he'd like it better if it was just him and his plants, testing his own capabilities by lamplight. Unfortunately, people didn't value the same things that he did, so he'd have to work on his plant on his own time.

Down in the lab, the androids seemed to be doing just fine, each one of them eager to get started. Nasra passed out tablets and within a few minutes, everyone was engrossed in their work. Aiken continued to run tests, just to make sure that it was perfect. He was a little worried. He was, after all, an earth science major, and doing anything other than earth science was new territory.

Most importantly, he was terrified that Astra, and-or Nasra, would yell at him if something went wrong. He pulled nine vials out of the case and gingerly set them in the test tube holder. Nasra looked over his shoulder.

"Are you sure this is going to work?"

"Not necessarily, but the simulations all seem fine."

"Yeah, but those are simulations. This is a test on growing a human body, are you absolutely positive—"

Aiken grimaced. "Nasra, we are trying to do the impossible here, so you can imagine the kind of stress I might be under. It works on plants. It'll probably work on humans."

"What if it doesn't?"

"We can try again!"

"Well what if all those tries don't work and we're just stuck with empty promises, huh? What then?"

Aiken sighed. "Nasra, I promise that I am doing my best. It should work. And even if it's slow, we got this, okay?"

Nasra nodded and rubbed her eyes. "I'm sorry, I'm just a bit worried, you know?"

"I know, I am too. But you have to focus. So, please go worry about the people that actually need your supervision."

Nasra laughed. "They're doing pretty okay actually."

Aiken glanced over to where the others were working. Sure enough, they seemed to be doing just fine. "Okay, okay, so they're doing good. I just— wow. This is a lot, Nasra. Look at what we're doing." He smiled, ignoring the worries that had built up in his head. He could deal with them later.

Nasra nodded. "I know. It's beautiful and dangerous. I just don't want anything to go wrong."

"I don't either. I'll keep running the tests, we have nothing to worry about." Nasra walked away and Aiken mumbled the phrase to himself as he worked. "We have nothing to worry about, we have nothing to worry about…"

* * * * * * * *

Henry oversaw the androids as they built their own DNA structure. He was shocked at how well it was turning out. "Astra, are you seeing this?"

She nodded. "I know. You're doing great."

"Don't have such a plain reaction! Like, this is amazing! We are doing something absolutely extraordinary." He gave a low whistle. "Wow. Imagine if this was our actual project for the end of our degrees. That would be amazing."

Astra shrugged. "It still could be. I mean, just because Parkes is gone, doesn't mean that it's a free for all. Someone has to take over the school. No one just graduates with perfect marks and then moves on. We still have to work for it."

"Yeah, but what about all the legal stuff?" He added William's

DNA codes to the database. "I mean, how come no one is asking why he's not at the school anymore?"

Astra flared her nostrils in annoyance, glad for the fact that her back was turned so Henry couldn't see her. She grit her teeth. "I'm not really sure," she said stiltedly. She did know, and maybe it was a good thing that Xavier and the others decided to clean up that mess. They were still scouring the surrounding area looking for him and once they found him, well, she wouldn't want to be him. Whether it was a thank you, or a goodbye gift, she was lucky she didn't have to deal with it. "Maybe they're more concerned with all the crimes he committed."

Henry frowned. "Parkes was a criminal?"

"Among other things." She turned around, holding two beakers. "You'd be surprised, the authorities care more about the fact that he's missing, rather than why he left."

"Huh."

Astra laughed. "He'll get what is coming to him. Take these?"

Henry grabbed them. "Speaking of which, how is Elena feeling? She spent the most time with Aiken. She seemed sad."

Astra turned to see Elena helping Willow with her codes. "I think it did affect her for a while. But she's good at distracting herself, and she'll deal with it in her own time. She's empathetic. She'll be fine."

"You say that with so much confidence."

"I know that I'm right, and I don't have to prove that to you. Now if you excuse me, I have to set up some synthetic wombs."

Henry snickered.

"What? That's what they are. Do you want us to just throw lab grown babies into a big tank randomly? No! They have to be perfect, have all the right conditions. We don't want anything to be messed up." She huffed and walked away.

Henry shook his head and went back to steadily uploading the DNA that the androids created. Nasra came up behind him and set the test tube holder down on the table next to him. She sighed. "This is it, isn't it?"

"Yep." He typed rapidly on the computer. "We're just waiting on Astra to finish."

Nasra stared across the room to where Astra was messing with the smaller tanks that would hold the infant clones as they grew. "I still can't believe this is a thing. I mean, I went from doing research on growing human bodies to actually doing it."

Henry smiled and gave her a thumbs up. "And we're very proud of you, so keep up the good work."

"Is it weird that I don't feel proud of myself?" she questioned.

"What do you mean?"

"Like, I keep thinking something's gonna go wrong, and then it doesn't and we're okay, but then I still keep worrying. And I know what we're doing is groundbreaking, but I can't help but think that something might still go wrong. I just don't feel like I should be proud of myself for something that hasn't actually happened yet."

"Well, I mean, it's normal to be worried, but you gave it your best shot and that's all that matters."

Nasra shrugged. She opened her mouth to say something, then closed it, deciding to keep her other concerns to herself. "Thanks for that. I'll do my best."

Henry smiled and gave her a thumbs up. "It will work. Okay, look how far we got. It's gonna be okay."

Nasra nodded and echoed him. "It's gonna be okay."

Astra came up behind them. "Are you guys good?"

Nasra straightened. "Yeah, we're fine, just looking at the tests."

"Good." She gave them a curt smile. "We're ready."

42

Test Tube Babies

Nasra stared at the open pods. She trusted Astra to know what she was doing, but she still wondered if what they were doing was going to be safe.

Beside her, Zola fidgeted. "Are we sure it's right to put them in there?"

Nasra swallowed. "We have to. They were out for the process of designing their DNA. That was all we promised them. We never said they could be there for the synthetization process. It was a unanimous decision that we made. We can't go back on it now. Besides, they'll be safer in there." It was only after she stopped talking that Nasra realized she was just speaking to her own fears.

Zola sighed. "I know. I just—" she trailed off, biting her lip nervously. "They look so helpless and sad."

Nasra nodded. "I know," she whispered.

The two girls watched as Astra, Zola, and Henry moved the androids and turned the pods on. Finally, Astra closed the lid on the last pod, Isaac's, and looked up.

She smiled. "Alright, they're in a temporary sleep mode. Their systems are off so nothing can be uploaded, but as long as no-one hits the kill switch, they're going to be fine."

Nasra breathed a sigh of relief, pushing her thoughts to the side. The faster they finished the cloning process, the faster the androids would be released. "So, synthetization?"

Astra nodded. "Synthetization."

Nasra and Alyssa got to work. The two spent three days working on the process of cloning and perfecting the cells that they needed. DNA was complicated. Sometimes it didn't want to move and work properly. And the process of breaking the genes apart and overlapping them took way longer than expected.

Sure, the genes were malleable, all they had to do was put them together. But it was harder than it seemed in the beginning. It seemed fitting that the androids would get human bodies this way. Test tube babies, they were called. Nasra almost messed up a few of them just by zoning out and thinking about it.

Nasra ran the simulations dozens of times until she was satisfied with them. Then finally, all nine of them were ready. Each was made exactly as intended, and they were going to be fine. She didn't have to worry unless the codes went wrong, or the tanks malfunctioned, or the transfer didn't work. Nasra winced. *'Shut up,'* she told herself. *'You need to stop worrying.'*

Astra walked up behind her. "How's it going?"

Nasra jumped. "Astra! Don't sneak up on people like that!"

Astra stared at her. "I didn't sneak, I announced my presence, you just weren't paying attention."

Nasra rolled her eyes. "Okay, whatever. It's going fine."

Astra just shook her head. "In what way?"

Nasra handed her two Petri Dishes. "They're ready."

* * * * * * * * *

Nasra looked down at her tablet and adjusted the temperature settings of the tank. "Okay, go on."

Astra carefully inserted the last of the cells into the tank. "How is it?"

"It seems to be stable. Yeah, they're holding." Nasra gave Astra a thumbs up. "Alright, everything is looking good. Aiken! You're up!"

Aiken shivered. He wiped his sweaty palms on his pants, washed his hands, and put on gloves. Then, he hooked up the vials to the tanks. He tapped his foot anxiously while Zola started the program.

"It's online."

Aiken sprinted over to where she was standing. "Zola, did it work, did I do too much of a dosage, what if I grow them too fast and they die?”

“They’re fine Aiken, it released the proper amount you wanted.” She showed him the screen. “You did great.”

He breathed a sigh of relief and placed a hand over his heart. “Woo! That was nerve-wracking.”

Zola stared at him. “Uh-huh. Okay, so, you’re on tank duty tonight to make sure the serum is working, so why don’t you go take a nap? Nasra will watch them until you come back. Drink some water or something man, you look like you’re about to pass out.”

Aiken nodded and saluted her before running off.

“Henry, you might want to go with him, just to make sure he doesn’t get kidnapped again,” Astra added.

Henry rolled his eyes. “Why am I always on babysit Aiken duty?”

“He’s your roommate.”

“Okay, guess I can’t argue with that logic.” Henry ran after him and left the girls in silence.

“So.” Mary turned away from her screen. “How will we pass the time? We’ve got nine days to grow them to infants, and a couple more days to grow them to the ‘ages’”—she put air quotes around the word—“that they were supposed to be. As Astra so lovingly mentioned, we still have projects to finish. Will we even have time for that?”

Astra shrugged. “Probably. I mean, we can work down here, and I’m going to be taking care of the legal stuff, though the board of directors will probably appoint a new dean. Everyone just has to focus on graduating, getting the androids grown, and getting out of here. As soon as the transfer happens, we have to destroy all the evidence of it.”

Mary frowned. “Why?”

Zola rolled her eyes. “Because. If the authorities found out that Parkes not only ran experiments down here, but that Delilah wasn’t the only android, the others would be taken away. All of our research would probably go towards some horrific military weapon, and Elena might go to jail for assault."

"Elena's not going to jail." Astra's voice was firm. "That's the one thing I can promise. But Zola is right. No one can know they were androids. We have to get rid of everything. Burn the files, burn the lab, burn his research. We can finally give a proper reason for why this area was restricted in the first place because they're probably going to search it anyway."

Alyssa shivered. "Oh, man. I can only imagine what they'd do to them if they knew what we were doing here."

"To them?" Katya stared at her. "Girl, imagine what they'd do to us! Our work, yours and Aiken's serums, Zola, Astra, and Henry's codes, Nasra's research. Imagine what they'd do with that. They could even make weapons out of the android's bodies."

Mary frowned. "Does that mean that we have to destroy Delilah too?"

Astra sighed. "Unfortunately, we, and by we, I mean Zola, did not dispose of Delilah's parts properly, so she is already in the hands of the local police. Not for long, I'm sure, but still. They'll have enough time to look at her and go through her files. Well, that is, if they're smart enough to crack the codes and get inside her head. But, so far, I don't think we have to worry. It's hard to believe that anyone is going to slip up about the androids. Because apparently, we're not the only ones who know."

Zola's eyes widened. "What?"

"Yep," she said, popping the *'p.'* "Every student that came here before us was part of the grand scheme of making the androids assimilate into human society. They were kept silent under threat of failure, sabotage in the job hunt, and even death. It's in the earlier files, I spent a lot of time reading them. Though I wonder, all these people, all this time, and somehow, we're the only students who thought, *'let's mess this whole thing up, why don't we just actually make them human?'* Though we might not be the only ones who wanted to mess with the experiment, we have just been the only people who didn't get caught."

"Pfft." Zola laughed. "I'm glad it was us, even if it was terrifying in the moment. We defeated the whole purpose of wanting humanoid robots. We're doing the exact opposite of what he wanted, and that is amazing."

Katya nodded. "She has a point. What I want to know is, how did he make them so realistic? Like, they act so human, they talk like humans, they feel pain, show emotions. That programming must be absolutely perfect to make them mimic human experiences at that level. He must be incredibly smart."

Astra smiled stiffly. "No, he just stole something that didn't belong to him."

Zola spoke up. "Speaking of which, I meant to ask you this, since Henry told me that you created Delilah, how did the androids not know they weren't human?"

Astra sighed and looked down. "Programming. I made her so she would look and act like a human, she even had a synthetic stomach with acid that would dissolve anything she 'ate.'"

"Wow. That seems complicated. I can't believe you were able to do that."

Astra shrugged. "I had help. Besides, she was never meant to be that real. She looked down. "When Parkes stole her, he did something he wasn't supposed to and reaped the consequences of his own actions. Machines can't truly be human, ever. He tried to amend that, by building a bridge between humans and not, and while he might have succeeded in some ways, it wouldn't have lasted. We may be the eleventh control group, but we wouldn't have been the last. He would have just brought in another set. He wouldn't stop the trials, even if he thought it wouldn't work. Even though he knew it wouldn't work."

Elena raised an eyebrow. "How do you know that?"

Astra stood up, headed towards the door. "Because I happen

to know the type of person he is, and Leroy Parkes isn't the type to quit until he's gotten the results he wanted"—she paused and turned around to face them—"or he's dead." She shut the door quietly behind her.

43

Reflections

Astra drifted down the hallway, lost in thought. With the clones well on their way to being done, she had to do something about their memories. She had taken great care to make sure that no one had gotten to the files first, and luckily, no one had really paid attention to them. The clones. They were a great idea, but they came at a cost. She still had morals, no matter what they said about losing yourself in the divide. She of all people knew the exact implications of what they were doing.

She remembered the warnings when she left. She remembered the pain, the dull aches, and the numbness that settled in. It lived in her brain, in her blood, and in her bones. That numbness would soon turn to brutal burning anger, if she didn't keep herself in check. Of course, she took all the necessary precautions, but she couldn't help but wonder if it would be enough.

Astra unlocked her study room door and flicked on the lights. A computer sat on one of the tables, and next to it was a box full of jump-drives. The android's memories. No one really cared about what she did in the lab, so taking them was easy. Astra sat down and turned the computer on. She uploaded all the files to the computer and started to scroll.

Astra wasn't entirely sure what she was looking for, or even if her worries would turn out to be true, but she kept on scrolling through the files and videos. She scanned through hundreds of thousands of memories, from the creation of the androids, to now. Her mind drifted as she did so. The longer she scrolled, the more relaxed she became. Maybe she didn't need to worry, maybe her worries were just that, worries that had no cause. She was smiling until she spotted a video among the last few files. Her heart dropped. This was it.

She clicked it. Sure enough, behind Parkes, in an old familiar basement, was a soft blue glow. Astra facepalmed. She had always suspected that he had started working on the androids even before he left. However, it seemed he had been planning for a long time, much longer than she or anyone else had realized. They couldn't recognize her in it, but the tell-tale light was too much of a risk to be left.

Astra sighed. She had always been too curious for her own good. Ares had laughed when he found her creeping around the lab at night. She had been so naive as a child. Astra hovered the mouse over the button. She didn't know why she hesitated. Click.

And that was it, the file was gone. She had always been taught to cover her tracks. And maybe she shouldn't have, maybe she should have let them wonder. Unfortunately, habits were hard to break. Still, she thought that deleting the file would have given her a sense of relief. It didn't. Astra continued to sift through hundreds of thousands of files and made sure to delete those that she deemed too dangerous to be kept.

She checked further and dug as far as she could into the past. However, that one video had been the only true evidence. And after hours of scrolling, she was done. Astra leaned back in her chair. Of all the things she could have spent time doing, and she had to do this. Luckily, she had the night to herself, well, besides Aiken who would most likely be down in the lab, watching over the young clones.

Aiken. She narrowed her eyes. He stood in between her and her goal for the night. However, she didn't expect it to be hard to sneak past him. Even if he was watching the doors, she could take one of the many passages underneath the school. Astra shut the computer down, hid it and the drives in a small cabinet, then left the room. Poor Aiken. Poor all of them. Her friends, this school, they had no idea what they were dealing with. Somewhere in her mind, she knew the group would be lost when she disappeared.

However, unfortunately for them, she had a duty to fulfill.

Now that she had gone through the android's memories, it was time for the bigger problem: what to do with the empty seat that Parkes had left. Xavier had messaged her one last time, a promise that Leroy Parkes, no longer how long it took to find him, would be charged as a criminal. A thank you for a job well done, and a reminder that she had a new task. Her final job underneath them. She had to appoint a new Dean.

Ultimately, Astra was glad that they gave her that choice. If it was anyone else, she wasn't sure that she'd agree with them. Even though it was such an easy thing to do, to choose a person to lead, she couldn't help but overthink it. What if she chose the wrong person? And what if that person had no idea what to do, or worse, turned out to be just as evil, if not more?

She huffed. *'They just had to give me this job,'* she thought sarcastically. Astra wanted it, she had fought to get here, to be responsible for everything that happened. For some odd reason, now, she was annoyed that they granted her that wish. Even if she was used to this sort of behavior. The Dukes never dealt in apologies; they only gave compensation where they saw fit. It was in this gift of power that Astra realized this was their apology. It was the only thing they knew how to give. It was compensation for her time in their home, her work for them, and her knowledge. They had no other way to thank her.

After all, if there was anything that the Duke family had on this earth, it was power. Astra was grateful for that power, the freedom it gave her when she lived under their roof. They had money, they had gifted their children places to live, but when it came to feelings, they were helpless. It was a blessing and a curse for them. Something Astra knew all too well.

Either way, this last favor was one that she did not intend to waste. Astra didn't regret her choice to leave, it was much easier for her that way. They would be angry at her, she was their weakest link as Xavier had said, but she knew she was also just as treasured as the other children. But she had already planned to leave, and soon enough she would just be another person passing through the halls of the Duke family mansion. At least the goodbye wouldn't be as painful for them.

Her brothers and sisters, her friends, and her allies. She would miss them, in a way. She knew they would miss her. Astra truly wasn't bitter, even though maybe she was at first. She had long since learned how to crush her bitterness. After all, you can't really expect humans to be perfect. You can't expect anyone to be perfect.

Astra walked down the stairs towards the lab, each step soft so Aiken wouldn't hear her coming. The faculty files, as well as all of Parkes' physical files, were kept in the lab. It would take most people weeks to go through all of the filing cabinets and papers tossed aside. Luckily for her, Astra wasn't most people, and she knew exactly what she was looking for.

She wiggled her way inside one of the vents, and carefully crawled over the open lab space where Aiken was sitting and staring at the tanks. Astra held her breath as she crossed over to the other room. She jumped down from the vent and landed silently on the floor below.

She feared that Aiken might have noticed, so she ducked behind one of the android pods. She was wrong though, he hadn't seen. He was just sitting there, zoning out. Astra narrowed her eyes at him, then scampered through the door on the opposite side of the room. Her breath caught in her throat as she stared at the room. The arching ceiling and perfect rows reminded her of home, and she smiled.

She scanned the room for the identifiers on the front of each row of filing cabinets. She spotted the letter F and ran towards it. She opened as many drawers as she could. As she scanned each page, she muttered a name under her breath. Each one of the teachers and staff were corrupted by Parkes. She couldn't instate any of them. Astra flopped on the floor and sighed. She rubbed her eyes and fought the urge to scream.

This was completely and utterly pointless. How could she appoint someone she knew was working for her enemy? It didn't matter that he was dead, someone else would just take his place to ruin the life and work of the Duke family. She, of all people, knew of loyalty. She would do anything to protect her colony, and she knew the Dukes would do the same.

Astra pulled out her phone. The least she could do was warn them. She clicked on Xavier's icon. She hesitated, then called him. She owed them this much. She held her breath as the phone rang.

"Hello?"

Astra closed her eyes. "Hello, Xavier. I have a problem. So, apparently, every single one of the staff members I could have chosen was in allegiance with Parkes. His influence goes deeper than we thought. I can't think of anyone right now that would do a good job, and I definitely don't want one of yours so don't even suggest it."

"I'll look into it. What are you going to do now?"

"I'm not sure. I'll find someone. If worse comes to worst, I'll call one of you."

"You really think we have time to babysit a school whose dean you had killed?"

"I did this on your orders. You owe me a favor."

"I owe you nothing."

"Your messages say otherwise, what you have done says otherwise. You owe me for everything I've done and will continue to do for you. You owe me for cleaning up your messes, and you promised me this in compensation. You of all people should be able to honor a promise, shouldn't you? Don't you know anything about loyalty? Or do you want me to burn your house to the ground when I leave?"

She heard him sigh. "Fine. If you are unable to find someone who is a suitable fit, then you can call in one of us for a favor, and we'll find someone to take the job."

"Thank you."

"Don't thank me for common courtesy. You're right, I do owe you something. Now, if you excuse me, I have to make sure that the authorities stay away from you guys while you work, and Astra?"

"Yes?"

"If you find Parkes before me, hand him over. I want his head mounted on my wall."

44

In Loving Memory of Arya Jade

Astra stared at her dorm room wall in silence. Today was day eight of the cloning process, and in a few minutes, Henry would come bang on her door and tell her to come out to watch the tanks. Astra checked her watch. She had a few moments of silence, a little bit of time to herself before her plan would be wrapped up.

She wanted to enjoy that silence, but per usual, that never happened. Not when she had things to do. Her notebook with the list of tasks she had to do tonight was already in her bag. Astra glanced over at the bottles of water sitting in stacks in the corner of the room.

She'd give one to Henry when he came to get her like she had given one to everyone else. More than one, she had gone through hundreds of bottles of water. They needed water to survive, and what a pity that they couldn't drink the water that made up most of the earth's surface. She had spent several days buying water and making sure that everyone was sufficiently hydrated. Most of the time, they were too tired to fight her on it.

Astra sighed and sat up, picked up one of the water bottles, and opened the door before Henry had a chance to knock. "Right on time." She handed him the bottle. "Drink up, I can't let you die from dehydration."

Henry raised an eyebrow, hand still raised in the air. "Hello to you too I guess." He took the bottle. "Way to lower the plastic consumption of the school, Astra."

She rolled her eyes. "Relax. If you return the bottles to me, I can clean them out and reuse them. Or give them to Aiken, he uses them to grow flowers."

"Wait, really?"

"He's very big on saving the environment, I'm surprised he's not vegan.”

Henry chuckled. “Yeah, but that’s because he actually likes his plants and doesn’t want to eat them.”

“Huh.” Astra moved past him. “Alright, get out of here, go to bed. I have a long night ahead of me and I don’t really want to waste it on pointless conversations. I’d fall asleep too quickly.”

Henry laughed. “Fair enough. Good luck Astra, and goodnight.”

Astra watched him trudge down the halls before she turned towards the lab. Tonight, she would have the underbelly of the school to herself, and she’d need that time to execute the next phase of her plan. In hindsight, she should have waited until tonight to look at the files in the lab, and not have snuck in. She berated herself for not thinking of that earlier. Sleep deprivation would do that to you apparently. She was used to not sleeping for long periods of time, but she was not used to the headaches and dizziness that came with it.

Though, there were positives. She could go and look through even more files, hopefully, there would be someone outside of Parkes’ influence. Not necessarily in the school, but outside? Astra had several people who owed her favors. It wouldn’t hurt to use some of them. She’d be leaving them soon, cashing in favors was just the kind of thing she needed to do, especially if she was unsure of her own return.

Astra arrived at the lab. She dropped her bag, and a small mechanical spider darted across the floor. “Hey!” Astra quickly grabbed it by the leg and held it up in front of her face. “What am I going to do with you?” She considered flicking it, but that might do more damage to her fingers than it would do to the spider. Astra had been carrying the thing around for the past two years, unable to let it go.

Every so often, the stupid thing would try to escape the confines of her bag, and she’d have to put it back in there. Originally, it was made to dispel a gas form of a liquid that could send someone to sleep almost instantly, but Astra had decided it would be too dangerous as the person who tried to use it might accidentally knock themselves out. So, she turned it into a camera, and it was perfect for the kind of life she lived.

Astra threw the spider back into her bag. Until she wanted to let it loose to record more footage, it would stay in her bag. She couldn't risk it escaping and being found before its part in her plan was over. She plopped down in the closest chair and stared at the tanks. The eight-month-old infants were growing fast, though the rate of growth was far slower than it was a week ago. Just one more day and they'd be ready to be removed. Astra blew a strand of hair away from her face. Elena would be watching the tanks tomorrow. She didn't have much time to waste.

On one side of her split-screened computer, Astra read file after file of people she had met, none of which popped out to her. On the other side was a list of all the parts she'd need from the androids. The rest would be properly disposed of. By disposed of, of course, she meant she would need to hand them over to Xavier, but what he wouldn't know is that she'd be keeping their chips.

She needed them after all, it wasn't like she was doing this to snub him, or to get revenge. He'd be disappointed once he realized, but of all people, Astra knew that deep down, her rule-following, stern, older brother of a former best friend, was still the reckless child that she had met so long ago. He would understand exactly why she needed them, and he wouldn't tell. Besides, by the time anyone found out, they'd assume the chips were lost among the archives in storage and wouldn't suspect a thing.

Astra smiled to herself. Her old memories would be cherished, valued just as much as she valued the chips that would seal her freedom. But they wouldn't get in the way. Astra's smile dropped and her eyes narrowed. Feelings weren't something she needed at this time. She had survived too long to let them take over now.

Astra typed rapidly on the computer. She filled in pieces of her codes that were missing and made mental notes of places on the maps of the school where the final phase of her plan would take place. There was an old observatory that was on the outskirts of the school grounds that would work perfectly. There were also multiple spaces underneath the observatory where she could fit in extra wiring if needed. It was the best choice, she just had to get everyone there. Astra checked her trackers. Sure enough, everyone was blinking on there, eight red dots in various dorm rooms. All except Henry had blinking green lights as well, an indication that the codes had come online.

Henry's would take a bit to settle into his system. While the nanobots had been built for effectiveness, they still took about 20 minutes to get in place and turn on. Astra closed the screen out; she would let the program run its course and not bother to watch. "A watched pot never boils," she whispered. She distinctly remembered one of her sisters saying that to her, and she remembered writing it on Arya's grave when she died.

The funeral was years ago, and yet Astra could still remember how bright and cold the day was, and how she was tasked with giving the eulogy. "So the stars will be remembered, and even when they die, they'll shine bright forever in our skies, so close and yet so far," she recited. It had been years since she had thought of that, and Arya Jade was the first person she had ever sung it to.

Astra hadn't cried when they buried her, having long since passed the point of grief. All she wanted then was revenge, and she had gotten it partially, though it had taken a toll on her mental and physical health. All she wanted to do at that point was to destroy everything. If it wasn't for Xavier and the rest of the Duke family, she would have.

Arya had taught her everything she ever needed to know about coding and blending in with other people. As Ares Duke's daughter, she was the only person who was always home. She rarely ever left her room; it was even rarer to see Arya grace the gardens or the town. She seemed to love to stay within four walls, and whenever Ares wasn't home to make sure Astra wasn't making a mess, Arya watched her. It was an insult to Astra's very being not to remember the older girl in the traditional way, even if she wasn't the kind of person to be emotional about anything.

She wasn't home when Arya died. She wished that she was, it was part of the reason Astra had been so angry at Arya's death. *'An accident,'* came the whispers in the hall. Someone had given her food she was allergic to. *'Murder,'* Astra's brain screamed. Arya had been poisoned, hadn't she? Astra was right in the end. And she knew exactly who was to blame. This was revenge.

Astra continued on with the codes, and as she did so, she whispered the final verse of the song under her breath. "For years to come, and years to live, under your light, we'll shine. From ages past to ages present, we'll keep you close to mind. Even when you fade away, your presence will be ever close. You will never leave our hearts or thoughts, for you, we love the most. In the center of our city, in the altar of the sky, may you rest forever peacefully, and may we never forget your life."

45

The Final Stage of Growing

Alyssa stood in the lab and took notes of the clone's vitals. Behind her, Aiken prepped more doses of the serum.

Aiken huffed.

"What's wrong?" Alyssa questioned.

"I'm a bit scared, these are more than, I don't know, like 30 times stronger than what I gave them last time. What if they have developmental problems? I don't want them to die if it turns out wrong."

Alyssa turned to him and pat him on the shoulder. "Relax. The larger tanks will accommodate them even if they turn out bigger than what you expected, and we can always try again."

"We're growing real people Alyssa; it doesn't matter that they're clones. If we mess up, it's kind of rude to just let them die, or grow up and then strip them of whatever identity they had before we transferred consciousnesses to their bodies. If we make a mistake, we're gambling real lives, it doesn't matter how old they appear. At least this way they wouldn't have any time to think about who they are."

Alyssa shrugged. "I suppose it makes sense like that."

"Of course it makes sense like that!" He set his tablet down. "Do you really think this is the right thing to do?"

Alyssa frowned. "I mean, we're already almost done, how are you having regrets now?"

"Because it just seems wrong. Like, if we mess up, we are obligated to take care of them until they die. Or if the bodies don't survive the transfer, we have a promise to the androids we have to keep." He stared off into the distance. "I keep wondering if it's okay to just leave them in their pods forever. I mean, they're not really human. We wouldn't be hurting them."

Alyssa facepalmed. "Maybe think about that later? Or you should have thought about it before actually." She threw her tablet down on the table beside him. "You made a choice; they made a choice. And it's on you if you decide later that you don't want to do it." She gestured to the tanks. "Look at them! They're developed, they're ready to be grown to full size, are you really going to stop now? Because you're scared?"

Aiken frowned. "I'm not scared, I just," he paused and dropped his head into his hands. "I think it's morally wrong. This technology, we're talking about a huge discovery, people will breed themselves to be perfect, to look exactly how they want to. If people find out about this, what's stopping them from changing every little thing, huh? What's stopping them from just growing another clone and leaving an empty shell behind?"

Alyssa opened her mouth, then closed it. She had nothing to say. He was right.

Aiken pointed at the tablets. "It's different with them, the androids. Their bodies aren't human, their shells can be recycled, but for the clones, if this goes wrong?" He looked up at her. "They'll die. And we'll have even more blood on our hands."

Alyssa took a deep breath. "Look. I know you're worried. If it helps, we can wait a bit before doing the transfer, just to make sure that the growth serum didn't have any negative effects, okay?"

"What if they're long-term? What if they die too soon or live too long, or they turn evil or something?"

"Then we'll deal with it when we deal with it." Alyssa picked up her tablet. "Nasra and Zola will be here any minute now to help move the clones into the new tanks." She looked at him in sympathy. "No one will blame you if you mess this up, Aiken."

"Maybe you won't," he said miserably. "But I'd blame myself."

Alyssa pretended she didn't hear him, so she walked over to the tanks and stared at the closest clone. He had a point. The child was so small, and yet she knew that if they just let them be, took them out of the tank, cleaned them off, and let them live properly, they'd be normal children.

Albeit, clones. They'd be carbon, human, copies of androids, but children all the same. Maybe he was right. Maybe they shouldn't go through with it. Unfortunately, it was too late for Alyssa to even consider those things, because Nasra and Zola had arrived, and there was no time for regrets.

Alyssa looked back at Aiken. He seemed normal, and no one had asked him how he was feeling. Everyone seemed to go with a *'wait for him to come to you'* mentality. Aiken looked tired, and she felt bad for him. She also thought of Elena, cooped up in their dorm, refusing to speak to anyone. Alyssa considered asking Aiken how he was feeling, but ultimately decided against it and turned towards the tanks.

Nasra checked the clones' vitals, while Zola set up her codes. They all worked in silence for a few minutes. Alyssa winced. She considered dropping her tablet, backing Aiken up, and voicing her own concerns. But she didn't. And now it was too late. Zola called them all over to show them her screen.

"This will regulate the dosage on an even more precise scale, okay?"

Aiken nodded. "Explain that in simple terms, please. I'm panicking, and when I panic I can't understand English very well."

Zola rolled her eyes. "It will work perfectly, exactly like the simulation did. It'll only allow the exact dosage to go into the clone for every hour that you tested. That way, it will be impossible for there to be any mistakes."

Aiken made a face. "Impossible?"

Zola stared him down. "Impossible."

"You promise?"

"I promise."

"Okay."

She turned around. "Alyssa! Resident doctor wannabe. Would you mind transporting the babies to their new tanks?"

Alyssa laughed her worries away. "Yes ma'am."

"Let's go."

It was a careful process. Nasra drained the tank halfway so they could take the top off, and Alyssa lifted the child out and moved it to the other one. She did this nine times and was on pins and needles throughout the move.

Finally, the last top was closed, and the new tanks came online.

Nasra clapped. "We did it!"

Alyssa breathed a sigh of relief. "I don't think I could be a mother if this is how I carry children."

Zola scoffed. "I wouldn't even trust you to hold my cat."

Alyssa shrugged. "Fair enough."

"For a future doctor, you don't really have steady hands," Zola quipped.

"I was nervous! I'll develop surgeon hands eventually."

"Isn't that something that's supposed to come naturally?"

Alyssa tsked and threw an empty water bottle at Zola's head. "Shut up," she yelled playfully.

Aiken shook his head. "Ladies, if you could restrain from making loud noises while I am finishing up, that'd be great."

The two exchanged glances before running up to watch Aiken work. They all held their breath when he pushed the button to start administering the serum. Aiken slowly smiled. "Vitals are holding. The dosage isn't too high."

Zola slapped him on the back. "See? I told you that it would work. You're fine!"

Aiken nodded. "I guess so." He turned to her, smirking. "Unfortunately for you"—he thrust a tablet into her hands—"it's your turn to watch the tanks."

46

Waiting

Zola decided that tank duty was almost as bad as if she had been asked to watch paint dry. She almost nodded off. Every so often, she would jerk awake and see the clones a year or so older. It was both fascinating and boring at the same time. She hit her head on the table and sighed dramatically. Suffice to say, she was bored.

She checked her codes, just to make sure that they still worked, and then got distracted with homework. It was a wonder that the professors just kept on teaching as if their boss hadn't just died a little more than a week ago.

Zola typed the last words of her paper, then saved and closed the document. She'd review and revise it in the morning, that is if she revised it at all. It was very tempting to just print the paper and turn it in without looking over it.

There were whispers in the hall, theories about what had happened. No one was even close to the truth, and no one had found Parkes's body yet. Zola scoffed. It was better for her not to question where or how Astra had hidden the body, or even if she had destroyed it. There were just some things about the girl that no one was allowed to know.

She didn't delve too deep into those theories. One, she might slip up, and two, there wasn't really any point in knowing what other people thought about what happened. She also didn't have time, since she spent most of her afternoons and evenings in the lab. She had to study, and within that time, she thought about how she would break the news to the androids that Parkes was dead. For some reason, no one had told them.

While that was a concern, Zola was more concerned with how the teachers acted. They taught as if nothing had happened. They broke apart groups who theorized in the hallways, and above all, they were skittish, and they all watched their backs with wide eyes. Zola narrowed her eyes at the thought, squeezing her pencil until it snapped.

She needed to find out what they were hiding, the curiosity gnawed at her conscience until it was the only thing she could think about. Sometimes that was a bad thing, curiosity killed the cat or so they say. But it was her curiosity that got her into this school, and she wasn't about to let it go.

Zola glanced at her watch. It was 11 p.m. The bodies had grown past pre-teen years and were beginning to look a lot more like their android selves. Zola clicked the call button on the first icon that popped up on her phone. Henry.

He picked up, and the first thing out of his mouth was an annoyed, "What do you want?"

"I need you to watch the tanks now."

"Absolutely not."

"I'll buy you food for a week."

"Suddenly I am wide awake, I'll be right down."

Zola smirked. She hung up the phone and stood up to stretch. In the corner of her eye, she noticed that the door to the back room where the android pods were kept was slightly ajar. She narrowed her eyes.

"I'm here!"

Zola turned to see Henry burst through the doorway, slightly out of breath. He leaned down on his knees. "That was fast."

"I heard you'd buy me food?" he panted.

"Yeah, but I didn't expect you to get here that quickly."

"Yeah, well—"

"—what's going on?"

Zola and Henry turned to see Elena standing in the doorway.

"I just saw Henry sprint past, and I was a little concerned."

"You might need to be," Zola said. "I was just about to ask Henry if that door was open this whole time." She pointed at the cracked door leading to the back rooms.

Henry looked at it. "Huh. It was closed last time I was in here, but someone might have opened it in between."

Zola glared at the door suspiciously. "I could have sworn it was closed when I last came in here."

Elena made a face. "Are you going to check?"

"Are you two coming?"

"Of course I am, you aren't leaving me in here alone if you die or there's a ghost," Henry said.

Zola laughed. "Ghosts don't exist. Come on." She gripped the pepper spray in her pocket, and the two moved closer to the door.

Elena followed hesitantly. "Are you sure this is a good idea?"

Zola shrugged, quickly throwing the door open. "No clue. Henry, check the pods." Zola looked around the room and behind the door, immediately noticing the other door was also open. "Guys…"

Henry turned around. "Oh, you've got to be kidding me."

"What's behind that door?" Elena asked.

"Do I look like I'm the kind of person you should ask that question to? And no, the pods are all active, they're still in there," Henry said.

Zola breathed a sigh of relief. "Good." She moved closer to the door. Henry peered over her shoulder. "Well, no one is out over here." She opened the door and stepped inside the room.

Elena grabbed a scalpel off one of the lab tables and slipped it into her pocket as she followed the two into the room.

Henry shivered. "What is this room doing here? Also, why is it so cold? We should call for backup, call Astra or something, this is creeping me out."

Zola rolled her eyes. "Oh, come on you coward. It's just air, and it looks to be some sort of storage room. Look at all these filing cabinets."

Henry sighed. "Yes, you go smart girl. Congratulations, you

know what this place is. Now can we get out of here?”

“Nope.”

Henry made a face. “That’s it, I’m calling Astra.”

“Henry, don’t.”

“Too late.”

Zola sighed. “Great.”

Astra picked up rather quickly. “What?”

“Hi, Astra, sorry to interrupt on anything important that you were doing, but we have a problem. Do you happen to know of any storage rooms in the lab? Cause we found some doors open.”

Astra’s heart sank. She had been very careful to shut all the doors. Someone else must have been there. “I do, but the doors were locked, to make sure the androids didn’t get out. Did you check the pods?”

“That was the first thing we did. They’re all fine.”

Astra closed her eyes. “Good. Um, I’ll be right there.”

She took the stairs two at a time, and with every footstep, she felt sick. Something was wrong, something was terribly wrong. She reached the storage room and nearly ran into Henry.

“Sorry,” he jumped to move out of her way.

“It’s fine. Okay, tell me everything.”

Zola shrugged. “I just looked up like five minutes ago and re-alized that the door was slightly open.”

“Well did you fall asleep?”

“Maybe, I’m not sure, I could have.”

“Ugh! Zola, I expected better from you.” Astra turned towards the lines of cabinets. She took a deep breath and called out into the room. “I know you’re in there! Whoever you are, I will find you! You might as well give up now!”

47

Cassidy

Astra stared out into the storage room. There was no reply. She scanned the area for any sign of movement. Zola, Elena, and Henry watched her, trying to figure out what she was thinking.

"What?" Henry asked.

She huffed. "What do you mean, what? That didn't work, though I honestly don't know what I was expecting. Whoever it is must be further into the room. Which means I have to go looking for them. Guard the door." She disappeared between the shelves without waiting for an answer.

Zola and Henry looked at each other in shock.

"Did she just?" Elena asked.

"Seriously? I'm gonna go follow her," Zola said.

Henry grabbed her hand. "Zola, you shouldn't go after her, you don't have a weapon, and you have no idea what or who could be in there. Especially if it's a teacher." Henry glared at her. "I'm serious, you have no idea what is in that room, or what we're up against."

She stared at him. "Neither does Astra. What if she gets hurt? Let go of me."

Henry laughed and dropped her hand. "No offense to you, but Astra is the scariest thing in this room, and probably the whole school. I'm sure she can take care of herself."

Zola made a face. "That doesn't matter. Doesn't stop me from being worried. No matter how powerful or smart you are, there is always going to be someone more powerful and smarter than you are."

"You act like she's going to die immediately," Elena stated, rolling her eyes.

"What if she does? Do you want to be left without the protection of the girl that you claim is the scariest person in the school?" Zola questioned.

Henry sighed. "Fine. I suppose you have a point. If she isn't back in ten minutes, you can go after her. But be careful. I'm not losing two friends in one day."

Zola whipped around and narrowed her eyes at him. "Fine. Start a timer." She looked back towards the aisle that Astra had gone down. "You're not gonna lose either of us. I swear." She sighed and closed her eyes. "I really hope that there's nothing there."

* * * * * * * *

Astra made it to the middle of the room before she heard noises. She quickly crouched down. If she could make herself as small as possible and blend in with the shadows, she could sneak up on whoever it was. She peaked around the corner. A few steps forward and-

"Astra."

She whirled around, ready to punch whoever it was, only for the girl in front of her to catch her fist.

"Astra, what have we told you about sneaking around?"

Astra wrenched her arm out of the girl's grasp. "To not announce my presence?" she asked sarcastically.

"Exactly."

"What are you doing here Cassidy?"

"Xavier sent me to look for the files that you so graciously told him about. We still need to sort out this mess, and considering you have all the evidence we need to convict Parkes' helpers, we need them."

Astra rolled her eyes. "You could have told me. I would have gotten them for you."

"That takes the fun out of it. I haven't been out of the house in ages." Cassidy walked past her and beckoned for her to follow. "How did you even know it was me?"

"You left the doors open," Astra said. Her words came out flat.

"Oh." Cassidy raised an eyebrow. "You figured that out all from some open doors?"

"I didn't expect it to be you. I thought it'd be a teacher, then I heard the footsteps. Only a few people I know walk like that. It had to be one of you."

Cassidy laughed. "Oh yes, the good old-fashioned, make no noise rule, except we can still hear each other's footsteps if we listen hard enough."

"That, and your bracelet was jingling. I get that you like jewelry, but that was just plain stupid." Astra stared at her pointedly. "Weren't you the one who told me not to wear anything like that on a job?"

Cassidy tsked. "So maybe I forgot to take it off. I wasn't expecting anyone to notice I was down here."

"You're wearing white, and you broke into the basement of one of the most renowned tech schools in the entire world, and you *'didn't expect anyone to notice you were down here.'* Cass, that's just simple logic. I didn't think you had it in you to use flawed logic."

Cassidy fake yawned. "Well, I think you would know that even if I was caught, the person who found me would be dead."

"You're full of yourself. You better be glad that I got here first, because most teachers have guns."

Cassidy snickered. "I may be wearing white, but at least I have a bulletproof vest on."

"Good."

"Stop being so pretentious. Since you're here, you might as well lead the way."

"With that attitude?"

"Astra."

"Have you forgotten that you're not the boss of me anymore?"

"For old times sake." Cassidy put an arm around Astra's shoulders. "Just play along."

Astra pushed her away. "I'm not in the mood for that."

"Oh, come on."

Astra whirled around to face her. "Get it through your head Cass, I'm not your friend. Just." She paused. "Take that aisle, you'll find the faculty on the second to the bottom shelf near the end. Then leave, and don't bother saying goodbye."

Cassidy hummed. "Angry are we?"

Astra scoffed. "I'd like to see you try to make me angry."

"Well, I'd rather not right now, given as I have a deadline so-" she shooed Astra away- "why don't you go back to your friends, your stupid school, and the life you've chosen. How do you sleep at night knowing what you've given up?"

Astra looked her straight in the eyes. "I just think about all that I'm looking forward to. At least I can sleep at night knowing I've made up for what I've done. What can you say about that?"

Astra turned around and walked down one of the other aisles, not waiting for Cassidy to answer. A few rows down, she ran into Zola.

"Astra! Oh good, you're alive. I thought you had died or something."

"Died? That quickly?"

"You were gone for twenty minutes."

"That's nothing. My siblings have left me in places for days."

"That's awful! My brothers won't leave me alone in a grocery store for five minutes!"

Astra laughed. "That's because your siblings actually care about you."

"That's really depressing? Like, are you ok?"

"I know it is, and yes I'm perfectly fine."

"Did you find anyone?"

Astra hesitated. "No, I didn't. Let's go make sure no one snuck past Henry. They might have already left before you got here."

Astra grabbed Zola's hand and pulled her along behind her.

Henry's eyes lit up when he saw them.

"Well?"

"Nothing," Astra said.

"What she said. I thought I saw something earlier, though I might have been wrong."

"Ok then, I guess whoever it was must have already left." Astra walked past Henry into the lab. "So why don't we go back to the problem at hand, the fact that no one was watching the tanks!"

Worry flashed across Zola's face and she ran past Astra towards the computers. She and Astra checked the clone's vitals while Henry checked to make sure that no one tampered with the tanks.

"They're ok," Henry reported.

Zola nodded. "All fine over here."

Astra sighed. "That's good. But both of you were being irresponsible. You shouldn't have left them."

"Well I'm sorry, I got suspicious about the open doors!" Zola threw her hands up. "I can never win with you!"

Astra glared at her. "Well, maybe you should have left Henry to watch the tanks."

"I tried to; he didn't want to stay by himself."

"Yeah," Henry chimed in. "What if Zola died, and then someone came in to kill me?"

Astra facepalmed. "You're too paranoid, calm down."

"I will not."

"And where's Elena?" Astra asked.

"I don't know, she followed Zola, I thought she would've been right behind you guys," Henry said.

Astra opened her mouth to respond when a loud scream cut her off.

Zola gasped. "Is that Elena?"

Astra's eyes narrowed and she ran off in the direction of the noise without responding.

"Astra. Astra!" Zola yelled. "Wait!"

"Oh come on!" Henry groaned. He ran after the girls. "If this was a horror movie we'd all be dead," he yelled.

Astra followed the sound of shuffling and Elena's angry voice until she found the two in one of the aisles, Elena struggling to pull her arm out of Dean Parkes's grasp. He desperately attempted to cover her mouth.

"Astra!" She shouted.

Parkes looked up, surprised, and Elena took that opportunity to slip her hand into her pocket and pull out something that glinted silver in the dim light.

Astra looked on in shock as Elena raised the scalpel with a shaky hand.

"This is for Aiken," she said.

"El no!" Zola yelled.

Elena ignored her. "Don't you ever"—she grunted as she drove the scalpel into his chest—"ever, hurt my friends again!"

She continued to stab him, about a dozen times before the anger finally ran out. Elena dropped the scalpel. She stood there for a second as Dean Parkes stared at her before toppling over, dragging her down with him. Elena sat there in shock, blood splattered on her face and clothes. Her head spun as she realized what she had done.

"What just happened?!" Henry yelled.

Astra turned just in time to see Henry leaning against one of the cabinets throwing up. She shook her head and stepped towards Elena, pulling her to her feet and away from the body. She was staring blankly into the distance, and Astra didn't even bother to try and comfort her. "Zola?"

"Hm?" She looked dazed.

"Help Elena to the dorm, ok? Henry, please brush your teeth, drink some water, and all of you rest. I can take care of the rest."

Zola nodded. "Ok." She slowly reached out to grab Elena's hand and pulled her along, leading her towards the door.

Henry hesitated, but eventually said goodbye and left.

Astra watched them turn the corner and fade out of sight, then turned back towards Parkes's dead body.

Cassidy appeared at her side. "So, need a hand with the clean up?"

Unconventional Ideas

Astra walked into the lab and let out a sigh of relief. She was more tired than she had ever been in her life. It almost felt like her bones were weighing her down. Cassidy's visit was unexpected, but she wasn't going to let that ruin her current plans. She retreated to the nearest chair and stared at the tanks. They looked so real, even though by all rights and purposes, they were technically dead. Not that they had ever been alive.

It was their features that threw Astra off the most. She had gotten used to the androids, and she already knew what synthetic skin looked like. These were human bodies, and she knew that too, but the fact that their faces belonged to machines made her feel something. She didn't know what it was, all she knew was that it was an unpleasant feeling. After all, she of all people should know the difference between being and looking human.

Astra pulled her phone out of her back pocket. She pulled up her codes and typed in a series of commands. About five minutes later, she heard a clanking in the vent behind her, and her mechanical spider crawled across the floor and up her leg, carrying her bag. Astra smiled.

The spider was one of her favorite projects, small and agile. It usually sat in the top corner of her room, watching and waiting for someone to come in and tamper with her things. With a household like hers, pranks were common, and Astra didn't like being unprepared. She rarely ever left the house without it when she was young.

It was one of her first inventions, and had almost grown a mind of its own, moving when it wasn't supposed to, but still following its basic programming. She had lost it during the first semester's finals. It had slipped out of her bag, and she almost thought she would never see it again. She hadn't left it out of her sight once she found it, not until she reprogrammed it.

Astra was surprised to see the amount of footage the thing had recorded. She didn't realize how much storage space it still had left. She had spent a couple of days going over the videos, and it gave her a few ideas. Astra didn't usually care for the ethical approach. In her line of work, that often caused more problems. So, she used the spider to administer the trackers.

That part was harder than she expected, though, to be fair, being stabbed with a small needle in her sleep would probably wake her up. But that's what sleeping pills were for. Astra pulled her notebook out of her bag. She surveyed her list, and the most recent crossed out line. *'Eliminate the Glitch.'* Her job here was done. If she wanted, she could leave without any regrets.

It wasn't like she didn't want to leave, but she had made a big impact here. It was hard to incorporate her training and just disappear when she would be leaving so many people who knew exactly who she was. She didn't feel comfortable doing that, not when there were people who would kill to find her, simply for what she knew.

Astra sighed. Unfortunately, she would be staying here a bit longer, just until she could tie up her loose ends. She closed the notebook with a light snap, let the spider crawl into her hand, and stood up. She was done working for other people. It was time to put the final phase of her plan into motion.

* * * * * * * *

The next morning, Katya arrived at the lab early. To her surprise, Alyssa was already there.

"Hey," Katya greeted her.

Alyssa looked up, startled. "Oh, hi, Katya. What's up?"

Katya shrugged. "Not much, just the usual, couldn't sleep. You?"

"I was anxious, you know?"

"Neither of us are going to be fully awake later, are we?"

Alyssa scoffed. "I don't think that was ever the case during the entirety of our stay here."

Katya hummed. "You're probably right."

Alyssa frowned. "Hey, did you see Astra on the way down here?"

"No, I didn't, why?"

"Well, she was in here when I arrived, and she basically made me stay here to watch the tanks so she could go back to her dorm."

"And?"

"I kind of assumed she was going to come back, but maybe she went to sleep."

Katya shook her head. "No, I can't see that happening. Most likely she just got distracted doing something, like working on her project."

Alyssa groaned and dropped her head onto the table.

"What?"

"Our projects, we still have to finish them."

Katya made a face. "Yeah…" she pat Alyssa on the shoulder. "At least your research and serum is useful, I got a big telescope, that's it."

"I guess so. I just wish we could like, I don't know, combine them. That would make it a whole lot easier."

Katya pursed her lips. "That's actually a pretty good idea."

Alyssa looked up. "Wait, really?"

"I mean, yeah. We have quite the range of skills and projects. Combining them would not only give us the chance to work in areas that we normally wouldn't, but we might even discover something that we find interesting."

Alyssa grinned. "I mean, I'd love to do it, but we'd have to get everyone on board with it, especially with this 'unconventional idea.' The school and the board of directors won't like it if we do this."

Katya scoffed. "Oh, come on Alyssa, we practically are the board of directors. I mean, what are they going to do about it? The Dean is dead, and that means all bets are off. I'm sure no one will care."

Alyssa shrugged. "Let's ask everyone first, but I have no problem with this. In fact, I really want to do it."

Katya nodded. "Okay, so in"—she checked her watch—"three-ish hours, we present this idea to the group?"

"Sounds good." Alyssa turned back to the tanks. "Do you think that the transfer will go well?"

Katya smiled. "Of course it will. Alyssa, you're one of the smartest people I know, which is a very big accomplishment. It'll work."

"Doesn't stop me from being worried," Alyssa mumbled.

Katya nodded. "I know, but hey, cheer up. At least you've got help."

Alyssa still looked apprehensive. "Yeah, I guess so," she said slowly.

49

The Transfer

Zola sighed. Today was the day. Even though the clones were ready the day before, there had still been a lot of work to do. At this point, judging by the look on her face and how quickly she had drunk five cups of coffee, Zola wasn't sure that Alyssa had even slept.

"Are you okay?" Zola questioned.

"M' fine, just a little tired," Alyssa mumbled. "Can you get me more coffee? Also, that briefcase has my serum in it, so be very careful with it, Aiken! Thank you."

Zola pursed her lips. "If I get you coffee, will you take a break?"

Alyssa frowned. "A break? We just started?"

"And? You look like you're about to fall asleep on your feet!"

Alyssa turned towards the tanks. "Sleep is for the weak."

Zola raised an eyebrow. "Yeah, and after this you're going to sleep for a week," she whispered under her breath.

"What?"

"Nothing! Getting you coffee right now." Zola sprinted out of the room.

"Huh." Alyssa placed her tablet on the table. "Okay, so this stuff has to be controlled very carefully, Henry?"

Henry nodded. "Yeah, as soon as Zola gets back we can start the process, but this thing right here," he placed a small black metal box on the table. "You'll put the serum in here, and then you connect these wires to the pod, and these wires to the clone, Zola's code will do the rest."

"That simple?"

"Well, I mean, not really, but, science!" He laughed awkwardly.

"Really?"

"Look, I don't really know how all of this works, it's not my area of expertise. Isn't this your project?"

Alyssa nodded. "Yeah, it is. I mean, all I've ever done is been able to read the minds of animals. I'm not exactly sure how it'll react. I mean, technically, it should work, but…" she trailed off.

"But what?"

"What if we lose them? I mean, it's never been tested on a human before, if it doesn't work, what then?"

"Astra has the backups, you're not going to lose the memories, or the programming."

"And if it fails? Over, and over, and over? I can't deal with not keeping promises."

Henry sighed. "Look. I have full faith that the transfer will go smoothly. I mean, so what if it's only worked on animals? Zola is capable of dealing with any and all problems, Astra could probably figure something else out even if the serum doesn't work. Not to mention, you're so smart that you made this serum, something that is still fantasy for some of the most famous scientists in the world. Besides, brains are pretty similar anyway, so who's to say that it won't just work exactly the way we planned? And, to make things even better, if anything goes wrong, you've got some of the best minds in the world ready to fix things on the fly."

Alyssa nodded. "I guess so. I'm still worried."

"You're always worried. I don't know what it is with you people and not being confident, when you've gotten this far. I mean, even being able to read an animal's mind, to some extent, is a feat all on its own. That's a big accomplishment for someone who came into this school for health science. I mean, think of what good you could do with this when it works."

"If it works," Alyssa corrected.

"No, no, we are not having negative attitudes, not this early in the morning. When it works."

"Okay, so, when it works. But what about the bad stuff? Like the government getting a hold of it, or it being used to start wars?”

“Consider this, don’t let them know.”

“I’m not capable of fighting the government to keep them from taking my research.”

“Well, not on your own, but you’re not alone anymore.” Henry nodded towards the tanks where Mary and Aiken were checking the vitals of the clones. “You’ve got them, you’ve got me, and Zola, Astra, Katya, Elena, Nasra. We’re all ready to stand by you if anyone tries to hurt you or steal your research.”

Alyssa laughed. “It’s weird.”

“What?”

“How close we’ve become. We spent the last year and a half being distrustful of each other, but you have one crisis, and suddenly everyone is best friends.”

“Well, that’s the thing about shared trauma. Brings people together.”

“Yeah, you’re right. But you know what else brings people together? Shared interests in, I don’t know, movies. Books, games, music, stuff like that. Why couldn’t we have all met each other normally?”

Henry snorted. “First of all, we all come from different countries, so yeah, have fun trying to think of alternate ways we could have met each other. Second of all, meeting normally? Really? Where’s the fun in that?”

“Where’s the fun in what?” Astra asked,

Alyssa and Henry turned around to see Astra and Zola, both holding a couple of coffee cups.

Alyssa smiled. “Not much, just how we all met each other, and my concerns for today’s events. Is one of those for me?”

Zola nodded. “Yes, and please take one before I drop them.”

Alyssa snickered. “Here, Henry, you take some, the rest can go on the desk. So, are we ready?”

Henry raised an eyebrow. “Bold question for someone who

was having doubts a couple of minutes ago."

"Oh, shut up man, let me at least pretend to have some form of confidence in myself."

Henry raised an eyebrow and took a sip of his coffee. "No, I don't think I will."

Alyssa huffed. "It doesn't matter, But, are we ready?"

Astra looked at Zola. "Are we?"

"I mean, I'm ready, are the clones? Mary, Aiken, how's it going over there?"

Aiken ran up to them. "Their vitals are holding steady, so, ready when you are."

Astra frowned. "Okay, where's Nasra? It would be great to have the literal expert on this subject available before we start."

"I'm here, I'm sorry, I was compiling a list of things we have to do." Nasra waved a piece of paper in the air. "Okay, so, Henry, Aiken, you're going to need to roll the pods in here, Katya, Mary, there's a closet over in that room, there are a couple of stretchers, can you bring those in here? Thanks. Astra, Alyssa, Zola, I'm going to need you three at the computers, you guys are the most important part of this operation, everything rests on your shoulders."

Alyssa inhaled. "Well, that makes me feel so much less nervous."

Nasra gave an awkward smile. "I'm sorry to put all this pressure on you, it's just that, I do need to put that much pressure on you. This may be my research, but the technique, that's all you. It's my theory, you're proving it correct, so all power to you, just go over there and get to work. Look, we have a lot of preparation to do, so I'm counting on you to set the serum up while we set up the transfer space. Okay?"

They nodded. "Got it."

Nasra grinned. "Thank you." She turned around. "Okay, Henry, Aiken, be very careful. Mary, Kat, you can put the stretchers right here. Since it will take a long time to do the actual transfer, and there's no guarantee that they'll wake up right away, it's important that there's space for us to walk, so try not to put them too close to each other, we need to be able to monitor their vitals as well, okay?"

Astra raised an eyebrow. "Wow, leadership really suits her, huh?"

"No kidding," Zola said. "But you heard her, let's get to work." She grabbed the box off the table. "Astra, you and Henry built this, so tell me how it works."

Astra took it from her. "Okay, so the serum goes in here. Alyssa?" Alyssa placed one of the vials in the box and Astra closed it. "These wires will connect to the pod, as well as the brain of the clone. This little port right here is where we uploaded Zola's codes, which can be controlled from the computer."

"Huh." Alyssa stared at it. "Such a small contraption, but it has such an important job."

Astra nodded. "Yep. And we have eight more to set up. Zola, this is box number one, it's meant to go to Cassian, please check the computer to make sure it's connected."

"Yes ma'am." Zola took the box from Astra and walked over to the computer. Astra placed the other boxes on the table, and she and Alyssa began assembling the rest of them.

Alyssa strode over to Zola. "Alright, nine boxes of mind transfer juice ready."

Zola paused and stared at her. "Why'd you say it like that?"

"Why not?"

Zola scoffed and shook her head. "Alright, they're all synced. I'm pretty sure they're labeled, so all you have to do is match the box to the pod."

"Seems simple enough."

"And yet it's easy to mess up."

Alyssa glared. "Stop. I'm beginning to think you're all saying stuff like this to make fun of me."

Zola grabbed two of the boxes. "Alyssa, you don't need to worry. It's going to go great."

"Yep!" Astra bumped Alyssa with her shoulder. "You should be proud of yourself. Now go hook these two up to Willow and Morgan, will you?"

Once the clones were hooked up to the pods, the group gathered around the computers.

"Hey, hey, hey." Zola glared at them. "Give us some space, I know it's exciting, but that's not an excuse."

There were mumbles of apologies as they backed up.

Astra grabbed one of the tablets. "Alright, Zola, ready when you are."

Zola smiled grimly. "Lovely. Uh, just a sec—" She typed rapidly. "Alright, Alyssa, want to count off?"

"Uh, yeah, sure. Um, one, two, three."

Zola clicked enter. Nothing happened.

Alyssa raised an eyebrow. "Did it work?" she questioned.

"I started the process. It's not going to happen right away."

"So that was anticlimactic," Henry quipped.

"Yeah, yeah, yeah, whatever." Zola rolled her eyes. "Nasra, how are their vitals?"

"They're fine."

Aiken wiggled his way to the front. "Okay, how long is this going to take?"

Astra looked at Zola. "Yeah, how long is it going to take?"

"Could be a couple of hours, could be a couple of days. We can monitor their vitals through the tablets, or someone could stay in here for the whole transfer, what do you guys think?"

Henry raised his hands in defense. "I'm not babysitting again, the whole *watch the clones grow* thing was enough for me."

Astra pursed her lips. "So, no one wants to stay and watch the clones? Are you sure?" She looked pointedly around the room. "Okay then, tablets it is."

Katya raised her hand. "Okay, so, does that mean we get to work on our projects now?"

Astra smiled. "If everyone's in favor, yes. And I know just the place where we can do it."

50

Misconceptions About Final Projects

Katya kicked the lab door open. "Alright!" she yelled into the room.

Aiken jumped and clutched his chest. "Gosh, when did you become so loud? You scared me."

Katya made a face. "Sorry Aiken. Maybe you should practice being less paranoid."

"Excuse me?"

She ignored him. "So, here's what we were thinking. Earlier, Alyssa and I were discussing combining our projects. Given that all our projects are very diverse, I was thinking, we should try to find things that we have in common, and go from there?"

Astra pursed her lips. "Zola and I did coding."

Henry nodded. "That would work with my computer, which I think might be able to work with your telescope Katya."

Katya nodded. "So, we might be able to do something with those?"

Astra hummed. "A giant telescope?"

Henry's eyes widened. "My computer can support this."

Zola smiled. "And my codes can control it, maybe like, a warning of some sort, for asteroids? Passing comets? Observing other planets better?"

Astra hummed softly. "We'd still need some kind of support system, and a place to put the thing."

Katya turned to the others. "So, Alyssa, Elena, Mary? What do you have?"

Mary smiled. "I've got something, and boy am I glad you asked!" She whipped out several tubes and rolled them out across the table. "This is what I have so far, I'm still working on it, but I have a place nearby where we can start building."

Elena looked over Mary's shoulder. She frowned at the plans. She picked them up. "Mary, where did you get these?"

Mary looked at her confused. "What? They're mine, I made them."

"No, Mary, these are mine. Which means you stole them."

Mary frowned. "No. I didn't, they're mine, I've been working on these for the past year. I never touched your plans; I never even saw them."

Alyssa looked on, worried. "Please don't fight here."

Katya elbowed her in the ribs. "Fight? This is more than a fight, Elena is accusing her of thievery, so Elena, are you sure these are yours? And Mary, are you sure you didn't take them?"

Elena glared. "Shut up, Katya, I know my work when I see it. All this time I thought I was just imagining it, and it was you who went in there and stole my plans?"

Katya frowned and made a face but didn't argue. She grabbed Mary's plans and walked away to look for Elena's.

Mary squared her shoulders. "No! I don't know why you think these are your plans, but they're mine, and I know they're mine cause I've been thinking and dreaming about them for a long time! You can't just claim someone else's work!" She stomped her feet on the verge of tears. "You can't!"

Alyssa's eyes widened, realization flooding her thoughts at Mary's words, and her heart skipped a beat.

Elena clenched her fists. "You can't just steal my work and deny it! I know what I did, and those"—she pointed at Katya and Zola who were comparing the two plans in the corner—"are mine! So you stole them!"

Mary glared at her. "I stole nothing, and I mean nothing, from you!" she screamed. "And if you think you can accuse me of stealing, if you think I would do anything like that, then you obviously don't know me at all!"

"Well maybe I don't!" Elena lowered her voice. "I know what

I've created Mary, and it's sitting right there on that table."

Alyssa jumped in the middle. "Wait! El, Mary didn't steal your prints. I actually think I did."

"What?!" The two glared at her.

Mary stepped forward. "You stole them?" She frowned. "That means you helped Delilah. What, how, and most importantly, why did you do it?"

Alyssa jumped backwards and tried to get a hold of her words. "No, that's not what I mean. Uhhhhh." She backtracked and stumbled over her words. "Delilah stole the physical plans. I didn't steal the plans intentionally." She looked down. "At least I don't think I did. See, since my project was a serum that allowed a doctor to basically read an animal's mind, it was meant to be very diluted. It wasn't supposed to help me read a human mind. But it was too strong at the beginning. I must have accidentally read Elena's thoughts, and I must have let them spill into Mary."

"That explains why I dreamt them up, after you started testing! The rest of it was mine though, I promise." Mary looked at Elena. "I'm really sorry El. I'll find something else to make."

"No you won't!" Katya jumped in. "We actually need both of your machines. For Henry. We want to put them together. Zola and I just looked at Mary's prints. Besides the accidental dreaming of El's things, she also has all of ours. The thing is, she didn't build it, you did, and we need that power source. El, will you help?"

Mary frowned. "Wait. So none of what I made was actually mine? What?"

Elena ignored her, staring at Katya thoughtfully. "What will I get out of this?"

"A lot of credit. This is the first time that things like this ever happened, and I don't think anyone expected Alyssa's serum to do this."

Alyssa nodded violently. "I swear I didn't mean to steal."

Elena waved her arm and rolled her eyes. She sighed. Now that she was done yelling, it felt almost useless to fight. Everything was so insignificant now compared to what she had done. "It's fine, it's not your fault. You're very lucky I built it and didn't just do the prints. Alyssa, we may need to have a talk later, but for now, I will accept that you managed to create a genius item that I trust you won't let fall into the wrong hands?"

Alyssa gulped. She saluted Elena. "Aye, aye, captain."

Elena laughed. "You look scared. This is a completely valid explanation, a strange one that I need time to process, but at the moment, I'm not mad, just in shock. Expect anger later."

Katya clapped her hands. "Great! Well, not the anger part. Let's just get to work!"

That was easier said than done. The project they decided to tackle was a bit of an uphill climb. Henry's computer had slots he had no idea what to do with, slots that fit together perfectly with the other projects.

Elena smiled at Mary. "I may be a little angry that you accidentally took my plans, but I have to thank you for perfecting them."

Mary nodded. "You're welcome?"

Elena snickered and turned around. "Of course, you wouldn't have gotten here without me, so maybe you should be the one thanking me."

Mary raised an eyebrow. "How very petty of you. But thank you, I guess. I appreciate the help."

Henry pat Mary on the shoulder as he moved past her. "Hey, it really isn't your fault, and she'll get over it, okay?"

Mary sighed. "It's still a bit weird."

"Everything we've done here is weird, we've literally done things that I wouldn't have even imagined of a few years ago. If you'd told me that I was going to be in Canada building a telescope after literally killing my dean, though I didn't do it, I would have looked you in the eyes and asked if you were drunk."

Mary giggled. "I guess I can't really blame myself, can I? But you're right, I should be used to weird by now, shouldn't I?"

"Absolutely. And if you're going to be blaming anyone, you might as well blame Alyssa."

"She's already worried about Elena blowing up at her, so I think I'll leave her be."

Henry shrugged. "Suit yourself." He passed a bag to Astra. "Put these in, will you?"

Astra nodded, and opened a panel, turning her back so she could hide what she was doing. She pretended not to hear anything as she listened in on the rest of the group bicker and poke fun at each other. She carefully slid Henry's control chips into their respective slots, as well as a few of her own. She was very glad Henry had brought her that chip last year, she was one short after someone dropped her bag on the floor, snapping one in half. She closed the panel and sealed it off. It would come into use later. Astra was just glad no one would suspect her.

Against her better judgment, she had gotten a little attached to the group. More than attached. In fact, she might have said that she had grown fond of them, even though she knew that wasn't a possibility. They weren't her people, the ones that she desperately needed to return to. Maybe Xavier was right, it was a bad idea to let them get to her. But, she didn't care. She didn't mind that they had wiggled their way into her head.

She started connecting wires and inserting some of her own codes with Zola. She smiled softly. It wasn't that she was feeling happy or anything. Or maybe she was. This was her first time away from the colony, and she had no idea how it really worked. Zola noticed her smile and elbowed her playfully in the ribs.

"You're warming up to us I see."

Astra chuckled. "Maybe. Or maybe I'm faking it, you'll never know."

Zola shrugged. "I think I'd know." She moved away to get more parts.

Astra sighed. "No, you wouldn't," she whispered. "You never would."

After a few days, each one full of laughter as they built, small cuts and bruises while they tinkered, and taunts after the last few adjustments, they were done. Katya mounted her telescope on the top, traced wires, and made sure that it worked like it was supposed to. The old observatory was a perfect fit for the telescope.

Katya wasn't sure why it was there. She didn't care either. All she knew was that she was grateful, especially to Astra who had found the place. Grateful for her friends, and their support, grateful that their project would be useful for studying the stars. She stepped down from the platform and turned to the others. "Well, it's operational."

They cheered and took turns hugging each other. They met the newly awoken clones outside, each still slightly tired and groggy from their consciousness transfer. Getting a new body and getting your heart jumpstarted makes one tired apparently.

Cassian made his way over to Nasra and gave her a thumbs up. "I guess I underestimated you. You really did get to change the world."

She smiled. "Yeah, and I'm glad we managed to get all your memories back."

He nodded. "That is a pro, though it's kind of weird to know that I was just, you know, built."

"At least you have a body now. A human one."

"That's true. And hey, you got to make a place for yourself. Isn't that what you wanted?"

Nasra nodded. "I got more than I bargained for though."

"Well, I think that's an added bonus."

The group crowded together outside in order to decide on food choices, choruses of congratulations greeted each of them. It had been a successful year, a job well done, and now there were new opportunities for the coming years.

Unlike other students, they decided not to transfer to another university, instead staying at the school to do more research and help out with new students. They also took over the school as a student council—after all, with Dean Parkes gone, someone had to do it. Against Astra's better judgment, they decided not to destroy Parkes' research and the lab. They wanted to use it for their own research, and she had gotten outvoted anyway.

Eventually, they would get around to the new applicants, and they would get to encourage new students to work on new ideas and ways to help the world. But today was a day to just have fun, so they headed towards the town.

Astra grabbed Isaac, keeping him just out of hearing range of the rest of the group as they walked.

"What?"

Astra hummed. "I know you're 'J'. That you're the one who left the message on the wall. Jaejin Kim huh? They nicknamed you Isaac according to your file though. I didn't think Leroy had it in him to be sentimental with names."

Isaac didn't look shocked. "I didn't either. I surprisingly prefer Isaac though. I mean, I liked my handler, but I didn't like my original name. Leroy called me Isaac. He didn't call me anything else, and so the rest of the staff followed. And I'm honestly not surprised, about you finding out that is. You were in charge of our memories, if anyone was going to do it, it was you. But..."

"What?"

"Can you keep it a secret? I don't want anyone else to know, and at this point, I'm hoping they'll all forget about it."

"Forget about it? Why?"

"Because there's just too much they don't know. I'd rather not have to explain to them, but you would know, wouldn't you."

Astra looked down. "Yeah, I know. Isaac, the name you carry is important, even beyond what you know. It's his brother's name, you know that, but I know what Isaac Parkes did. I know why

Parkes named you that, and I know who killed the original Isaac. I know that you don't want them feeling guilty for his long-forgotten humanity, he didn't have much in the first place, so don't worry too much. I also know what you did to sabotage him, and I have to thank you for that. Without you, we wouldn't be here."

"You shouldn't thank me, all I did was glitch his system, I should thank you for saving us. I never wanted to be a weapon."

"Still, it's admirable, and kind of ironic that it was you, I mean, you were his favorite, right?"

Isaac shrugged. "I guess. But can we get back to the point?"

Astra hummed. "Yeah, yeah, I know. I've kept your secret this long, there's no harm in keeping it forever, but Isaac—" Astra stopped in the middle of the road. "There's another problem. You know what I am."

Isaac looked away. "Yeah, about that—"

"Look, I don't need to know how you found out, all I need is for you to keep quiet. Only you know, so let's keep it that way, okay? A secret for a secret?" She held out her pinky.

He stared at her. "That's a little childish isn't it?"

Astra raised an eyebrow. "The world was built on children's dreams Isaac, don't be pretentious. What do you say?"

Isaac hesitated, then locked his pinky with hers. "Deal."

Epilogue

Astra slipped away from the group, back to the machine. She breathed a sigh of relief. She had done it. She had been doubted, taunted, but she had proved them wrong. Her siblings would be proud. Especially Xavier. He knew what she'd be up against when she came here. He knew it would be her most difficult mission yet. He also knew that she did not plan to return.

Astra had been so careful to not share her family name, her family plans with the group. She had been so closed off. Destiny proved to be a bump in the road, but no one had figured it out. They only knew that she was evil. They didn't know what Astra knew, and she hoped they would never find out.

Of course, wishes didn't always come true. She learned that the hard way. Even with the help, the plans, and her own research, she had almost fallen short. Almost. She didn't like almosts. It made her skin itch with the reality that she could fail if she didn't work hard enough. Even if she did work for it, sometimes those failures crept up on her and swallowed her.

She definitely didn't like failure. That made her frustrated, and frustration led to anger, and anger would corrupt her. She didn't have time for that corruption. If she wanted to return, if she wanted any of her work to be worth it, she couldn't focus on the almosts. It was something she was still learning.

She was finally going home. Her leaving the Dukes was inevitable, but Xavier's harsh words pushed her over the edge. Despite everything, she'd miss him most of all. She remembered telling him her plans before she left. At that time, he seemed so proud of her. She didn't know what he'd think of her now.

'When I no longer work for you, and I'm ready to go home, I think I want to talk about what I did here. It's a long time away, so

I can stay here as long as I want, but who knows, maybe I can take you with me.'

'I think you'll do great, but still. Do you have to talk about it right now, Little Star? You know I can't go with you.'

Astra opened the door to the room where the machine was sitting. Her heart pounded. It would take a while before the signal would ever reach its intended audience, and even longer to dispatch someone, if they chose to do so. But she didn't mind the wait.

Astra trailed her fingers over the machine. They only thought it was a supercomputer-powered telescope, something that could warn people of asteroids, see the stars in a different way, and control satellites. But it was more than that. Astra did it for a reason.

Manipulation. The human brain was just a code, easily nudged in the proper direction, especially with the help of nanobots. Their research backed it up. Nasra's study of the human cell. Aiken's growth serum. Zola's code which could control everything it needed to, like a virus, Henry's computer, Elena's batteries, the way they spilled over in Mary's dreams. All of their work was good, they just needed a push over the edge.

Best of all, it was her idea. And what a brilliant idea it was. She could've done it without help, but this made it faster. She edited Zola's codes when the other girl wasn't looking, so she would finish quicker, changed Elena's blueprints, altered Alyssa's project, made sure Mary heard Alyssa's thoughts, and it was hard. But she did it.

They would hate her for it, if they ever found out. Sure, she hadn't planned everything. She didn't know about Aiken's serum, she had planned on coding her message, expecting it to take months. With his serum, it could take days, or maybe even as little as hours. She didn't expect Henry to have the computer, and certainly didn't anticipate Katya's telescope. She didn't know they would decide to build the machine, she thought she would have to do that in secret.

Her plan actually worked better, with all of these pieces in place, her true motive buried under good intentions. By the time they figured it out, if they even figured out the original purpose of the machine, Astra would be long gone.

She inserted a jump drive into the side of the machine, proud as she uploaded the code she had so longed to use. It was her prized work. Such a shame she couldn't share it with the others.

"You coming? We have a lot of work to do today, so I don't know why you're just standing around."

Astra jumped. She turned around to see Morgan standing in the door. "Yeah, just a second. I want to check something."

"Okay, but hurry up." Morgan left the room.

Astra turned back to the computer. She pulled the drive out and slipped it into her pocket. Finally, she inputted the last instructions and pressed enter. Astra pulled a Band-Aid out of her pocket, and winced as she sliced her finger on one of the sharper sides. A little droplet slid down her hand. She caught it with the open vial of Aiken's serum, dumped the contents of another vial into it, and then slipped into place near the keyboard.

Astra hesitated for a second as her instructions streamed across the screen and disappeared. She carefully wrapped the bandage around her finger as she exited the room. "Okay, now I'm ready. Let's go."

Worry flashed across Morgan's face. "Wait, what happened?"

"Oh, just cut my hand on a piece of the machine. It's okay."

Morgan frowned, but didn't seem to dwell on it. She slung her arm over Astra's shoulders. "If you say so. You have got to be more careful." They followed the others down the hall, joking around, catching up with the others and laughing.

Astra was lucky she didn't look back. Otherwise, she would have seen the bright white computer screen, a multicolored star blinking in the middle. She would have heard the incessant beep-ing caused by the serum, as it began to spread throughout the machine. With each pulse, it sent out an encrypted signal, powered by a single drop of blue blood.

To Be Continued In...
CLANDESTINE

O

Prologue

There's not much that a person can do when they're stuck indoors. Astra didn't realize how hard it would be to fight off the urge to fall asleep. She was currently quarantined in her dorm room, under several thick blankets, due to yet another experiment gone wrong. All hell breaks loose when you leave Alyssa Clark by herself, apparently. Of course, Astra was a stubborn girl who didn't let the supposed sickness keep her from working. Sniffling once in determination, she tapped away at the keys until she was satisfied with her word count, then set the computer aside. It was getting late, and she knew no one would bother her anyway.

She fished her notebook out of her bag and opened it. Ever since she and her friends had taken over the school, Astra had been going through the leftover files in the room underneath it. There were thousands of them, and Zola had told her it would take years for someone to even begin to put a dent into the to-be-read pile. Luckily, Astra wasn't a normal person, and after a week of scouring, she was almost halfway through.

Then, Alyssa accidentally loosed a disease into the school, causing the infected students, Astra included, to be confined to their rooms. Every so often, Astra would employ Henry to bring her some files, and she continued her hunt at a snail-like pace. At least it kept the boredom away. Meanwhile, Astra knew that Zola was off firing all of the old staff and putting out ads for new employees. Nasra was in charge of finding and interviewing every single student who ever knew about Parkes' old experiment, and the rest of the group were left to their own devices.

She was upset to be stuck in her room, angry that her immune system wasn't kicking in. She knew it was a side effect, but she hated it all the same. She'd get over it as soon as Alyssa was able to come up with a cure. Still, it had been days since she was ordered to stay in her dorm, and she hated the idea that she had to be there and not work. Of the files that Henry had brought her, there wasn't much to be found. Still, she took notes, steadily weeding through Parkes' journals, lab notes, employee records, and experiments.

Every single time she found something related to Destiny, she'd have to stop and collect herself to keep from punching the wall in her anger. Parkes never should have been trusted, but they were all too naive to have seen it. If it weren't for Isaac…

Astra paused. Getting lost in her memories wasn't good for her work ethic. She pulled the most recent stack of files out from underneath her bed and got to work. Most of it was useless. There was nothing out of the ordinary for Parkes, just records, thousands of them. He was very organized, she had to give him that. She skimmed through most of the records. They weren't interesting to her anyway.

It wasn't until she pulled out a file labeled *Project Checkmate* that she realized. It was an old tradition, playing chess. She had learned it from her parents; she had even played the game with Parkes once, back when she was younger. Mostly, he played with her father, who claimed all of his kids' work as his own in front of guests and allies. It was for their own safety, after all. No one had to know what they did.

She read through the file carefully, and couldn't keep the hatred from welling up inside her. She picked up a cup and threw it across the room. Astra never allowed herself to get angry. It was a risk she couldn't take. Still, she granted it to herself just this once. She had to. Her technology wasn't just in Parkes' hands, it was spread across the globe. It was recycled, used, and then retired to a facility to be studied, kept safe, once Parkes had to go into hiding.

Syn's Technology Research Facility, he called it. After synergy, because he and so many people had worked together to make it happen. Astra scoffed. Parkes must have thought himself so brilliant. She didn't often make mistakes like this, underestimating her opponent. If anything, she overestimated. So how could she have overlooked the thought that Parkes hadn't destroyed the designs that came before his last project? The android's predecessors, shut off and dismantled though they were, were trophies. And this facility was the biggest trophy case that ever existed.

Authorities had spent years trying to convict Leroy Parkes of the crimes he had committed, but they had no evidence. When he died, that was perfect for them. They couldn't take his work, and that made things harder. She could easily break into a police station and remove her tech. But to infiltrate a research facility that prized its work and rarely hired anyone, was strict on its internships, and would have her file on hand? That was risky. There was not a lot she could do.

She had to tell someone. She couldn't do this on her own. Astra's eyes narrowed, and she made a split-second decision as she grabbed her phone.

Xavier Zhang didn't like surprises. He was no stranger to secrets. He kept them loyally his entire life. Then again, it wasn't like he had a choice. Now, in the wake of his father's death, he was without a mentor, surrounded by people he barely knew, trying to recall his siblings back from their various locations across the world. He was tired, of course. Days cooped up in a darkened conference room trying to put your father's affairs in order would do that to a person. He had finally gotten around to it, after the disasters of last year.

It was tedious work, but he did it without complaint. Well, without complaining out loud. When his phone rang, he was grateful for the distraction. He picked up without bothering to check the caller ID. "Hello?" All that he could hear on the other end was static. He frowned. His eyes widened in recognition when he heard the breathing, a rhythm he could recognize anywhere. "Astra?"

"Hello, Xavier. I have a favor to ask of you."

Acknowledgements

A lot went into this manuscript in order to make it the book it is today. I started it back in 2019 (Or maybe 2020, at this point I can't remember), but at that time, it didn't even have a plot, it was just a vague idea. If it wasn't for the group of people that I was so blessed to have help me, I would probably still be writing it today.

First off, I want to thank all of my friends and family who beta read this book for me, you all are amazing, and I couldn't have done it without you. Especially my mother who read the first edition of this book in a week so that I could have a proofreader. In fact, I need to thank my mother who helped me cultivate my imagination, and taught me that turning in essays that are anything less than my best is unacceptable. You taught me that my writing doesn't have to be perfect, but I'm still a perfectionist anyway. Thank you for your support, and encouragement. Thank you for editing the most and making sure that everything I said made sense. I love you!

Secondly, I would like to thank my cover designer, Jessica. Thanks for putting up with me while I struggled to put my thoughts about the cover into words. You're the best. I'd also like to thank my Creative Writing professor for his lectures, and for his wonderful criticism. Thankfully, I passed his class. Without him, I would probably have published this book way later, or never published it at all.

Finally, I'd like to thank everyone who made this second edition possible. So many people put their hearts into feedback, sharing my posts, buying merch to help fund this, and so much more. Especially Effie and Riley who did my cover and interior formatting since I couldn't figure out how to make the original files fit. I literally couldn't have done it without you. Every bit of fanart, every comment, every meme that was sent to me, you guys are awesome. I'm so thankful for my little community of sci-fi nerds.

Ad Astra Per Aspera!

Pronunciation Guide and Glossary

Astra Aracelli (As-truh Are-uh-kell-ee): Computer Science, Engineering, and Programming/Data Analysis Major

Aiken Frost (Aye-ken): Earth Science Major

Nasra Dabiri (Nas-ruh Dah-bee-ree): Neuroscience Major

Elena Valdivieso (E-leh-nah Val-dee-vee-eh-so): Mechanical Engineering Major

Hanbin 'Henry' Lee (Hen-ree): Computer Science Major

Zola Reed (Z-oh-lah): Computer Networking and Communications Major

Alyssa Clark (Ah-lis-ah): Health Sciences Major

Marilyn Anne 'Mary' Newman (Mare-ee): Civil Engineering Majorr

Katya Leonova (K-ah-t-yah Lee-oh-noh-vah): Astronomy and Astrophysics Major

Leroy Parkes (Lee-roy): Dean of Students

Delilah Hayes/Destiny Duke (Dee-lie-lah/Des-tin-ee): Information Technology Major

Willow (Will-oh): Engineering Major

William (Will-ee-um): Accounting Major

Morgan (Mor-gun): Chemical Engineering Major

Cassian (Kas-ee-un): Chemistry Major

Castor Allen (Kas-tor): Environmental Engineering Major

Isaac Kim (Eyes-ick): Computer Engineering Major

Enlai 'Eric' Huang (Air-ick): Engineering Major

Nara 'Nicole' Arai (Nih-kole Ah-r-eye-ee): Physics Major

David (Day-vid): Molecular Physics Major

Xavier (Zay-vee-er): Astra's brother. Not a student.

Cassidy (Kas-a-dee): Astra's sister. Not a student.

Kyan (Kee-on): Zola's oldest brother. Not a student.

Jamal (Juh-mal): Zola's older brother. Not a student.

Bonus Content

Alternate Prologue One

Light streamed through the window, casting shadows on the carpet floor. Two people sat cross-legged in the middle of the room. In between them was a low wooden table with an old chessboard sitting on top.

"Hmm," Ares mused. He picked up one of his knights. "Knight to B5," he said finally.

Astra smiled. She tapped the board, indicating one of her bishops. "Bishop to B5."

"Hmm. You sure?"

Astra nodded. The light glinted off the buttons of her black sweater. "I am sure."

"Always double check your moves Astra," Ares said, taking her bishop with his queen.

Astra smiled wider. "I know." She moved one of her pawns forward. "You say that every time."

"The point of chess is not to play—"

"The point is to learn, I know."

Ares smiled at her. "Good. So, let's talk this job that you want to take on."

"What, do you think I cannot do it?"

"I do not *'think'* anything, I figure it out by logic and facts. Regardless of how I feel, your skill and knowledge determine how good you are. Not me. It is the nature of the job and the people involved. Are you confident that it is not a project of passion?"

"Why would it be?" Astra questioned.

"You of all people would have reason to go, even when we have told you it is not a good idea."

"If I do not go, who will? Do I let everything go, sweep it under the rug like it is dirt and not disrespect?"

"Does it matter if it is disrespect?" Ares looked at her pointedly.

Astra sighed, pawn in hand. "I—" She hesitated. "Everything matters, intention, words, facts, feeling. These make up motivations, reasons. Feelings inform thoughts, which inform choices. That is why everything is considered the way it is," she said finally.

"But…" Ares prompted.

"But rash decisions are bad—"

"Not bad."

"Ill-advised," Astra said quickly. "If logic is to dictate my choices, then at some point, they will slip up. I will win." She placed her pawn down.

Ares took it swiftly with one of his. "Of course, that does not mean that your skill level will not cause you to make a mistake."

"That would invite a question of *your* skills," Astra retorted. "Considering you trained me."

"I am merely a mentor. Your failure is not a reflection of my own, just as your success is not a testament to my greatness. You alone are in charge of what you do. My teaching simply gives direction."

"What a good father you are," Astra said sarcastically.

"Do not be rude," Ares chastised. "Being responsible for your own fate is important. Nothing is set in stone. Your ideals will change as you grow older."

"If everything is my responsibility, then what is the reason for discipline?"

"Love," Ares said simply. He moved one of his castles. "Your move, daughter."

Astra stared at Ares, jaw clenched. "Love," she repeated.

"Yes."

"Love?"

"It is mercy, Astra."

Astra scoffed, rolling her eyes. She captured his other knight with one of her pawns. "What is the point of teaching us to ignore emotion when going into a job if *love* is how one defines the reason for punishment."

"Discipline and punishment are different. Punishment is for anger, discipline for teaching."

"And one teaches out of love?"

"Why else would you grant someone knowledge?"

Astra shrugged. "Kindness, goodness? Just because?"

Ares laughed. "Both come from love, Astra. No one does anything just because they want to, there is always a reason, whether you're aware of it or not."

"I thought that emotion meant weakness."

"Weakness? Have you forgotten everything you learned in school?" Ares asked incredulously. "It is not weakness; it is a strength. Different circumstances beg for different skills. Just because certain jobs require more knowledge than others, doesn't mean you forget emotion completely. You cherish it. It has a place, just not everywhere."

"Is that why we're taught to save ourselves?" Astra asked, moving her bishop across the board.

"Sacrifice is required to grow Astra," Ares said gently. "Part of sacrifice is admitting when you're wrong, because there will be times when you are."

"So, if I win, will you let me make my own choice?"

Ares raised an eyebrow. "About the job?"

"Yes. If I am to be responsible, independent, if I am to force my own destiny, make my choices based off of logic and proof of skill, then that is my request."

Ares nodded. "Okay. If you win, then you may go."

Astra grinned. "Perfect." She moved her queen into place. "Checkmate."

Alternate Prologue Two

The sounds of footsteps in shallow puddles of water on the concrete bounced off the wall, mixing with the soft splashes of water dripping from the pipes. A middle-aged man sprinted down the narrow passageway, ducking to avoid the pipes above his head. Though he was still far ahead of his pursuers, his pace was slower than he wanted. Unfortunately, there was not much he could do about it.

He was carrying two bags full of parts, and a bunch of cash stuffed into his pockets and shoes. He could hear shouting behind him. It only made him run faster. He had built an empire off of stealing, he wasn't about to let that all crumble down now. The sound of his name slowly became more evident.

"Leroy! LEROY!"

He only ran faster. This was a game, a game of chess, and he was winning. Leroy rounded the corner, nearly running into someone. "Isaac!" he hissed. "Are you serious? I almost ran you over."

The younger man shrugged. "Sorry. You told me to wait here."

"Not in the way!"

"Leroy!"

The sounds of his name got louder. Leroy glanced back towards the way he came. Light glinted off the puddles of water the closer they got. He reached behind him, pushing Isaac. "We've got to go."

Isaac didn't budge. "About that. Where's the exit?"

Leroy looked at him, incredulous. "What do you mean, where's the exit?"

Isaac stepped aside. "You told me to quote, *'go down there and wait.'* This is a dead end."

Leroy groaned and dropped both of the bags. He pulled a gun out of his waistband and passed it to Isaac. "Here. I hope you don't have to use it." He stepped forward and pressed his hands against the wall. "There's got to be a secret door here somewhere."

The footsteps got ever closer, and the sounds of his name were like roars in his ears. As he found the seam in the wall, they came around the corner.

"Stop!"

Leroy turned around to see three men with flashlights and pistols. "Really Ares? You're going to shoot me? Are we not friends?"

"We stopped being friends when you started stealing from me," Ares replied.

"It's not really stealing," Leroy said. "Think of it as a gift, for all I've done for you." He stepped forward, shielding Isaac from the men in front of them."

"All you've done for me? You've done nothing. I've given you everything. You sat at my table, you ate my food, you've been my ally." Ares put his gun into the holster on his hip and raised his hands. The other two men followed suit. "Just tell me why you did this."

"Why are you pretending like you're going to spare me?!" Leroy yelled. "We both know you don't do mercy."

"Consider it an act of good will. Between friends."

Leroy scoffed. "I doubt it. Come on Isaac."

Isaac didn't move.

Leroy turned. "Isaac?"

Isaac raised the gun shakily. "I'm sorry, I can't let you do this."

Betrayal lit in Leroy's eyes. "Isaac, please."

The man on the left drew his gun, aiming it at Leroy's back.

"Victor," Ares said in a warning tone.

Isaac's eyes widened as they flitted over Leroy's shoulder to Victor. "No!" Isaac yelled, turning his gun on Victor. "Don't kill him!" He shot him in the shoulder.

Victor screamed in pain, and the gun went off, up, hitting a clamp attaching one of the pipes to the ceiling. Leroy took the opportunity to grab both bags and push through the door in the wall.

The last thing he saw was the pipe swinging down and blocking
the men from following him, taking Isaac's head with it.

Sera Amoroso is the self-published author of The Makria Cycle. She's a freelance editor, college student, cosplayer, linguist, tea enthusiast, and avid reader. She spends most of her time at home with her dog, Minnie.

She has been writing stories since she was ten years old. Ever since she got her hands on books such as The Lord of the Rings, and Enders Game, she wanted to publish one of her own. Finally, multiple scrapped ideas and discarded drafts later, she did it.

Torsion, her debut novel, kicks off The Makria Cycle trilogy. She's also been featured in the anthology Aphotic Love, and the 2024 edition of The Dragon Bone Journal. When she's not writing, she can be found reading, creating languages, and playing games with friends.